TYGER!

TYGER!

TYGER!

TYGER!

RICHARD HOYT

A TOM DOHERTY ASSOCIATES BOOK
NEW YORK

TYGER! TYGER!

Copyright © 1996 by Richard Hoyt

Text for the poem "The Tyger" by William Blake is from a selection of Blake's poetry in The Laurel Poetry Series published by Dell. General Editor Richard Wilbur. Copyright © 1960.

This book is printed on acid-free paper.

A Forge Book
Published by Tom Doherty Associates, Inc.
175 Fifth Avenue
New York, NY 10010

Forge® is a registered trademark of Tom Doherty Associates, Inc.

Design by Lynn Newmark

Library of Congress Cataloging-in-Publication Data
Hoyt, Richard.
    Tiger! tiger! / by Richard Hoyt.
      p.   cm.
    "A Tom Doherty Associates book."
    ISBN 0-312-85804-3
    1. Endangered animals—Fiction.   2. Serial murders—Fiction.
3. Tigers—Fiction.   I. Title.
PS3558.O975T5   1996
813'.54—dc20   95-42569
                                          CIP

First Edition: April 1996

Printed in the United States of America

0 9 8 7 6 5 4 3 2 1

for John Henley, bookman nonpareil

The Tyger

Tyger! Tyger! burning bright
In the forests of the night,
What immortal hand or eye
Could frame thy fearful symmetry?

In what distant deeps or skies
Burnt the fire of thine eyes?
On what wings dare he aspire?
What the hand dare sieze the fire?

And what shoulder, & what art,
Could twist the sinews of thy heart?
And when thy heart began to beat,
What dread hand? & what dread feet?

What the hammer? What the chain?
In what furnace was the brain?
What the anvil? What dread grasp
Dare its deadly terrors clasp?

When the stars threw down their spears,
And water'd heaven with their tears,
Did he smile his work to see?
Did he who made the Lamb make thee?

Tyger! Tyger! burning bright
In the forests of the night,
What immortal hand or eye,
Dare frame thy fearful symmetry?

—William Blake

TYGER!

TYGER!

1

12 June 1957, Hamburg

The circusgoers in Hamburg on that Saturday afternoon
had not come to see Roberta, the woman with the curly piglike
tail that poked out of the back of her skintight slacks—suggestive
of truths unacknowledged—or Conrad, the man with a tiny green
fedora perched atop his cucumber head, or Louisa, the girl with a
face like a morose toad, complete with warts and large, protrud-
ing eyes.

And neither, yawn, were they especially impressed by scant-
ily clad girls in see-through outfits riding galumphing elephants
around the ring. Or later, the same sexy girls on galloping camels,
this time dressed up in slightly tattered harem-girl outfits, and in
fact looking like escapees from a Shriners' convention.

And were the clowns really that funny? Or was there not
something else about them? The people watching them had all
been bopped on the head at one time or another, some of them numerous if not countless times, and not merely by plastic hammers
or foam rubber baseball bats either. And when they got whacked
on the rump and sent flying, it was not by a playful broom. They
did not always bounce right up from these conks on the head or
blows to the rump to hurtle forward to the next outlandish disaster.

The exaggerated, Chaplinesque pratfalls of the painted clowns
with their sad faces served to remind the assembled spectators of
how unfunny, and therefore hilarious, life really was. The clowns
forced them to look life straight on, and they laughed because of

the awful truth. What the clowns said through outlandish mime was simple enough: Good intentions were fine, but Murphy's Law everywhere obtained—when something could go wrong, it would.

So, when one sad clown sent another morose clown tumbling across the sawdust, everybody laughed. Being a clown was serious business; to be eternally serious, while perhaps righteous, was in fact to be a clown. And what of the clowns with outsize, bulbous noses and the absurd, ear-to-ear smiles that consumed their entire faces? No matter what happened to them, these clowns smiled on. But their smiles were patently bogus, painted on. To go to the circus was to take a giddy dip into the truth.

The spectators watched the trapeze artists and high-wire artists for the same reason they bought overpriced tickets to formula 1 automobile races: to see the rare lethal or crippling crash. But trapeze artists, no matter how awesome their flips and spins and twists, performed high above nets. There were no nets outside to save people. When they crashed from life's high-wire, they screwed into the ground up to their armpits, and that was it.

And while it was titillating to imagine that the female aerialists were nearly naked instead of wearing skin-colored tights, those daring ladies of the big top were clearly unattainable and so not very provocative to dads sitting in the darkness with their wives and kids. The dangers of entrapment by desire and possession were far more real, if less exotic.

So, while aerialists were entertaining, it was the tigers who lurked in the darkest recesses of the human imagination.

The promoters of Captain Prince–Cox's International Circus, understanding the thrill of genuine risk, billed Lothar Neumann, the death-defying Lothar the Magnificent, as the main attraction. The handsome Lothar, tiger master, was the featured star touted by the many posters plastered about Hamburg by the circus's advance men. A tamer of tigers was this handsome German. Here, clearly, was a man who knew what danger was all about.

So when the mellow-voiced ringmaster announced, with as much drama as he could muster, the appearance of the *"greaaaaatest tiiiiiger maaaaaster in hisssssstory,"* next in the center ring, the crowd hushed.

This would be, they were told in solemn tones, a death-defying *"perforrrrrmance"* they would tell their *"grrrrrrrandchildren"* about. In fact, those with bad hearts might be advised to skip this act.

No sooner were those with bad tickers given fair warning, than the tent was plunged into darkness, enabling the crew to erect the tiger cage in the center ring.

The most excited group of spectators was perhaps FC Baltic, a youth-league football side for eleven- and twelve-year-olds who, having recently won a championship cup, had been rewarded by the team coaches with tickets to the circus. They were seated less than five meters from the edge of the cage, and when Lothar Neumann stepped from the entrance to the center ring to await his introduction, several of the wide-eyed young footballers handed him circus posters to autograph, Neumann graciously obliged. Then, it was time to be introduced. Lothar, having finished with the autographing, licked his lips and took a deep breath.

The announcer warned the crowd against making sudden loud noises because Lothar the Magnificent was engaged in dangerous business. A startled tiger could cost Lothar his life, the announcer said. When Neumann was introduced, it was fine to applaud, but lightly please. Anybody violating this simple requirement for the performer's safety would be escorted from the big tent.

This was not the time for the steam calliope to play "Entrance of the Gladiator."

This was serious time.

Tiger time.

A single snare drum began the build-up: *bum-diddy, bum-diddy, bum-diddy, bum; bum-diddy, bum-diddy, bum-diddy, bum.*

Suddenly, a single spotlight, in the center ring, focused on a man with a whip: Lothar Neumann, a tall, lean man, blond-haired, blue-eyed, and with rugged, intense, Sean Connery good looks. He wore white shoes, blue, formfitting tights, and a red, sequined tank top that showed his powerful biceps and hairy chest. Lothar the Magnificent was no accountant; he was a tiger trainer and looked like one. He had presence, and commanded attention.

The crowd, following its instructions, applauded lightly.

Then, a second spotlight.

Before them: a tiger sitting on a stool.

Then, a third, fourth, and fifth spotlight. Then six and seven, until six handsome tigers were revealed, each sitting atop a stool, on massive, tensed haunches. The spotlights caressed these feline beasts, their muscles like great cords of rope. They were cats. Silent stalkers. Killing machines. Their yellow killer eyes looked disdainfully out at the darkness beyond the lights. A lion was merely big. A tiger was quick and strong and mean with razor fangs.

Neumann popped his whip over each tiger and bowed, and the crowd again applauded lightly.

Then the center ring was slowly flooded with light, stronger and stronger, at length revealing that Neumann and his tigers were in a circular cage.

Neumann popped his whip above the head of the first and sixth tigers and they hopped off their stools and traded places. Without pausing, he did this with the second and fifth tigers, and the third and fourth. *Pop-pop-pop! Pop-pop-pop!*

Thus tigers were rearranged. When the cat master demanded, the tigers obeyed.

The crowd applauded.

Neumann snapped his whip again, and the tigers hopped off their perches, pacing, while assistants raced into the cage and retrieved the stools.

Then Neumann held up a large yellow hoop. He cracked his whip and the tigers lined up and jumped through it in a single file.

Lothar the Magnificent threw the hoop aside and took a bow. The crowd applauded.

Next, he made the tigers hop onto a large barrel, one after another, and roll it around the ring, while the other tigers took turns running through it.

Then his assistants rolled six large, colorful balls into the cage— red, green, blue, yellow, white, and orange—and the tigers hopped atop them, with Neumann popping his whip above their heads. The tigers began rolling the balls around the ring with their huge claws.

Suddenly, without warning, the cat above the green ball jumped off and took a single neat swipe at Lothar Neumann's throat.

Just like that.

A casual slash. A feline oopsie. It was unclear if the tiger was being playful or whether he was demonstrating his resentment at having to put up with a whip being popped over his head.

No matter. Lothar Neumann dropped, blood spurting from a severed artery.

The crowd, stunned, was momentarily silent. Was this part of the act or was it was real? When the spectators understood it was real, the panic began—and the screaming.

Squirt, squirt, squirt.

The tiger who had made the lethal swipe, looking bored, returned leisurely to the green ball as though nothing had happened. He had slashed the throat of the man who made him sit on silly stools and jump through hoops and roll a stupid ball.

This was not part of the act.

Squirt, squirt, squirt.

This was not bogus blood. This was a shocking, nearly surreal crimson.

Squirt, squirt, squirt.

It was the real thing.

This was unexpected.

Real life.

Squirt, squirt, squirt.

An assistant raced past the stunned young football players into the cage, keeping a wary eye on the bored tigers atop their balls. He grabbed Lothar Neumann by both wrists and dragged his blood-soaked, dying body, quickly through the door.

Squirt, squirt, squirt.

In the cage, the six tigers continued rolling their colorful balls around the cage as though nothing untoward had happened. See here, they seemed to be saying, we know how to roll these balls. This is an easy trick, no big deal. We don't need anybody popping a whip over our heads.

If the tigers felt any emotion over the loss of their master, they didn't show it. In fact, there were those who later maintained that the tigers rolled their balls with exceptional enthusiasm. One observer described them as playful, like overgrown kittens having fun atop colorful balls of yarn. Certainly, they were indifferent to the fuss and confusion attending the untimely death of Lothar the Magnificent, the greatest tiger master the world had ever known.

2

Bhagalpur, India, 1995

On the porch outside, a monkey, scavenging for food, peered in between the glass louvers at the living room of the cottage. The monkey, who looked like a wizened old man, cocked his head with curiosity. Inside, a wide-shouldered, dark-haired man in his late fifties, wearing sandals and shorts, but no shirt, swore at the monkey in German. The monkey, chastened, bounded off.

Before the German, a slender, naked Indian girl, with dark brown, nearly charcoal skin, waited beside a stool with a towel draped over the top rung.

The girl had a finely boned face with an aqualine nose and extraordinary, large brown eyes. Her straight black silky hair hung to the small of her back. She wore dangling black-white-and-orange earrings. She had long, slender legs and a dimunitive torso. Her tiny rib cage had delicate ribs. Her breasts too were small, but with dark brown nipples as large as a man's thumb. She had a proud carriage with narrow hips above long thighs, and an exquisitely shaped rump. If she had lived in Europe or North America, she would have been a fashion model working the ramps for high bucks.

She stood before a full-length mirror mounted on the wall.

The German retrieved a cold beer from the refrigerator, studied the girl, and squeezed ropes of red, yellow, raw umber, and white paint on a palette which he put on the stool.

Then, with the naked girl watching in the mirror, he began marking her body with a felt-tipped marker. He started at the base of her slender neck and moving down either side of her elegant spine, outlining what appeared to be irregular horizonal stripes, some larger than others. When he reached her lower back, he continued down the inside of her buttocks, then down her slender thighs and the calves of her legs.

The German periodically wiped the sweat from his forehead and belly and ribs. His model appeared to be unaffected by the heat as, following the German's English instructions, she turned this way and that, positioning and stretching her body to help him with the work. As she did, she watched herself in the mirrow.

When he had finished with her back, he got another bottle of beer and walked around the girl to examine his project. Then he outlined the same stripes, only smaller, on her ribs and face.

It took him a half hour to finish marking her up with the felt pen.

The curious monkey returned, possibly wondering what was going on in there. The German grabbed a shotgun from the corner and stalked angrily onto the porch.

The monkey, squealing, scurried up a tree and disappeared.

The German put the shotgun back in the corner and considered his model. He got himself another beer, then began mixing the red, yellow, and raw umber until he arrived at a muted buff-orange that satisfied him.

Then he began painting her back the buff-orange, filling in the space between the spaces he had outlined with the felt-tipped pen, leaving stripes of the girl's charcoal-brown skin. He painted her back this color, her extraordinary butt, and the backs of her legs.

As he moved to the sides of her slender limbs and torso, he added white, turning the yellowish orange increasingly pale.

He paused to admire his work, and squeezed another rope of white onto his palette. He painted the front of her legs white, as well as her narrow belly and small breasts, blending the white into the pale yellowish orange on the sides of her ribs and legs.

The girl giggled and murmured something in lilting Hindi-English as he ran his brush across her breasts. He grinned and flipped her nipple with his finger.

He saved the front of her throat and her face for last, painting the front of her face white, with a patch of white above her eyes. He returned to the off-orange for the middle of her forehead, her nose, and beneath her eyes, leaving tiny stripes of dark skin.

When he was finished, the German burst into a broad grin. The Indian girl, thus painted, was nothing short of stunning. He motioned with his hand for her to turn, showing him her profile.

The girl smiled as well. Watching her tiger reflection in the mirror, she turned, showing off her legs; below the elegant curve of her spine, her provocative, striped tiger rump.

Outside, insects clicked and whizzed and buzzed in the afternoon sun.

The German spoke to the tiger-girl. She listened, then put her chin up and dropped her long arms to her sides. While she suppressed a smile, he painted whiskers, thin black lines, outward from the base of her nose.

When her whiskers were finished, he once more mopped the sweat from his ribs and belly with a towel. Then, beer in hand, he walked slowly around her, admiring his handiwork. He told her she was beautiful, and she laughed.

He was finished, and they were both thrilled with the results.

The German went to the sink and ran water on a small whetstone. Then, he wet the large blade of a Swiss army knife and began sharpening it, admiring the tiger-girl as he did.

He also had an erection. His cock strained at his walking shorts. The tiger-girl kneeled, looking up at him with her brown eyes, ready to take care of him with her mouth.

He shook his head no. Not yet.

He retrieved another bottle of beer from the refrigerator. Mopping his forehead with a handkerchief he slipped a photographer's vest over his short-sleeved shirt, and grabbed a tripod of aluminum telescopic legs and a Hasselblad camera.

Then the tiger-girl, her entire body a beautiful mosaic of charcoal stripes with a sandy buff-orange background, led the way outside, her colorful earrings dangling.

The sun was now low in the west.

The German, his trousers still bulging, set up his tripod and snapped the camera into place on top. He motioned with his hands as he gave her instructions for her first pose, at the base of a huge tree with bark like dry, crusted mud.

The Indian girl was an exotic beauty to begin with. Painted like a tiger, she was exotic in the extreme, bordering on the surreal.

The curious monkey watched from his perch in the tree. The insects buzzed and clicked and whirred.

The German, his thumb on a remote that triggered the camera shutter, framed his first shot. Then, following his instructions, his model turned her sinewy tiger-body this way and that, as the German snapped off shots on the Hassleblad: *click-clack, click-clack.*

Such a gorgeous, exotic tiger was this lithe and limber beauty, so slender she was and oh so sinewy. She was feline, there was no other word for it. Sinewy. Feline. Sexy.

3

Her name was Marta Fuentes. Her husband, Oscar, a butcher by trade, had died of tuberculosis three years earlier. She was forty-three years old, with six of her eight children—ranging in age from five to fifteen years old—still living in her tiny house on Lorega Street just up from the slaughterhouse where her husband had worked.

She cleaned fish in Carbon Market close to downtown Cebu City, in the Philippines, for which she earned 110 pesos a day—about four U.S. dollars—depending on business. It took fifty pesos a day to buy the two kilos of rice it took Marta to feed her family each day. If she were to add meat or vegetables to her rice, that was extra.

After she bought clothes for her children, and their school supplies, there were precious few pesos left. Were it not for the help of her brothers, sisters, aunts, uncles, and her many cousins, Marta would not have made it. In the Philippines, families stuck together; their survival depended on it. To those who say that behind every successful marriage there is a determined woman, the Filipinos can say, with pride, that they are a nation of determined women.

When Marta first began having heart pains, she turned to the only doctor she could afford. At the public clinic, after a four-hour wait, a doctor took her blood pressure and listened to her heart. He said not to eat overnight and come back the next day to have a sample of her blood taken, a wait of just two hours.

* * *

James Burlane, aware that the old Chinese was watching him, nevertheless took his time browsing the colorful bottles and boxes and cans on the shelves of Beijing Medicinal Works, one of numerous shops in San Francisco's Chinatown that sold traditional medicines. The Chinese were much given to red, which Burlane knew brought good luck. He figured everybody who had something physically wrong with them needed a little luck, whether they were trying to hedge their bets with western medicine or with Chinese homeopathic medicine.

In order to find out what worked and what didn't, the Chinese had been using the time-honored system of trial and error for thousands of years. Ordinarily, Burlane put his trust in the scientific method that had evolved in the West, but once in a while . . .

An old Chinese man, the proprietor, watched him, his face a blank mask.

Burlane found himself standing in front of what seemed like an entire wall of medicines that contained ginseng. The night before he had read from cover to cover *Prescription for Extinction,* the report on patented oriental medicines published by TRAFFIC US, an organization concerned about the use of endangered species in these medicines. That report listed more than 180 brand names of medicines containing ginseng.

Since Burlane did not read Chinese, he couldn't appreciate all the brands on the wall. But there were several with English names that looked interesting: *White Monkey-Lungs Crystalize, Dragon Man Pills, Essence of Frog and Ginseng, Leung Chi See Sea Dog Pills, Powerful Deer Penis Capsules, Healthy Brain Pills, Prosperous Farmer-Spleen Qi, Sea Horse Genital Tonic Pills, Turtle Mountain Tonic Dragon's Brew, Trisnake Itch-Removing Pills.*

Burlane assumed that *Dragon Man Pills* were intended to induce dragonlike performance in the bedroom. He thought momentarily of buying himself a bottle, but thought no, what he needed more were *Healthy Brain Pills. Prescription for Extinction* had listed a half dozen ginseng compounds that also included tiger bone, such as *Tiger Bone Glue* and *Tiger Bone Limbs-Strengthening Pills,* but he did not see any of these among the offerings of the Beijing Medicinal Works.

Looking at the ginseng compounds, Burlane said, "I was curious about what else is good for the problem of ahhhh . . ." He let his voice trail off. He already knew the answer. Penises were an important ingredient for their purported aphrodisiac qualities, the Chinese being in the market for the dicks of antelopes, crocodiles, sheep, seals, deer, horses, donkeys, dogs, and tigers.

The proprietor said, "Check the section to your left."

Burlane did. This was a wonderful section. Here, the Works offered the *Crocodile Penis Potency Capsule,* made in Lanzou, China. *Dragon Man Pills,* made by the Wuzhou Drug Manufactory, contained, among other things, ginseng, milk vetch, and both deer and fur seal penises. Not to be outdone, the United Pharmaceutical Works of Kwangchow marketed *Wo Lung Wan,* containing penis of Sitka deer, fur seal, and tiger, in addition to tiger bone and ginseng, but it was not represented on these shelves, as far as Burlane could see.

Burlane could easily understand why the Chinese male, given his druthers of fucking like a sheep, donkey, or dog, might well have his heart set on a tiger penis. But the aphrodisiac qualities of penises were not universally agreed upon by the Chinese themselves.

"Which of these are the best?"

The proprietor looked thoughtful. "The Tianjin Li Sheng Pharmaceutical Factory holds that dog and deer penises are best for sexual energy, with the maximum benefit coming from a combination of the two."

Burlane saw that the Guangzhou Pharmaceutical Industry Corporation apparently agreed; on the shelf in front of Burlane was a bottle of Guangzhou Pharmaceutical's *Powerful Deer Penis* capsules.

The old man said, "The musk of the Sitka deer is good, too. Your own western scientists say that in small doses musk stimulates the heart, uterus, and central nervous system, but in large doses, it does the reverse."

"Do you carry it?" Burlane asked mildly.

The proprietor shook his head. "It's on the endangered species list."

"I see," Burlane said. He continued browsing, quickly encountering a section with medicine containing bile—the bitter, yellowish green secretion of the liver. There were pills with the bile of pigs, dogs, bears, crocodiles, and snakes.

"Do you believe in traditional medicine?" the Chinese asked.

Burlane said, "I know there have been clinical studies that show red wine is good for the heart, and that garlic is useful for reducing cholesterol. I used to scoff at ginseng, too, because all the stupid western magazines claimed there was no such thing as an aphrodisiac."

Burlane did not add that cannabis worked just as well if not better. Both ginseng and cannabis stimulated the senses and lowered inhibitions. He was glad that Americans scoffed at ginseng; if they had discovered that it worked, professional moralists—who apparently couldn't sleep for the thought that somebody, somewhere, might be having fun—would have long ago opposed its use in order to get themselves elected to public office. The American political syllogism was amazingly simple:

First major premise:
Righteous people are good.
Second major premise:
Good leaders are righteous.
Minor premise:
Sensual pleasure is not righteous.
Conclusion:
Good people vote for candidates who oppose sensual pleasure.

In Burlane's opinion the minor premise was flat absurd, which screwed the entire logic. He was amazed that politicans hadn't gone after the authors of cookbooks, but apparently nobody had yet told them that eating good food was a sensual pleasure, as was listening to music or enjoying the smell of an aftershave lotion. The Chinese were lucky the federal government hadn't attempted to ban ginseng.

"Are you a journalist?" the proprietor asked.

Burlane looked surprised. "Me? A journalist?" He laughed. "No, nothing as fancy as that, I'm afraid. I market solar panels for heating water."

The proprietor cocked his head. He had to be over eighty. "Do you have a particular problem today?"

Burlane massaged his left bicep. "Lately, I've been getting a pain in my arm here and my shoulder. I think it's probably arthritis. I always regarded arthritis as a disease of old people, old people being everybody older than me. Now my shoulder aches, I've tried aspirin and Advil and Tylenol and the rest of it, but my shoulder still aches."

"It could be arthritis," the proprietor said.

Burlane said, "I read a magazine article that said that Chinese traditional medicine containing tiger bone was good for arthritis. Something called *Musk and Tiger Bone Plaster* was recommended."

Prescription for Extinction listed seventy patented medicines that contained parts of tigers and their factory names and locations, most of them in China. Of these, sixty listed tiger bone as the principal ingredient; seven listed unidentified parts of the tiger; and three, presumably the most expensive, listed tiger penis. Some were mixed with other ingredients of traditional Chinese medicine. The most popular generic name for these medicines, eleven in all, was *Musk and Tiger Bone Plaster*.

"We don't have anything containing tiger bone. The tigers are an endangered species," the proprietor said. He had been warming to Burlane, who seemed to be open to the properties of homeopathic medicine. Now his face returned to a mask.

Burlane didn't think there was any doubt he was lying. He would have bet money, marbles, or chalk that there were plenty of compounds containing tiger bone in the back of Beijing Medicinal Works. Maybe not a whole lot of tiger bone, but for sure a wee teeny bit. "Do you know where I can find some?" Burlane said.

"I have no idea," the proprietor said.

* * *

When James Burlane got back to his hotel room on Van Ness Avenue, he looked up *Sea Horse Genital Tonic Pills* in *Prescription for Extinction.* He learned these pills, manufactured in Hebei, Tianjin province, China, were marketed to the Japanese and contained a miscellany of penises and testicles of several animals which Burlane could not identify owing to the use of Latin names.

One that he did recognize was *Os Tigris,* bone of the tiger. If sea horses were actually used, Burlane wondered who removed their genitals and how?

According to *Prescription for Extinction,* clinical tests showed that tiger bone did, in fact, have an anti-inflammatory, analgesic effect on arthritis induced in laboratory animals. There were numerous other medicines that had anti-inflammatory and analgesic properties.

Curious about how much tiger bone was actually in the many tiger-bone plasters listed in *Prescription for Extinction,* Burlane checked the appendix on formula verification. He learned that the *Natural Musk and Tiger-Bone Plaster* manufactured by the Fifth Chengdu Pharmaceutical Factory in Chengdu, Sichuan province, contained fifty grams of tiger bone for 108,000 packets; each packet contained five sheets of plaster. An entire tiger skeleton weighed from thirty to forty kilograms—a kilogram being a little over 2.2 pounds. At the current black market price of thirteen cents for a gram of tiger bone, the actual tiger content of a five-plaster packet is worth only three thousands of one cent.

That wasn't much tiger bone, but when nearly a billion Chinese believed it helped relieve arthritis pain, they were capable of going through a whole lot of *Natural Musk and Tiger-Bone Plaster.*

Burlane wondered: Even if clinical injections of tiger bone in arthritic rats proved of some benefit to the suffering animal, could that small amount of tiger bone actually do anything for a human being with arthritis?

Even then, almost none of the patented oriental medicines generically known as musk–tiger bone plaster actually contained hydroxyapatite, the inorganic compound found in bone. Bone could be identified by taxonomic family, not species. The main ingredient in these medicines was zinc, believed most likely to come from Smithsontium—zinc carbonate—found in limestone areas of China.

If it was zinc that provided the relief and not bone, was it not possible for the Chinese to break the news to the public and educate people to treat their ailments with something less exotic than tiger bones?

Or if bones it had to be, was it not possible that the bones of other animals had anti-inflammatory, analgesic properties?

Why not grind up the bones of butchered cattle?

Most of the companies manufacturing patented oriental medicines, some 220 of them, were in China. Another forty were located in Hong Kong, and a half dozen or less were located in each of Singapore, Malaysia, Taiwan, Korea, and San Francisco. Burlane found it interesting that only three listings were given for Taiwan, which in 1992 had suffered U.S. trade sanctions for trafficking in endangered species. The U.S. refused to import any product from Taiwan that contained products of wild animals, a sanction that cost the Taiwanese millions of dollars a year in lost revenue.

In pursuit of bones and penises, the Chinese had already killed off nearly all their own tigers. The people who had hired Burlane had concluded, logically enough, that for all these Chinese-made medicines to contain tiger bones, somebody had to be buying and shipping poached tigers to the manufacturers. They had to be imported, probably from the Indian subcontinent, the Indochinese and Malay Peninsulas, Sumatra, and Siberia.

Some supplier had to buy the tigers in the first place.

Who was doing this?

Burlane flipped through the indexes listed by TRAFFIC Network. One of these contained some two thousand ingredients of patented oriental medicines. Most of these were plants with Latin names that Burlane couldn't understand without a good dictionary.

Burlane felt he could have used some *Ching Chun Bao Recovery of Youth Tablet*—made from asparagus roots—manufactured by the Hangzhou Chinese Medicine Factory #2. Surely asparagus was not an endangered species. Maybe a couple of tablets would reinvigorate him for the task ahead.

4

Below the Northwest Airlines 747, in shifting Rorshach banks of gray and white clouds over the Pacific Ocean, James Burlane saw tigers running, horizon to horizon. He saw a magnificent tiger growling. He saw a defiant tiger snarling at the sun. He saw a tiger crouching, as though it were lurking, unseen, watching the passing plane. Once, as the plane passed a blue hole of ocean, the sunlight reflected white off the decks of a merchant vessel on the water; to Burlane it was a piercing tiger's eye looking up at him.

Then Burlane saw, clearly he thought, the lonely, melancholy visage of a mighty tiger stretched out above the Pacific, facing its Asian haunts. This clearly was a tiger of consequence. Was it resignment or despair that Burlane read on the cloudy tiger's face?

Was this tiger dying?

Or was it already dead?

The clouds shifted. Slowly, the windblown tiger-cloud raised its head, seeming to look directly at him.

Was it calling out? Yes, it was. The tiger, clearly, was addressing him.

Saying what? Was it asking a question? Was it pleading?

Then the clouds faded and the ghost-tiger dissolved into a blur, vanishing into the shifting mists above the ocean that was a chasm between East and West.

Burlane hated transpacific flights; they seemed to go on for unendurable lengths of time. The Korean man next to him, a representative of the makers of the Hyundai automobile exported to the

United States, spoke only rudimentary English, so anything approaching a satisfactory converation was impossible.

Burlane stretched his legs under the seat in front of him, trying to get the blood going. He had read magazines until his eyes were exhausted. He had played solitaire with miniature cards. He was tired of drinking red wine; beer made him pee, and going to the toilet was a chore, an odyssey topped off by having to stand with a full bladder staring at the OCCUPIED light. The movie, a moronic love story, had failed to grip his attention. It wasn't that Burlane was a callous hard-ass male, incapable of enjoying a love story, but this one was just plane dumb; he couldn't identify with the male, and had no interest in the female. Now there was nothing to do but think.

The Bali tiger went under in the 1940s. The Caspian tiger went out of business in the 1970s. There were no more tigers on Java after the 1980s. The estimates are that maybe thirty to eighty remain in South China. Conservationists said the South China tiger is next, of course, followed by the Siberian tiger, then the Sumatran tiger. There are an estimated 650 Siberian tigers left, and perhaps a couple of hundred more than that in Sumatra. Then there are thirty-five hundred to five thousand Bengal tigers remaining, and maybe a thousand to seventeen hundred Indochinese tigers.

Tiger, tiger.

What was to become of the tiger?

Was the answer to the fate of the tiger somehow kinetic, action-oriented, as in the boom-boom movies? Or were the problems of the tiger's future deeper and more complicated, rooted in a culture that was beyond the ability of western tiger lovers to change, however thrilled they were by this wonderful beast and however well-intentioned their concern over its future?

Burlane, his mouth dry, pulled down the plastic shade over the window. He closed his eyes.

Burlane tried to go to sleep, but he could not. He could not take his mind off the tigers in the clouds.

James Burlane believed the tiger was most likely being strangled by the snarl of history and cultural differences. An important part of untangling the snarl lay in understanding the religious and philosophical roots of the Asian imagination.

Burlane, an Asian hand of some years, knew that whereas Europe had been dominated largely by Catholics in the south and Protestants in the north and west, the religious landscape of East and Southeast Asia was more complicated. Muslims had overrun the southwestern flank—Indonesia and Malaysia. Even the Philippines, dominated by Roman Catholics, was Muslim in the south, on Mindanao and in the islands of the Sulu archipelago. In China, Confucianism, less a religion than a philosophy of life, lay heavy on the moral landscape.

But for the rest of Asia, Buddhism, with its many schools and philosophical off-shoots, was the predominant religious influence. While the Christian Messiah had made his appearance in Palestine to the east of Europe, the reverse was true for East and Southeast Asia; the Buddha had sat under the bodhi tree in India, to the West.

Burlane knew that the Theravada or southern school of Buddhism dominated Cambodia, Laos, Burma, and Thailand, whereas the Mahayana or northern school held forth in Korea, Mongolia, Japan, Tibet, Nepal, Vietnam, and China. Followers of the Theravada school believed in reincarnation and that the way to eliminate *dukkha*—almost every screwed thing that can happen to an individual—was to eliminate desire.

The love of tigers is desire.

To eliminate desire is to eliminate *dukkha*.

Historically, Mahayana Buddhism split into several schools: early on, salvation was offered through faith in Amida, the Buddha of the Western Paradise; then, through faith in the Lotus Sutra, the Buddha offered salvation to all animal life; later sects promised salvation through self-reliance, self-discipline, and meditation. In Zen Buddhism—whose roots were in twelfth-century China and which later flourished with the Japanese—one sits in meditation, *zazen,* and achieves intellectual self-discipline through nonsense conundrums, *koan,* which lead to character building and to sudden enlightenment, *satori.*

For the Buddhist the nature of the present is clear: Individuals and individual egos have no meaning; they rise from the whole and sink back into it, nonentities, part of the endless chain who have risen and fallen before, and life continues.

Thinking of this, watching the clouds, Burlane invented two *koan:*

What is the sound of a dead tiger crying?
What is the odor of conservationists sighing?

A student of Zen Buddhism who actually tried to answer those impossible questions risked getting slapped about by his master.

Burlane, for the moment fancying himself a *zen* master, gave two possible answers:

Who cares what happens to the tiger?
Why care?

A student who understood that both *koans* and their answers were irrelevant was closing in on the territory of *satori.*

Whether they were of the Theravada or Mahayana schools, Buddhists did not believe that history and the human condition could be improved or, in the present case, that vigorous, logical human invervention could somehow save the tiger.

Or did the issue of the tiger have to do with "face," that is, of personal and cultural pride? In Asia, from Singapore to Ulan Bator, the critical notion of face, of keeping or losing it, everywhere obtained.

The idea of face was difficult for North Americans and Europeans to understand, Burlane not excluded. The tiger was an Asian cat, not a North American or European animal. Yet Burlane's employer—CITES—had arrogantly dispatched him to run down the buyers of poached tigers in Asia. He was in fact a kind of hired gun, and the act of hiring him was western hubris, there was no denying it.

Burlane wondered: How would the Americans feel if a consortium of Chinese and Japanese conservationists had dispatched a professional investigator to Montana to track down poachers of mountain goats? Or how would the Europeans like it if the guy was sent to the Alps to run down bear poachers, if there were any bears left in the Alps?

And yet the awful, undeniable truth was that the Asian masses appeared not to give a flying fuck about tigers or any other wild animals for that matter; were it left up to them, they would push endangered species out of business pronto: the orangutan; the panda; name the beast. This was a difference between the European and Asian imagination that Burlane felt few people appreciated.

The Chinese did not respond to President Bill Clinton's calls to improve "human rights," which to the Chinese was an alien concept forced upon them by arrogant, busybody, high-minded westerners meddling in the internal affairs of a country halfway around the planet. The rights of wild animals? This was enough to make a Chinese laugh, and they usually only laughed when they were embarrassed or in pain. How on earth was anybody to believe the Chinese would yield on the necessity of saving the tiger? The very idea was absurd.

One thing Burlane did know: The amazing tiger, ranging all the way from tropical Indonesia to freezing Siberia, was an adaptable cat if there ever was one. If given a little help, he was convinced, the tiger just might have a chance. But then, Burlane was an American mongrel, a product of the western imagination; although he had grown up on a small farm in eastern Oregon, he was an intellectual descendant, ultimately, of those wonderful ancient Greeks who believed in logic, vigorously applied. Burlane was flat pissed that human stubbornness, stupidity, and horseshit pride might cause his grandchildren to have to read about tigers in books or watch them on videotape instead of knowing they were out there at night prowling the forests on their great silent pads. And so he had accepted the assignment given him by the Convention on International Trade in Endangered Species, even though they were very likely deluded, same as he was.

James Burlane, traveling under his nom de guerre of Major M. Sidarius Khartoum, felt compelled to to do his damnedest on behalf of the tiger.

The clouds that had earlier yielded tigers in Burlane's imagination now thinned, revealing land up ahead. That would be Sakhalin Island, where, in the bad old days of the Cold War, So-

viet jets had knocked Northwest Airlines Flight 007 out of the sky.
Now, in more civil times, commercial airliners had Russian permission to fly over Sakhalin.

Burlane would start his investigation in the Russian Far East, where the fabled Siberian tiger was in imminent danger of extinction.

As the plane passed over Sakhalin, there were more clouds and more tigers. . . .

Later, as the 747 began its descent, the clouds thinned again, and Burlane could see the well-tended rural landscape below him. Soon he would be seeing the blue roofs. He did not know why the Koreans seemed to prefer blue roofs, and his ignorance bothered him. Was the preference because of some religion or philosophy, or because some company that made blue tiles had managed to strong-arm its way into a near monopoly?

Burlane wondered about such things. He asked questions. He couldn't help himself; that was the way he was. What had the tiger in the clouds been trying to tell him?

He twisted in his seat.

He thought: Tyger! Tyger!

Then came the inevitable questions. Questions, questions. Then the *koan:*

What was the syntax of saving the tiger?
How big were the feet of one fool trying?

5

Munich, January 1996

███████ There was no sense listening to the jabber from head-quarters, so Hermann Iversen drove the Opel sedan with the radio turned off. He knew where he was going. Better to concentrate on his driving. A cold rain had earlier given way to spitting sleet, but now that, too, had stopped. There was a thin sheen of ice on the pavement, making driving downright dangerous.

The streets were filled with affluent residents of Munich, all bundled up against the weather. They popped in and out of taxis, walking spraddle-legged on the icy sidewalks to keep from slipping; they were determined not to let the weather dissuade them from their Saturday night partying.

He drove down Muellerstrasse. His stomach rumbled. He hadn't eaten dinner, and he was hungry. His wife and daughter would have left something in the refrigerator he could heat up when he got home. Even when he called to say he was eating out, they always had at least a snack waiting for him. It was their female thing.

At Weinhartstrasse, Iversen turned right. Two blocks later, he turned left down a narrow sidestreet. He could see the squad cars waiting up ahead, two of them.

He parked the Opel behind the squad cars and got out, quickly adjusting the wool scarf around his neck. The cold wind cutting into his face. On the corner, behind frosted panes of a bar, he could hear the heavy *oompah-pah, oompah-pah, oompah-pah* of a baritone playing to a rolling beat of one-two-three, one-two-three, one-two-three, German drinking music at its best.

He buttoned his trench coat all the way to the top and pulled his dark blue stocking cap down over his ears. He stood, listening to the oompah-pahs for a moment, thinking what a world this was.

Down the sidewalk, a uniformed officer called his name.

Iversen pulled on the leather gloves his wife had given him for his birthday; then, tilting his head against the biting wind, he joined the uniformed officers. There were four of them, two from each squad car. Two kneeled by something on the sidewalk. The other two stood with their backs to the icy wind, breath coming in frosty puffs.

Iversen saw what was on the curb of the sidewalk between, a body, half on the sidewalk, half in the street. "*Sheisse,*" he said. He clenched his jaw.

One of the standing cops said, "You were quick, Lieutenant Iversen."

"Not far to drive," Iversen said.

"Have to be careful in this weather," the standing cop said.

Iversen, noting that a middle-aged woman waited in one of the squad cars, licked his lips and squatted with the two kneeling officers.

"Still warm," one of them said.

The second kneeling officer said. "She's still dry also. She got dumped after the sleet stopped."

The body, that of a young woman, a brunette with long hair, was naked. Before she was killed, somebody had painted her back and rump and the backs of her legs a ruddy orange, blending this into white on her stomach, chest, and the front of her legs. Over this base, he had carefully painted white trim and black stripes. The result was a human tiger. The paint was water soluble, acrylic probably, and the sleet was starting to mottle the tiger stripes.

Iversen's mouth turned dry. That could easily have been his daughter, Inga. She had long blonde hair like Inga's, and was about the size, five-feet-seven, maybe, and about the same age.

One of the standing cops, looking over Iversen's shoulder, said, "He pushed her out of the car and drove off. We've got a woman who caught a glimpse of his face." He nodded toward the woman who was waiting in the squad car. "Her name is Frau

Brant. She was just coming out of her flat to go to the greengrocers around the corner."

"Did he see her?"

"She doesn't think so, but she's not sure."

Iversen shifted his weight so he could get a look at the face of the tiger-girl. Her face was covered with paint, so it was hard to make out her features, yet there was something familiar about her. Iversen knew this girl. He was certain of it. He took his handkerchief out of his hip pocket and took a swipe of paint from her left cheek and down the side of her nose. Yes, he did know her! *"Sheisse!"* he said again, his eyes wide.

"You know her?" said the cop looking over his shoulder.

"Ja. I know her," Iversen said. He stood, looking grim. Down the street, he could hear the *oompah-pah, oompah-pah* from the bar. "You call the gut wagon?"

One of the cops who had been kneeling by the corpse stood, "It's on its way. Who is she?" he asked.

"I may have seen her at a family gathering once. I was a guest."

A family gathering? The cops all waited, curious, but didn't want to press him. If he wanted them to know who it was, he'd tell him.

Iversen said, "If it's who I think it is, I'm not sure you want to know." He dug a package of French Gaulois cigarettes from the pocket of his trench coat, and ripped open the top. His stomach gurgled. He was still hungry.

One of the cops on the sidewalk shifted positions so he could get a better look at the face of the corpse.

Hermann Iversen took out a cigarette and lit up. He said, "She's Bauer's niece."

The cop looked up, eyes wide. "Karl Bauer?"

Iversen inhaled. "His brother's daughter. Rolf, the orthopedic surgeon."

A half hour later, Hermann Iversen was standing in front of the downstairs entrance to the redbrick townhouse of the chief of detectives, Karl Bauer. The rain had begun again and lashed against

Iversen's trench coat. His stomach rumbled. He stubbed out his Gaulois and punched the yellow button of the intercom.

"*Ja?*" This was Anna Bauer, Karl's schoolteacher wife.

"It's me, Anna, Hermann Iversen."

"Karl said you'd called. We've been expecting you. Come right on up, Hermann."

The door buzzed as Anna unlocked it from upstairs, and Iversen made his way up the steep stairs.

One flight up, Iversen rapped on the inner door, and Anna opened it. He was engulfed in a sudden rush of warmth, and his glasses fogged.

Anna was in the middle of ironing and behind her, the Bauers' two teenage sons watched *bundeslige* football on television, Bayern Munich versus FC Hamburg.

As he wiped his foggy glasses with his handkerchief, Iversen answered the question in Anna's eyes by saying, "We've got a problem, I'm afraid, Anna."

"Karl's in his study, reading. Go right on in, Hermann."

Iversen said, "Who's ahead, Heinz?"

Heinz Bauer, the younger of the two boys, said, "Bayern Munich, one-nil. Stolz scored on a header. Gerhardt gave him a beautiful cross. It's a good match. How's Inga?"

Iversen managed a smile. 'Oh, she's fine. She's home struggling with her algebra." Heinz, he knew, admired his daughter Inga. Iversen didn't blame him. It might have been fatherly pride, but Iversen considered his daughter a real looker and a charmer as well. He said, "Inga's a football fan, too, Heinz. She's been nagging me to take her to see Bayern Munich. Would you like to go with us if we do?"

Heinz brightened. "Sure!"

Anna, grinning, said, "Would you like some coffee, Hermann? A cold night like this."

"Some coffee would be nice, Anna, thank you." Iversen went into the study. Karl Bauer was fascinated with detection and mysteries and his study was lined with shelves of books in both German and English on famous cases, serial murders in Atlanta, San Francisco, and Seattle, a famous rape case in London, an account of an Italian cop's efforts to fight the mob in Sicily, a book about the use of DNA as forensic evidence, name the book and Bauer had it.

Bauer, a rugged, balding, barrel-chested man, who had been sitting in an overstuffed chair reading *Der Stern,* put the magazine down. "What's up, Hermann?"

Hermann glanced back. "Anna's bringing us coffee. I think we should wait."

"Oh, sure. Have a seat, Hermann. You look cold."

"I'll thaw."

After Anna brought them their coffee, Iversen waited until she was gone, then cleared his throat. "A woman on her way out to shop found the body of a dead girl on a sidestreet off Muellerstrasse." He glanced at his watch. "That was a little over an hour ago now."

Bauer eyed Iversen over the rim of his coffee. This was no usual body or Iversen wouldn't have interrupted him at home. He said, "Go on, Hermann."

Iversen said, "Do you remember reading in the papers about a couple of odd murders, one in India and one in Indonesia, where the killer painted his victims like tigers before he murdered them?"

Bauer took a sip of coffee. "We have one of those on our hands, do we? A tiger murder? Here in Munich?" He looked puzzled.

Iversen nodded.

"But that's not all, is it? Or you wouldn't have come here straightaway."

Iversen cleared his throat. "No, I'm sorry to say it's not."

"Give me the rest then."

"You mind if I smoke, Karl?"

"No, no, go ahead, by all means. This isn't America quite yet, thank God."

Iversen retrieved a Gaulois and lit up. Exhaling, he said, "I knew the girl, Karl. I recognized her immediately, even with her face painted like a tiger. She was beautiful." Iversen swallowed.

"Who, Hermann?"

Iversen licked his lips. "I met her at a family gathering. At a Christmas party."

Bauer leaned forward. He cocked his head, the gesture asking, where? What Christmas party?

Iversen said, "Here, in this house."

"Tell me."

"It was Erika, Karl. Rolf's daughter."

Bauer blinked and said "No."

Iversen sighed.

Bauer paled. "Erika. You're sure of that."

"I'm sure."

Bauer's jaw fell slack. He was stunned.

"Her body was still warm. Also dry. The killer dumped her from his car and drove off. She was found by a resident on her way back from buying groceries. We do have one witness; a Frau Brant was on her way to the store when he threw the body out. She had a brief glimpse of his face. She's uncertain whether or not he saw her, but she thinks probably not."

"If he had, he'd probably have taken care of her right then and there, wouldn't he?"

"One would think so."

Bauer, shaken, stood and hobbled to a glass liquor cabinet, where he retrieved a bottle of schnapps. Then he limped to the door and opened it. "Anna, could you or one of the boys bring us some ice, please."

Iversen, watching him, said, "Flaring up again."

"It's this weather."

"Ahh."

"They've got me pumped up with steroids. I pop aspirin like candy. Nothing seems to work. It's like I've got sand in my joints."

They waited in silence until Heinz delivered them squat amber-colored glasses and a small tin bucket of cocktail ice. Then Bauer scooped up two glasses of ice, poured them each a long shot of schnapps.

Bauer took a pull on his glass, looking thoughtful. "I've dealt with murder all my adult life, Hermann. I wanted to be a homicide detective, and I made it. I was a good one, I think. Or at least, I did my best. How many times have I had to tell the parents that their son or daughter had been murdered by some asshole? How many times?"

Iversen shrugged. "Scores, at least. Maybe hundreds over the years."

"Many of those times you were with me, standing at my side."

Iversen clenched his jaw. "Terrible duty."

"We become calloused, Hermann. We never expect something like this to happen to us. To other people, maybe, but not to us. Not to my niece."

Iversen swallowed.

Bauer said, "Now I have to tell my own brother that his beautiful Erika is dead, murdered by some creep."

"I'm terribly sorry, Karl. What can I say?"

"There are times when we do what we have to do in the pursuit of justice, and we let nothing, but nothing stand in our way. It's what separates us from beasts."

Iversen, reflective, took a heavy hit of Gaulois.

"Raped, do you suppose?"

"I'd make book on it," Iversen said.

"That'll give us a DNA print, at least. And we've got a witness."

Iversen said, "Good for starters. If we can match a face with the DNA test."

Bauer poured them more schnapps. He tested one ankle and winced.

Iversen, watching Bauer's pain, said, "Your brains are up here, not in your ankles." Iversen tapped himself on the temple with a forefinger. "It's up here that counts, Karl. You've more than proven that."

Bauer clenched his jaw. "If she had been the daughter of a shopkeeper or government clerk, there's not much her family could do, except trust in us to do our job. But this is different, this is Rolf's daughter. My niece. Kill a cop, kill a cop's niece, same consequences."

"It could have been my daughter." Iversen lit another Gaulois and inhaled. "Erika was indeed beautiful, Karl. I remember thinking at the Christmas party, if I had been a young man and single, I'd have chased her to the ends of the earth."

"I want you to chase her killer to the ends of the earth."

Iversen nodded. "When I saw that body, I was thinking it could have been Inga. There was something familiar about her face, but I didn't recognize her because of the paint. Then I wiped some away from her eye and nose with my handkerchief, and I was stunned. Erika. Your brother Rolf's daughter. I could hardly believe it."

"If I could travel, I'd run him down myself, but I can't, so you'll have to do it for me."

Iversen took a quick hit on his Gaulois.

Bauer said, "With you, I've got the best detective in Germany on the job. You're like a determined hound, when you put your mind to it. Did I ever tell you that, Hermann?"

Iversen smiled grimly. "You have a lot of good detectives, Karl."

"No, no, Hermann. You're the best. I know that from being your partner all those years."

"Twelve years," Iversen said.

"That dead girl was my niece. If you were me, you'd feel the same way. I'm the chief of detectives. What am I going to tell my brother? Sorry, Rolf, but because of my ankles there's nothing I can do but sit and curse fate. I want to be able to tell him that I put the best detective in Germany on this man's ass, and he will not stop, never, ever, until he runs this pervert down. There will be justice, I swear it."

Iversen bit his lower lip. Then, he said, "We start tonight, while the scent is fresh."

Bauer said, "No sense putting it off."

"I agree."

Bauer said, "We begin the drill then."

"*Ja*," Iversen said.

"First, we have a girl in India."

"Dark skin turned into the tiger stripes," Iversen said.

"Where was that, do you know?"

"According to our computers, she was murdered in Bhagalpur; that's northeast of Calcutta and south of Nepal."

"Tiger country?"

"I'd bet on it."

"Then an Indonesian girl."

Iversen said, "Murdered in Padang, on the southwest coast of Sumatra, the northern most island in Indonesia."

"Also tiger country?"

"*Ja.* Has to be."

"From which we conclude what?"

Iversen said, "That the killer is a sexual psychopath with a thing about tigers. He travels." Iversen took another draw on the Gaulois.

"Why Munich?"

Iversen shrugged.

"A copycat? Different killer?"

"Could be," Iversen said.

Bauer stood, wincing, to scoop more ice from the bucket.

Iversen popped to his feet. "Here, I'll get it. Sit. Rest your joints."

Bauer, scowling, motioned for him to sit. "I'm not totally incapacitated yet. I can still make it to the office and back, and I can go have a cold beer if I want." He hobbled back to his desk. "It makes me furious that I can't do this myself."

"You don't have to be on the streets to be a good cop. Everybody knows that. It's good to have somebody in charge who knows what he's doing. You've been with us on the streets. We all appreciate that."

"I want to get this bastard," Bauer said.

"No more than me, Karl," Iversen said. "And I assure you, my wife and daughter will feel the same way."

"I think Heinz may have a thing for Inga, by the way. Have you noticed that?"

Iversen grinned.

Bauer said, "I want this killer for Rolf and for Erika. She'd turn in her grave if she thought her uncle Karl let her down on this one. I won't do it. I won't let her down."

Iversen took a sip of coffee. "I'll get him."

Bauer said, "Swear to it, Hermann."

"You know I won't quit, Karl. I'll get him, I swear it." Iversen thought for a moment. "But what if he's skipped the country, back in Asia somewhere? What do we do then?"

Bauer said, "First, you cover the territory here. If you get something solid to go on, there are plenty of ways to get you the money to travel."

Iversen said, "Everybody in the department will pitch in, Karl. You're one of us, and your niece was killed."

"Listen, Hermann, my brother Rolf is a bone surgeon. He owns one of the most successful medical clinics in Munich. He's got enough money to buy half of Bavaria. If it means getting justice for Erika, believe me, he'll hand you a signed check and let you fill in the numbers. Money's no problem, we'll come up with it. I'll see to it that you're given a leave of absence; nobody will argue with me. One thing we won't do is leave justice up to some crooked or lazy cop in the Third World somewhere."

Iversen said, "Interpol will help spread the word, so if the killer strikes again, the local cops will send me the details." He thought a moment, then said, "You know, Karl, I didn't have any supper tonight. Would you like to go with me to a bar somewhere? I feel like some bratwurst and maybe some fried potatoes with onions."

"And a couple of beers," Bauer said.

"Doesn't that sound good? I'll drive."

"There's a place just down the street," Bauer said. "My ankles aren't so bad that I can't have a couple of beers on a night like this." He stood and hobbled to the door, where his trench coat rested on a hook.

Anna Bauer looked concerned when her husband limped through the living room with his good friend and former partner. By the expressions on their faces, she knew something terrible had happened. She had been married to Karl Bauer for twenty-four years, and she knew that her husband would tell her about it when he was ready. But she knew from the anguished look on his face that this time, the tragedy was truly extraordinary. Even her two sons could see it. She could see that Heinz wanted to ask Hermann more about Inga, but Heinz knew that this was not the time for it. Frau Bauer was proud that her son was sensitive and considerate.

6

James Burlane's last trip to the Siberian city of Khabarovsk was ten years earlier, when it was still being run by Stalinist bureaucrats who had replaced the Bolshevik bureaucrats who had replaced the czar's bureaucrats.

Then the muddy rail station had looked and smelled like a cattle yard. It still did.

Then the ten-block-long Karl Marx Street, running from Lenin Square to a park overlooking the Amur River, had featured enormous, bright red paintings of Lenin on the sides of buildings. The portraits of the secular messiah were no more.

Then people had kept their distance, wary that a hint of friendliness might be interpreted by some horsebleep comrade as being traitorous to the wonderful Soviet cause. Now, they were friendly enough, as Burlane suspected they had been all along. So much foolishness and outright barbarity in the world had been committed in the name of high-minded abstractions, both religious and secular, that Burlane sometimes felt like puking at the thought.

Another difference in Khabarovsk now was that the camera-toting Japanese had arrived in their touristy packs, led by a guide fluttering the rising sun like a battle standard. In the last ten years, the Japanese, staggering under the weight of overstuffed wallets and on the make for good deals, seemed to have preceded Burlane everywhere. The Bushido businessmen had snarfed up the resort hotels along Waikiki, capturing with a surfeit of yen what they had failed to gain with their waves of Zeros in 1941. Aussie soldiers had stopped them in New Guinea, but they now owned the prime fishing and beach resorts in Queensland, on the northeast coast of Australia. They had scored the good beaches at Phuket in Thailand. Burlane had been pleased when the necktied Samurai had fallen on hard times in the early 1990s and had to sell off much of their captured territory at sixty cents on the dollar.

Now the determined Japanese were in Khabarovsk—in number. Burlane hoped the Russians had learned enough about the ways of capitalism to give the Japanese invaders a thorough screwing. The Bolshevik notion of an egalitarian society had always been a crock of manure, but Burlane had no doubt that the Russians were quick learners when given a chance.

Burlane did not believe he was being churlish in siding with the Russians; after all, what was the joy of Japanese triumph if there were no losses along the way? Did the Japanese not have a cultural fixation, dating from the days of the samurai, on the nobility of suffering? Their movies were filled with beads of sweat, tight lips, clenched jaws, and grinding teeth.

Before there had been no place in Khabarovsk to eat except the restaurant in the Intourist Hotel; now there was a scattering of small cafés, including the Sapporo Restaurant. Burlane had some time to kill before he talked to the Russian wildlife official Alexei Karpov at his office next to the post office on Frunze Street, about halfway between Lenin Square and the Amur River. So Burlane took a walk to the end of Karl Marx Street and then down the long flight of stairs to the beach. This was a river beach, not a proper ocean beach with sand, but narrow, rocky, and dirty. After a walk on the beach, he trudged back up the stairs for a stroll in the narrow park that flanked the river.

Burlane had grown up on the banks of the Columbia River, and, as a boy, he had thought there must be few rivers as large and grand as the Columbia. Now, looking across the vast expanse of the great continental Amur River, just below its confluence with the Ussuri, he had to grin at his youthful innocence. Here was a real river. It wasn't like the mouth of the Amazon; Burlane had been to Belém, at the mouth of the Amazon, and there the yellow-brown river was so wide it was impossible to see the other side.

The Amur, a vast, heavy, solemn, grayish river, was so wide it was easy to mistake it for an ocean bay.

On his last visit, Burlane had had his picture taken at the butt end of a cannon in the park. He had sat with his hands around the barrel so that it looked like an enormous erection. The Russians in the park had been amused, but had kept their distance. Finally, one man, grinning, had accepted the challenge and volunteered to take Burlane's picture with Burlane's diminutive German camera.

This time, he knew, he would have no problem at all finding someone to take his picture.

In a telephone call from Vladivostok the previous day, Burlane had offered to take Alexei Karpov to lunch, but he didn't want to take him to the overpriced Harbin Restaurant, financed by Chinese, or the Sapporo Restaurant, backed by Burlane's ubiquitous friends from Nippon. Burlane himself tried always to avoid the showy or pretentious, even if he was spending other people's money.

After casing the possibilities, he decided on the moderately priced Kafe Sonja on the corner of Karl Marx Street and Derzhinskikogo Street. He chose the Kafe Sonja for the perverse reason that the street was named after the former KGB monster, Felix Derzhinski. Burlane did not understand the logic of allowing a street to retain the name of a torture artist.

If Burlane had chosen by street alone, he would have taken Karpov to one of the interesting-looking outdoor kiosks on Turgenev Street, next to the river. Burlane felt Ivan Turgenev was the most underrated of the great Russian novelists—an objective, perceptive observer of the manners and morals of his day, not a religious or political nutball as were many of his more famous lessers.

A few minutes before the appointed time, Burlane dropped by Karpov's spartan office for their lunch and talk. Karpov turned out to be a large bearlike man with strawberry blond hair and an outsize mustache wearing blue jeans and a green-and-black checkered wool shirt. On seeing Burlane, he stood up behind his desk, which was a jumble and clutter of papers. A cluttered desk was a sign of character in Burlane's opinion. He extended his hand. "Alexei Karpov?"

In a deep, resonant voice, he said, "Major Khartoum, I bet."

"Me in the pink," Burlane said. Burlane glanced at his watch. "I say we talk on our way to eat. We'll knock back a few vodkas and talk a little tiger."

"Sounds fine by me. I'll just knock off for the afternoon, and we'll make a day of it."

"I'm relieved that you speak such good English."

"Thank you. English is essential these days if you have anything to do with international business. By the way, here in Khabarovsk we call it the Amur tiger, after the Amur River. Farther south and in Vladivostok, they call it the Ussuri tiger, after the Ussuri River. You've probably heard it called the Siberian tiger. They're all the same cat."

Burlane said, "I'll call it the Siberian tiger, so as not to offend local pride."

Karpov smiled. "It's about time CITES did something besides hold meetings. How did they come to hire you? Another committee, I bet. They have to come up with some reason to have a vacation in a fancy hotel."

"A committee headed by their chief tiger man in Asia."

"Heinz Tepe," Karpov said.

"You know him then?"

"Oh yes, I know him. He's a zoologist and former academic who has for years been a consultant on Asian animals for CITES. He has been here many times monitoring our studies. If I'm not mistaken, it was his research that persuaded the Americans to finally do something about the Taiwanese. Heinz knows his tigers, believe me."

Burlane said, "He lives in the Philippines on Mactan island."

Karpov looked puzzled. "I've often wondered about that address. Is that island near Manila?"

Burlane shook his head. "Just off Cebu in the central Philippines."

Karpov glanced at his watch. "I say we go eat. You pick a spot?"

"The Kafe Sonja."

"Good choice. We can relax there. They have good pork cutlets and a first-rate *ukha*." Karpov grabbed his coat from a hook on the wall.

"Which is?" Burlane said.

"A kind of fish soup."

"Sounds good. As long as the vodka's cold and there's no law against admiring pretty women."

Karpov laughed. "In Russia? Please, please, Major Khartoum, my friend. We're in Russia here, not America. We've learned our lesson about legislating the impossible."

James Burlane and Alexei Karpov left the government office building for the two-block walk down Karl Marx Street. As they walked, Karpov said, "Speaking of Heinz Tepe, have you met his wife?"

"His wife?"

Karpov, groaning, rolling his eyes, grabbed for his crotch. "Oh yes, the lovely Lily, a Chinese-Filipina."

"Mrs. Tepe is an extraordinary lady, I take it?"

"*Extraordinary* is hardly the word for it. She came with him on one of his trips here. She's tall for a Chinese and with a face and figure. Oh!" Karpov bunched his lips and shook his head. "She could be an actress if she wanted. How Herr Doktor Tepe wound up with her is anybody's guess. Are you going to see him on this trip?"

"After I do a preliminary survey of the problem here and in Hong Kong and India."

"Then you'll meet the fabulous Lily." Karpov groaned again.

"I assume so," Burlane said.

Karpov slowed his hulking stride to avoid crashing into a pack of Japanese tourists. "It's about time CITES and the rest of them did something like this. Talk, talk, talk. The Chinese and Koreans aren't paying any attention. Everybody knows that. Direct action is the only way. I wish you luck, I truly do, but to be honest, I don't think you stand much of a chance of accomplishing anything."

"It's a worthwhile cause, in my opinion. I'll do my damnedest, guaranteed," Burlane said.

They soon settled into a table at the Kafe Sonja. In Burlane's earlier travels the only places worth eating in had been the hotels, where the Soviets hustled hard currency from foreign travelers. There was an occasional snack bar here and there, but nothing else. The Kafe Sonja was rough stuff by American or Western European standards, but there were tablecloths on the tables and curtains on the windows. And, wonder of wonders, when they sat down, a waiter, looking polite, showed up to take their order.

Burlane deferred to Karpov, who ordered their food, a fish soup, pork chops with boiled potatoes, and a bottle of vodka.

Karpov said, "You know, Major Khartoum, it truly is foolish to try to stop the traffic at this end of the trade. You Americans know about markets, and how they work. Eliminate the market for tigers, and you eliminate tiger poachers. It's no use for people to come here complaining to us. We hardly have money enough to eat, much less buy vehicles and gas for game wardens. The British gave us some money, that's true, but it's not enough."

Burlane pulled a small notebook from his hip pocket and glanced at his notes. "Through the Tiger Trust."

"Correct. I hate to sound like a beggar, always having to whine for more money, but we're reduced to that if we are to have any chance at all. Look, Major Khartoum, this is a huge country; the Amur tiger now has a range of about eight hundred miles of evergreen forest. That's roughly the same as from San Francisco to Seattle or from Atlanta to New York."

"A lot of territory to keep an eye on." Behind Karpov, two slender, beautiful women entered the Kafe Sonja and took a seat.

Karpov said, "We figure about ninety tigers were poached last year, and it's still going on."

"How many do you have left? Do you know that?" Burlane asked.

Karpov pursed his lips. "Hard to tell. Some say as few as two or three hundred. Others say as many as four hundred. I don't think anybody knows for sure. But we're told that once the population dips below a hundred-twenty or so, the Amur tiger is doomed."

"How long do they have?" Burlane, watching the two human beauties, found it hard to concentrate on tigers.

"A few years if we're lucky. It may already be too late."

They waited while the waiter delivered a bottle of cold vodka. Karpov poured.

Burlane raised his glass. "Here's to the beautiful tiger. May they still be with us in five years."

"I'll certainly drink to that," Karpov said.

One of the women was dark; the other was redheaded. Watching them, Burlane said, "Why are the poachers picking on the Amur tiger?"

"The Amur tiger is the largest tiger in the family. The way the Chinese and Koreans see it, big tiger, big hard-on, long loving. Biggest tiger, biggest hard-on, longest loving of all."

"Shit!"

Karpov said, "The value of the tiger is apparently in inverse relationship to the size of the brain of the man who thinks it's going to give him better sex. The stupidest value the Amur tiger the most because it's the biggest, and the white Amur tiger even more because it's the rarest. Undersize brain is the only explanation that makes sense. Can you think of a better one?"

"None that would be acceptable in diplomatic circles, I suppose."

The waiter arrived with their fish soup, served in wide, heavy, shallow white bowls, and accompanied by chunks of whole wheat bread. Burlane saw chunks of cabbage and onions in the soup. The aroma was grand. He took a sip, then tried the bread.

Karpov, watching him, said, "Well?"

"Fit for a czar, I would think. Delicious. Americans don't appreciate a good soup because they've been raised to believe soup is something that comes out of a red-and-white can." Two more beauties entered the café, both blonde. This time, they had to pass Karpov to take a seat.

Watching them pass, an appreciative Karpov said, "I'm afraid most food in Russia is pretty wretched by your standards. It's hard to develop a tradition of good food when you don't have anything to cook. But if you have fresh fish and a little imagination, it's still possible to make a good soup." Karpov took a sample. "It is good. We suspect our wonderful neighbors to the south have been doing most of the poaching of the Amur tiger. We're right next door."

"Next door to the Korean peninsula," Burlane said.

"Correct. Look at the map. We share a common border with North Korea just southwest of Vladivostok. And a small boat can meet South Korean fishing vessels in international waters in the Sea of Japan. But the South Koreans are apparently the biggest buyers for the Amur tiger. They're the ones with the money."

Burlane said, "Like raiding your neighbor's chicken coop, eh? Just nip over, grab yourself a fryer, and hightail it back."

"That's right. China is next door to the Indo-Chinese peninsula and to India. South Korea openly imported tigers until July 1993, and so we have Korean customs statistics to show us the volume of the trade. When the people you're working for began complaining about the slaughter, the Koreans began stockpiling bones. Between 1988 and 1992, they imported between fifty-two and ninety-six dead tigers a year—with the number rising each year."

"I take it those are Korean figures, not yours?" Burlane concentrated on Karpov, trying not to stare at the women. There were now four of them. All young. All with long hair. They all were small boned, with exquisite carriage and finely chiseled good looks.

"Correct," Karpov said. "Finally, to appease the West, they announced the official end to the trade and stopped counting the bags of tiger bones crossing their borders."

"They were fearful of trade sanctions." One of the blondes was flirting with him, tormenting him.

"Of course. Just like the Taiwanese and the Chinese. But the real market is in China. One hesitates to guess how many poached tigers they imported."

Burlane said, "But the trade in tiger bones continues in all three countries." A troupe of four more young women entered the café, pausing to chat with the others as they made their way to an empty table. The Kafe Sojna was now packed with slender beauties.

"They're not about to give up their precious tiger-bone wine. Whatever would happen to their sex life?"

"They could buy cultivated ginseng from the United States and Canada."

Karpov, looking amused, said, "Speaking of sex and sex lives, I bet you're wondering about all these women."

Burlane said, "Well, yes, I am. I know we were talking about girl-watching back at the office, but this is truly extraordinary."

Karpov said, "They are ballerinas. There is a dance company from Novosibirsk in town for a performance. Aren't they grand?"

"They sure as hell are."

Karpov, watching the table of the newest four, sighed and said, "All the herbalists need to do is fool you gullible North Americans and Europeans. As you no doubt know, Major Khartoum, a lie isn't dishonorable to a Korean or Chinese, it's merely a tactic that might work or might not. Despite all their earnest pronouncements, Earth Trust and other environmental organizations have been able to buy tiger-bone medicines in all three countries. And yes, I've read the report by TRAFFIC Network. Tiger bones are supposed to disperse 'cold wind' and expel 'wind dampness.' You want to tell me what that means?"

Burlane shrugged. He couldn't stop looking at the ballerinas. Even sitting down, laughing and talking and gesturing to one another with their elegant little hands and slender wrists, they were extraordinary. So delicate they were. So graceful. So grand!

"And it's supposed to strengthen the bones and muscles. Right. If you look at the specific medicines in that report, tiger bone is almost universally listed as an ingredient in concoctions intended to relieve arthritis pains or bolster virility. How many of those actually contain tiger bone is another question. But enough do that it's pushing the tiger out of business."

The waiter arrived with their pork cutlets, which had been breaded with flour and deep fried, and replenished their supply of bread.

Cutting his meat, Karpov said, "You Americans and Europeans really should take this up with the herbalists, Major Khartoum. Get them to knock off tiger remedies and you save the tiger. Value lies in the eyes of the beholder. I say again, no!—I implore you, I beg you, to tell your employers to please, please understand that where there is no market for tigers, tigers won't be poached."

"And the Chinese and Koreans don't like us telling them what to do." Burlane said, chewing. "Good cutlets. You Russians must be having a renaissance."

Karpov smiled. "Being polite or appealing to reason or common sense won't get you anywhere, but there you have it: The unadorned truth, however unpalatable. Traditional Chinese herbal medicine maintains that a person's bones hold the key to what's wrong with him. To eat a potion made of tiger bones is to become as a tiger. Pills made from tiger eyeballs are supposed to cure convulsions. If you hang the nose or claw of a tiger above your bed, you will have a male baby. Tiger penis soup will enhance your virility. Tiger whiskers will give you strengh."

"And the anus?"

Karpov grinned. "A tiger's anus. I'm not sure, but I bet they've got some screwball notion."

"What about the cock of a white tiger? What would that bring on the market?"

Karpov laughed. "The way their minds work, I hesitate to think! The Chinese have problems with your government using the issue of human rights to push them around. They don't recognize any universal ethic with regard to the treatment of human beings, much less any sort of sentimental concern for animals, which they regard as an absurd western affectation. I haven't told you the really scary part, Major Khartoum. Did you tell me that you're scheduled to talk to Andrei Bure in Vladivostok tomorrow?"

"Yes, I did," Burlane said.

Scarfing up the last of his cutlets, Karpov said, "Andrei is one of our most committed and determined game keepers, Major Khartoum. He loves the tigers, and he has this disheartening theory that . . . Well, let me say it's not just disheartening. If it's true. . . ." Karpov paused, then said, "But perhaps I'd better let Andrei tell you himself. What do you say we go for a walk down by the river? There are some places down there where we can have more vodka."

"And some of those little meat pies."

Karpov grinned. "Of course."

"Sold," Burlane said.

"You know, Major Khartoum, we Russians may have lost our empire, but we still have our chess players and our hockey players and ice skaters and gymnasts. And we still have our lovely ballerinas. The Amur tiger is the largest and most beautiful cat in the world. Only the fate of the tiger is out of our hands. To preserve the tiger we must have help."

7

■■■■■Hermann Iversen began his investigation of Erika Bauer's murder by taking the logical first step of presuming the killer had a fixation with tigers. He went to Kruger's International, a company in Munich that had for years leased lions and tigers to circuses and to the movies. During the winter, off-season for the circuses, Kruger's trained and took care of the big cats.

He interviewed the director of Kruger's. The firm had almost no employee turnover, and, except for short holidays in Spain and Portugal, none had traveled abroad in recent years.

But the director suggested that Iversen talk to the owner of the now defunct Hesse's, a supplier of animals to zoos, which, despite its less suggestive name, was more far more international than his company. In its heyday, he said, Hesse's had had offices around the world, and was for years the company that had supplied Kruger's with the lions and tigers they trained for circuses and housed in the off-season.

Before going to Hesse's, Iversen ran a corporate backgrounder on the firm and learned that the company was named for its financial angel, Teo Hesse, a contractor who had made his fortune rebuilding Germany after the war. On the urging of his son-in-law, Orel Steinbach, a keeper of the Munich Zoo who had served as an enlisted tank driver in North Africa, Hesse used part of these profits to found an animal importing and exporting firm. The company, founded in 1950, had done quite well for thirty years, until the public attitude toward wild animals and the wilderness had changed dramatically.

Steinbach, now in his late sixties and with his father-in-law long dead, had liquidated his company's assets in 1991. He now lived in comfortable retirement, occupying his time tinkering with miniature steam engines and amusing Rube Goldberg mechanical contraptions that he made in a metal-working shop on the ground level of his brick townhouse.

Steinbach's plump wife, Anna, answered the door and ushered Hermann Iversen into the shop, which was filled with drills and presses and welding equipment. There her husband, his brows furrowed in concentration, was working on a small metal lathe, peeling bright curls of metal from a tiny shaft.

Seeing Iversen, Steinbach flipped a toggle switch, shutting off the lathe. An amiable-appearing white-haired man with a broad, intelligent face, he listened with interest as Iversen introduced himself, cocking his head and compressing his lips with concern as Iversen explained the nature of his investigation. Murder was a serious business, and under such circumstances, Orel Steinbach was a serious man.

When Iversen was finished, Herr Steinbach removed his gloves and sighed. "Such a world with perverts like that running around. How did you say you got my name?"

"I talked to the people at Kruger's."

"Of course. One of my best customers. Would you like a cup of coffee? I just made a fresh pot."

"Certainly," Iversen said.

Steinbach's wife headed upstairs, leaving them alone to talk.

"We can go upstairs also if you like. I've got proper furniture up there. All I have are stools down here."

"No, no," Iversen said quickly, taking a seat on a stool. "I like your workshop. The machines are fascinating. I'm a little bit afraid of power tools, to tell the truth, but I'm fascinated by them. It's difficult to know where to start with my questions."

"A young woman was murdered. If I can help, believe me I'm in no hurry." Steinbach poured them each a cup of coffee, and waited for Iversen to help himself to the cream and sugar.

Taking a sip of coffee, Iversen took a deep breath and let it out slowly. "Let's see, your main office was here in Munich, as I understand it."

Steinbach said, "The office here was mostly an administrative function, dealing with zoos and customers like Kruger's. We had a series of regional offices around the world through which we acquired the animals and arranged for their shipment to zoos."

"You had your offices where around the world?"

"A better question would be where didn't we have one?" Steinbach grinned. "The better zoos like to have the most dramatic and unusual animals from all continents. We had an office in Singapore to buy and ship animals from southeast Asia, but our Singapore representative found the government there so overbearing and the city so boring as to be mind-numbing, so he moved the office to Jakarta. Everybody knows the Javanese are consummate swine, but at least one can have a good time there and get laid once in a while."

"And the animals you got there?"

"The most popular were Komodo dragons, Asian crocodiles, and orangutans from Borneo. There are still animals left on Borneo and New Guinea, and even Indonesia, surprisingly enough. The Indonesians have managed to save most of their rain forests."

Iversen looked surprised. "Really? How did they do that?"

"They shoot people who cut down trees."

Iversen laughed. "I see."

"We had a representative in Sydney for kangaroos and wallabys, and koala bears and whatnot. Our Central American office was in San José, Costa Rica. The market there was mostly for exotic birds. Our North American office was in Toronto, Canada, but the most sought-after assignment was Rio de Janeiro."

"Oh?"

"Not because of anteaters, peccaries, or macaws, I can assure you, Herr Iversen. Because of the women's string bikinis. Some of those things were hardly wider than dental floss." Steinbach gave Iversen a lopsided grin.

"How about Africa?"

"Ahh. Africa. Of course. Mombasa, on the coast of Kenya, was the second-largest office outside our headquarters in Berlin. The Africans have elephants, of course, and lions and cheetahs, giraffes, zebras, rhinos, hippos. All big animals, and expensive to ship. Nairobi might have made more sense as a headquarters because it was centrally located and has an airport, but everybody wanted to live in Mombasa because that's where the beaches are. The stretch of coastline north and south of Mombasa has some of the best beaches in the world. Beautiful, white sand beaches. The seaweed can be a pain though, I have to admit."

"Mombasa for the beaches. Why not? What happened? I mean what caused you to sell out?"

"How do I begin?" Steinbach shook his head. "It was a long time coming, actually. My father-in-law started the firm in 1950. In those days zoos were pretty much jails for animals where you took your kids to stare at the monkeys and lions. This lasted through the 1960s, but by the 1970s, things began to change. More and more, zookeepers were learning how to breed animals in captivity."

Iversen said, "The public liked to see baby animals."

"Sure. If a male upland gorilla in Honolulu showed a willingness to copulate in capitivity, the Honolulu Zoo might loan him to Seattle. The same with elephants and giraffes and other large animals that were expensive to capture and ship."

"Fewer and fewer of the animals were coming from the wild," Iversen said.

"Unfortunately for us. That was the heart of our business. And when researchers in human reproduction began to make advances in artificial insemination in the 1980s, our stock really plummeted. The new ability to impregnate females with sperm from other zoos coincided with the rise of environmentalism in the First World countries. The zoos there were our best customers. The new emphasis was on saving endangered species by breeding them in zoos, which helped zookeepers when they asked their governments for more money. They had a new reason for being."

"Zoos as jails for animals were out."

"That's right. Now they were 'habitats' or 'environments' or some other euphemism. Then the worldwide recession hit, and zoos everywhere cut back, waiting for times to get better."

"And so eventually you sold out."

"In 1991. Now, if a zoo wants a pair of animals to begin their own breeding stock, it will send a specialist to the country of origin to negotiate with local game officials."

"You were considered old-fashioned and crass, and were eventually pushed out of the loop."

"Right. Incidentally, the snag in preserving species by breeding them in zoos is that they can't learn survival skills in captivity. When a zookeeper in Paris flops fresh meat in front of a baby tiger every morning, how is it supposed to learn to hunt game in the wild? A species that survives only in zoos is really a species that's out of business, isn't it?"

"More tigers in cages, but fewer tigers in the wild."

"That's about it. And you want to know something else, Herr Iversen? As I got older, I slowly began to lose my enthusiasm for zoos. I like animals, and it's true, what the critics say, zoos really are prisons. Some of them are perfectly abominable. Animals get neurotic when they're penned up like that, and you see monkeys so bored with nothing to do that they masturbate all day. I got so I just hated the idea of sending an animal to someplace where I knew it would be stuck behind glass or bars with absolutely no privacy. To be honest, I was ready to quit anyway."

Iversen said, "When I was a kid I could squash a beetle without a second thought. Not anymore. I think probably the older one gets, and the more one is forced to confront the facts of mortality, the more one values life in general."

Steinbach sighed. "I agree with that, Herr Iversen. But not all zoos are outrageous, mind you. The people who run a first-class operation like the one in San Diego take pride in giving their animals space and privacy, and as natural an environment as possible. But that's an expensive proposition, and most urban zoos just don't have the space or resources. There are zoos in the Third World that are just pathetic. The zookeepers can't afford to feed themselves, much less their animals."

"Where was your largest overseas office?"

"Mombasa, which was the main port of entry for the exotics in East Africa: gorillas, chimpanzees, name it. At our highest, I think we had six buyers in Mombasa. Some had contacts in Kenya or Uganda. Others knew people in Tanzania, Zambia, or Zimbabwe. Wherever there was game, our buyers had established relationships with local governments and wildlife officials. Some had an interest in a particular kind of animal."

"You must have shipped lions and cheetahs and leopards."

"We did."

"Did you have a specialist in cats, a cat man?"

"Yes, we did as a matter of fact. That would be Klaus Neumann. He had a way with cats. He wasn't restricted to cats only, but when somebody wanted a big cat or a rare cat, it was usually Klaus who made the arrangements. He knew how to capture them and how to take care of them en route to the zoo. He bought lions, tigers, pumas, jaguars, leopards, and cheetahs. If somebody wanted a jaguarundi, he'd take the job, but he left the bobcats and lynxes to others."

"A jaguarundi being?"

"A small reddish brown or reddish gray New World cat that looks like an otter and likes to swim. They're about a yard long or a little more and weigh ten to twenty pounds or thereabouts."

"Did Neumann show a particular interest in any one of the big cats?"

Steinbach grinned. "Klaus? Oh, tigers, clearly. He was a tiger man. He thought lions were overrated by the public, the king of beasts and all that. Lions operate in packs called prides, but tigers are loners, and Klaus admired that."

"You say he knew how to capture big cats. Did he do that himself?"

"Sometimes he helped, but mostly he taught our local contacts how to do it. That was part of his job, to build and train a permanent network of locals who knew how to capture the animals for which we had a market. In his case that was big cats."

"I see. Did you sell tigers?"

"Oh yes, of course. What's a zoo without a tiger?"

"Where was he based?"

"Officially in Mombasa, where we moved lions, snow leopards, and cheetahs, but he spent a lot of the time in India and the

Indochinese Peninsula and Sumatra because of the tigers and leopards there. It was a quick flight across the Indian Ocean to the Indian subcontinent. He occasionally went to Siberia if a zoo had the money for a Siberian tiger. They're the biggest and so the most expensive. He also bought big cats from South America."

Iversen made a note. "And the cats there?"

"Pumas and jaguars."

"I see. What can you tell me about Neumann? You know, his personal life, that sort of thing."

Steinbach said, "Klaus never married, as far as I know. He preferred Mombasa to Europe, but I suppose there's nothing unusual about that. He came here only to visit company headquarters once in a while. His mother lived here until she died recently, but I don't think he got along with her."

"She died how recently?"

"Three weeks ago, something like that."

"And his father?"

"He never mentioned his father. No wait, he once did, when I was visiting Kenya, and we were all drunk at a company party in a Nairobi restaurant. A tiger took a swipe through his throat in a performance in Hamburg. He was with Captain Prince–Cox's International Circus, which was big in Europe back then. We all knew what happened to his father, but Klaus never referred to it except that one time, when he was drunk. Klaus was a teenager when it happened."

"A tiger took a swipe at his throat?"

Steinbach said, "Severed a pumper, and Lothar bled to death with a tentful of horrified people looking on. Kruger's was where Lothar got his start, and was the outfit that had supplied the tiger that killed him. So when his son asked for a job, Kruger's hired him."

"I see."

"He helped take care of lions and tigers here in Munich in the winter, and worked as assistant to trainers during the off-season. But he wanted to travel, he said, and came to us for a job. He was just a kid then, but he had experience with the big cats, so we hired him. He was always a hard worker and earned his keep, I'll give him that. He was an interesting guy, actually. He liked to drink and tell stories with the rest of us."

"Did he have any brothers and sisters?"

"Not that he ever mentioned." Steinbach furrowed his brows, trying. "In fact, Herr Iversen, I think Klaus once mentioned that he was an only child."

"Raised by his mother after his father's death?"

"I think so."

"How old would he be now?"

"Klaus? Oh, I don't know. I should think he'd be in his fifties. He was a vigorous man who always looked younger than his actual age."

"So his father would have been killed when? In the late 1950s?"

"That sounds right. Something like that."

"What happened to him after your company went under?"

"That's a good question. I've kept in touch with most of my old employees. Some stayed put. They had married local women and liked the expat life. Some had bought property and had children in local schools. Some of them returned to Europe and got jobs in zoos or wildlife foundations of one sort or another. But Klaus just disappeared. I have no idea where he went or what he's doing. But if I were to bet money on it, I'd say it would be something to do with big cats. He seemed almost obsessed with them. That was clear from the day he asked for a job. Tigers especially. There was almost nothing he didn't know about tigers."

"What does he look like?"

Steinbach furrowed his brows. "I only saw him now and then when he was here or when I visited Nairobi. He was a big, rugged type. Brown hair."

Iversen grinned. It was a lousy description. "I don't suppose you have a photograph of him, or know where I could get one?"

"No, I don't. The only thing I can suggest is that you go to his childhood neighborhood in Munich. That's what I told the other guy."

"What other guy?"

Steinbach said, "Oh, I don't know. I can't remember his name.

He said he was an old friend of Klaus's and was trying to run him down."

"When was that?"

"Oh, I don't know. A week or so ago."

"How old was he, and what did he look like?"

Steinbach shrugged. "Middle-aged, I guess. In his forties. He had blond hair. I can't remember anything unusual about his looks. He said he was from Berlin."

"If I should go to Mombasa looking for Herr Neumann, whom should I talk to?"

"There's an engineer there, I've met a few times. He's been there for years. His name is Reiner Weithoff. He lives in a place called Mamba Village just north of town. You get off the bus and it's the second house on the right. You can't miss it. That's a good idea! If anybody knows how to find Klaus, Reiner will."

8

In James Burlane's earlier trips to Siberia, collecting information for the Company, the city of Vladivostok had been closed to foreigners; it was the chief Pacific base of the Russian navy. So Burlane had been forced to go through the nearby port of Nakhodka, which was used by Russian fishing trawlers, to conduct business with the comrades of the old regime. Even at Nakhodka, foreigners—always suspected of spying for the odious capitalists—had been hustled from the quay to the train station. There, observed by curious, broad-faced peasants, they were quickly dispatched north on the train, which circled Vladivostok at a safe distance.

It was on the train that Burlane had conducted his dangerous business of communicating with Company recruits inside the Soviet bureaucracy.

Now Burlane was able to stay in the bustling city of Vladivostok, which the Russians liked to compare to San Francisco. Indeed, it was a city of hills with beautiful vistas of the bay where the Russian naval vessels, now lacking the funds to train, were anchored, their hulls being slowly eaten away by the salt air. The Russians apparently loved comparing their cities to western metropolises. Novosibirsk was said to be the Chicago of Siberia. Uh-huh. Khabarovsk, it was held, was Siberia's Paris. Right.

Burlane had been to San Francisco many times, and he knew that any San Franciscan, upon hearing Vladivostok compared to their beautiful city, would burst out laughing. For here, as in

Nakhodka, all was rust and decay, except that now—with the power-loving comrades stuffed in history's trash can—the hustlers and crooks and creeps had taken over, managing the city's booming black market. The Russians were still poor, but at least now they could bitch about it without being thrown into labor camps.

The Vladivostok Hotel, likely dating from the late nineteenth century, was a large stone building, somber and gray on the outside, and cozy on the inside even if the elaborate green carpet was nearly threadbare. The restaurant overlooked Peter the Great Bay. While Burlane waited for his walk along the harbor with the game warden Andrei Bure, he drank vodka and had a snack of blinis, which were small pancakes or crepes filled with jam. The food in Russia was awful because a cook without ingredients was like an artist with no brush, a writer without paper. But the blinis, Burlane had to admit, were truly delicious. He didn't know if the Russians ate them with vodka, but he didn't care.

Burlane was amused at all the doom-and-gloom stories about Russia's dire straits. The truth was that the residents were far better off than they had been under the horses's ass comrades, anybody with half a brain could see that. The comrades had routinely exaggerated their successes for the benefit of the western press—these achievements being dutifully passed on to a gullible western public as the truth. Even the Company, motivated by the desire for larger budget, had gone along with the transparent ruse. To the Soviets, bigger was somehow better; a joke in the days of the comrades had been that the Soviets made the biggest microchips in the world.

Now that the Russian politicians wanted money from the western treasuries, the erstwhile Russian capitalists exaggerated their poverty. Where once they had bloated their economic numbers, they now underreported them. Woe is us, woe is us; give us more money or we'll go back to our old ways and aim rockets at you again; you wouldn't want that, would you? Once again, the western public was asked to believe the nonsense passed along by gullible television reporters, professional ignoramuses who believed passionately that good news is no news at all. Burlane assumed that the managers of the Company, their budgets shrinking with the declawing of the odious Russian bear, must be burning at this crass passing of the hat. The bankrupt state of the fledgling market economy was as much bullpucky as the alleged success of the state-run confusion had been.

The slick form of cadging by the Russians was no surprise to Burlane. The Russians on the street, having learned the pleasures of freedom and a market economy, simply didn't want to pay their taxes. Who the hell did? The thriving black market in Khabarovsk and Vladivostok, as black markets everywhere, was simply a device to avoid tax. Why should the Russian politicians be honest about their success if failure earned subsidies and good deals from the West?

There were drawbacks to the new Russia, of course. In the bad old days when the comrades were in charge, Burlane had never worried about his safety because a gentleman from the KGB was inevitably following him around. Now, with the gulag out of business, he kept a watchful eye on his wallet.

Below Burlane on Peter the Great Bay, the Russian warships looked so rusted and corroded, he bet the Russians couldn't give them away, much less sell them, as they were currently trying to do.

James Burlane and Andrei Bure both liked to walk, but they had different styles. The mustached Burlane, a man in his prime, walked with a long, determined stride. The bearded game warden, burly and black-haired—he reminded Burlane of a mountain man or a lumberjack out west—charged ahead with a distinctive gait, rolling from heel to toe.

They were both bundled in heavy coats and wore stocking caps pulled down over their ears. They pushed forward with their heads turned at an angle against the hard, icy wind that knifed in from the Sea of Japan. As they walked, buffeted by the wind, they looked out at the rusting, near-derelict remnants of the Russian Pacific fleet. As they walked, they talked about the disappearing Siberian tigers—Ussuri tigers, Bure called them.

Burlane started by saying that Alexei Karpov in Khabarovsk

had said that Bure harbored a particularly frightening theory, but Karpov refused to tell him what it was. That, he said, Burlane should hear from Bure himself.

Bure said, "First let me tell you about rhino horns. The Chinese believe rhino horn can clear the system of various forms of heat and fire."

"Fever?" Burlane stepped over a pile of rusted cable.

"That's apparently what they mean. By itself they say it can cure delirium, nosebleeds, and the vomiting of blood. They mix it with antelope horn to cure high fever and convulsions. You westerners can kick a fever with aspirin if you like, but they want rhino horn. The horn they like the most comes from the black rhino. Twenty-five years ago there were said to be sixty-five thousand black rhinos in Africa. You want to guess how many there are today?" Bure paused to make way for a forklift carrying a pallet of wooden boxes.

Burlane cocked his head and narrowed one eye, the gesture asking how many?

"Maybe two thousand at most, found in small pockets in South Africa, Namibia, Tanzania, Kenya, and Zimbabwe. Zimbwabe even went so far as to cut their horns off to make them less desirable to poachers. Still, in a two-year period between nineteen ninety-two to ninety-four, the population of black rhinos in Zimbabwe plunged from fifteen hundred to about three hundred. The reason for the plunge is spooky to us who want to save the Ussuri tiger."

"Why?" Burlane paused at a filthy window to peer into a large warehouse that was filled with used Japanese automobiles.

Bure took a deep breath and looked Burlane straight on. "Let me tell you frankly, Major Khartoum, there is solid evidence to believe that poachers are deliberately hoarding the horn of black rhino. They're getting about three thousand dollars a kilo now. Can you imagine what their stockpiles of black rhino horns would bring once the animals are extinct?"

"What about the horns the game people have cut off?" Burlane, his nose turning red, sniffed once and buttoned the top button of his coat.

Bure gestured with his right hand. "The horns are officially kept in government stockpiles, but that's like trying to carry gold dust in a sieve. It goes in the front door and out the back. There is plenty of evidence that the same people who are poaching the black rhino are behind the theft of government-owned horns. In any event, it's a useless tactic. A cut stump grows so fast that the animal becomes a poacher's target in just two years. Are you sure you don't want to go inside? It's cold out here, I know."

Burlane smiled. "Hey, when in Siberia.... If we just keep walking, I'll be all right. I like a good, hard walk." Burlane peered through another dirty warehouse window and inside saw piles of lumber.

"Can you imagine what the bones of an Ussuri tiger would bring once they're officially extinct? Outside of the saber-toothed tiger of the Ice Age, this is the largest cat who ever lived."

As they passed the edge of the warehouse, Burlane saw that the lumber was being put aboard a Japanese freighter. "Do you think somebody is trying to do that, poach the Ussuri tiger and stockpile their bones until they're extinct?"

"They may not have started already, but that's a tactic that we fear, Major Khartoum. The poaching has been unrelenting and mounting, as though whoever is behind it is completely indifferent to the future of the species. The numbers of Ussuri tigers are down to critical levels, as I'm sure Alexei Karpov told you. Suppose for a moment, just suppose, that the pressures of the last few years have just been a warm-up of sorts, lowering the population for a final, quick strike. It could be done."

Burlane said, "Before we continue, I need to get my bearings. Where are the tigers found, exactly? Can you show me that?"

"Of course." Bure pulled a map out of his hip pocket and unfolded it for Burlane's benefit. He turned his back to the wind, and ran a gloved forefinger along the map at the Sikhote-Alin Range that flanked the Siberian Pacific coast. "They're found all along here. That's a lot of territory for us to cover, let me tell you."

The northern end of the range was opposite Sakhalin Island—separated from Siberia by the Tatar Strait.

The southern end of the range lay opposite the Japanese island of Hokkaido; here mountains flanked the Sea of Japan.

On the eastern boundary, the Ussuri River flowed north to join the Amur River at Khabarovsk; the heavy, swollen Amur formed of the Songhua and the Shilka Rivers to the east, flowing out of Mongolia and Siberia.

Bure said, "Before, they could kill tigers close in to Vladivostok. No more. They've been thinned out to the point of extinction close in. But I suppose that's true of all animals close to urban areas. We've got three game reserves: the Kedrovaya Pad Reserve just west of Vladivostok; the Lazo Reserve, roughly one hundred miles east of Vladivostok; and the Sikhote-Alin Biosphere Reserve, in the middle of the eight-hundred-mile stretch of tiger range."

Burlane studied the map. "But surely all the tigers aren't found in the reservation."

"Not at all. We're just able to offer the tigers more protection in those areas is all."

"But they can still poach tigers."

"If they stay clear of the game reserves, they can still poach, yes. No problem. There's simply too much space for us to monitor." Bure folded the map and put it back in his hip pocket.

"If there is a conspiracy to put the Siberian tiger out of business, who is behind it, do you think? Your neighbors, the Koreans?"

Bure said, "I wouldn't put it past them, but no, I don't think it's Koreans. After it dawned on us what might be happening, but having no way to prove it, we waited until we got our hands on a poacher and went straight to the point. With vigor."

Burlane, looking out at a destroyer with great, reddish brown streaks of rust eating at its hull, smiled grimly. "You pounded on the miserable motherfucker until he talked."

Bure cleared his throat. "Uh, yes, I think that would describe it. He claimed, under some duress, that he was working for a Chinese operation, although he might not have known that for a fact. China always has been the major market."

"And maybe he was just trying to give you an answer that you would accept."

"Perhaps," Bure said. "We are all aware, are we not, Major

Khartoum, that the Chinese know how markets work. A Chinese is suspected of being behind the plot to drive the black rhino under. Perhaps it's the same man. There's a small café coming up, the Beijing Restaurant. Would you like to go in and thaw out for a while before we continue?"

Burlane grinned. "Sissy American, eh?"

"I'm cold, too, I have to admit. The Beijing serves a good noodle soup that's cheap and good. Big bowls, loaded with vegetables and pork."

"I had some blinis earlier, but that was just a snack. Let's go for it," Burlane said. "My employers are springing."

The only thing Chinese-looking about the Beijing Restaurant was a large dragon painted on the red door. But when they stepped inside, Burlane discovered, to his delight, that it had an interior of reds and golds and carved dragons that would have done justice to any American-Chinese restaurant. They settled in at a small table, near a window overlooking the street. Bure ordered in Russian from a Chinese cook.

"Order us a bottle of vodka, too."

Bure smiled. "That goes without saying."

While they waited for their order, Burlane said, "Did you ask the poacher who the buyer was?"

"He claims a man who spoke English with a German accent."

"And who is that?" Burlane asked.

"He said he didn't know. But he did give us what I think is a useful clue, if it's true."

"What was that?"

Bure said, "He said this German really knows his stuff. Knows all about tigers, and how to track and hunt them. He claims the buyer had been to the Sikhote-Alin Range a couple of times before. This was some years ago."

"Doing what?"

"Supervising the capture of tigers to be sold to zoos or circuses. This was all done with the connivance of the former comrades, whose territory this then was."

The bowls of noodle soup arrived together with their bottle of vodka.

Burlane, sampling his soup, said, "Good soup. Did this poacher tell his story to a judge?"

"He never made it to trial, I'm afraid."

Burlane winced. "Ouch."

Bure said, "We can see clearly what has happened to the black rhino. If this German is behind some kind of conspiracy to put the Siberian tiger out of business to drive up the price of its bones, somebody dammit has to do something, Major Khartoum. And this is Russia, after all. When we're cornered, it's easy to return to the bad old ways we learned from the czars and the commissars of fear."

"I'm not sure I want to know the details," Burlane said. "We Americans are squeamish about that kind of thing, me included."

Bure smiled. "I understand that. I wasn't going to tell you the details, Major. I assure you, I don't like what we did either. But we have pathetically inadequate resources to defend our tigers. We need all the help we can get. If this poacher was telling the truth, it's at least a start. Maybe it's something you can use."

Burlane took a hit of vodka. "Tell me, how does a poacher go about killing a tiger? Does he stalk them? Trap them? What?"

"The poacher first scouts a territory for signs. When he sees evidence that a tiger has been in the area, he finds a good spot to post as bait a young live animal. A goat or calf will do."

Burlane said, "This will usually be a place where his quarry often comes and goes, a waterhole, say."

"Right. Then he retreats to a perch in a tree at some distance to wait for the tiger. He's got a high-powered rifle with a telescopic sight so he's safe enough. The tiger will ordinarily make his approach at dawn or dusk."

Burlane said, "It's then that the poacher, if he is alert and skilled, can nail him."

"Correct," Bure said. "If you want to know about Ussuri tigers and tiger poaching, I'd suggest you talk to Heinz Tepe. Did Anatoly tell you about Tepe?"

"The CITES consultant in the Philippines, yes he did. And his wife. Tepe is in charge of the committee that hired me."

"The fabulous Lily!" Bure made an appreciative noise in the

back of his throat and poured himself some more vodka. "If you're going to all this effort to nail the poachers, Major Khartoum, I'd say a visit with Heinz Tepe and his wife is an absolute must. Lily'll make you lick your lips, I warn you. And you'll have to take care not to groan out loud."

Burlane grinned. "Maybe she has a sister."

"Say, maybe she does at that. Good thinking, Major Khartoum. Now you're using your head. Tepe's a collector, too, did Anatoly tell you that?"

"A collector? No, he didn't. Collects what?"

"Anything to do with tigers. Porcelain tigers. Old photographs. Paintings. Whatever."

Burlane blinked. "Did you say he both studies tigers and collects tiger memorabilia? Is that the word I want? Tiger crap, perhaps."

Bure held his glass up, urging Burlane to drink more. "Oh sure, big collector, always on the lookout for an old book that might have a print of a tiger in it. And CITES keeps him on the move, believe me. Gives him plenty of chances to do his collecting, I suspect."

"I think I'm getting drunk, Andrei."

Bure laughed. "Don't be afraid of the vodka, Major. It's good for you. Remember, when in Russia . . ."

James Burlane clenched his jaw and knocked back another hit of vodka. "I know. I know. To tell you the truth, Andrei, I'm beginning to think you Russians are more dangerous as friends than when you were supposed to be the evil empire. All we had to do then was match you rocket for rocket. Trying to stay with you hit for hit of vodka is too damn much."

A week after her blood test, Marta Fuentes returned to endure a five-hour wait, after which she was told what she suspected already: Her heart had gone bad.

She had high blood pressure and too much cholesterol in her system. She should not eat fat and should lower the amount of salt in her diet. The doctor prescribed two pills: one to reduce the cholesterol; one to lower her blood pressure.

She went to a Rose Pharmacy on Colon Street and learned that the cholesterol pills cost twenty pesos each, and blood pressure pills, ten pesos. Thirty pesos a day! One fourth of her daily pay. She had been told western medicines were expensive, but this, literally taking food from the mouths of her children, was just impossible.

9

Klaus Neumann had grown up on Oberstrasse in an older, but respectable working-class neighborhood of Munich, just far enough from the autobahn to Salzburg and the Austrian border to avoid the whiz and zoom of passing cars. A clean and well-kept area of narrow streets and small shops that had somehow escaped the Allied bomb runs in World War II, the neighborhood had obviously done well when the German postwar economy boomed.

This wasn't an area of flashy cars; there wasn't room for them, and Munich's system of modern buses was enough to accomodate residents who worked in other areas of the city.

Hermann Iversen quickly found the block where the young Neumann had lived with his mother before he went to work for Kruger's International and seek his fortune. Iversen scored quickly when he stepped into a meat market on the corner, smelling heavily of freshly cut garlic, that featured handsome sausages hanging in colorful ropes.

The proprietor, Herr Oscar Overmeier, a beefy, rosy-cheeked man with heavy-rimmed spectacles, wore a pale green apron and was cutting chunks of pork for his sausage grinder. Iversen showed Overmeier his detective's identification and told him he was chasing the murderer of the young woman he might have read about in the newspapers who had been painted like a tiger; as a part of the investigation, he was talking to all Munich residents, past or present, who had anything to do with tigers. He wanted to talk to Klaus Neumann. Perhaps Herr Neumann, through his long employment with Hesse's, might know something that would help solve the puzzle.

Overmeier put his knife down and washed his hands in a sink, looking thoughtful. Drying his hands on a towel, he said, "I read about that terrible murder. I'll help all I can, Herr Iversen. I do hope Klaus wasn't involved in any way. It's hard to imagine anybody you know doing something like that."

"I have no reason to believe that he did, but I can't afford to overlook any possibility. As it happens, the victim was a niece of a friend of mine, a member of the department."

Overmeier grimaced. "Yes, I remember seeing that on television. Frau Neumann was my steady customer for years. She and young Klaus lived just down the street here, but I suppose you know that."

Iversen said, "What can you tell me of the family, Herr Overmeier?"

"There's not much to tell, actually. Frau Neumann's name was Bette. Klaus's father was Lothar Neumann, who was a tiger trainer, billed as Lothar the Magnificent. But you probably know that story."

"He was with Captain Prince–Cox's International Circus. Killed by a tiger in the center ring during a 1957 performance in Hamburg."

"He popped the whip and all that. Made tigers jump through hoops and sit on stools and the rest of it. He got his start with Kruger's International that leases big cats to circuses. The tiger tore open Lothar's neck and severed an artery. He bled to death before they could get him to a hospital."

"How old was Klaus when that happened, can you remember?"

"Oh, I don't know, twelve years old, maybe, or thirteen. Something like that."

"That must have been hard on the boy."

"Oh, terribly hard. I remember Klaus was quite proud of his father. The owners of Captain Prince–Cox's circus were on financial hard times when Lothar was killed, and the furor following his death sent them under."

"They went bankrupt?"

"That's right. They sent young Klaus a framed poster promoting the final performance of the circus in Hamburg. It featured Lothar the Magnificent cracking a whip over the head of a snarling tiger. Klaus showed it to everybody in the neighborhood. He said he was always going to keep it on the wall of his bedroom."

"The final performance of Lothar the Magnificent."

Overmeier nodded. "And Captain Prince–Cox's International Circus. All of us could see that Klaus was crushed by his father's death. It was a terrible blow. It obviously changed him. He was less outgoing after that and never had much to say. He eventually came out of his depression, but it obviously wasn't easy."

"And how did the mother support herself and her son?"

"She owned the house where she and Klaus lived—it's just down the street here—and Lothar left her a small sum of money. But she made ends meet by working as a seamstress in a tailor shop a couple of blocks down the street, but that went out of business a few months ago. It's now a candy shop."

Iversen cocked his head. "How did Klaus get on with his mother?"

Overmeier hesitated. "Well, there you've hit on a sore spot, I'm afraid."

"Oh?"

"He didn't like his mother one bit. They constantly quarreled, and I think Klaus avoided her as much as possible. In fact, I'd go so far as to say he flat hated her."

"And the reason for that?" Iversen asked.

Overmeier cleared his throat. "Herr Iversen, Frau Neumann is better dead, and the past is the past. Let's put it this way: Bette Neumann was a lively, passionate woman. And a real looker in her day."

"Please, Herr Overmeier, this may be important."

Overmeier looked outside the window and sighed. "Her husband was on the road with the circus all the time, doing who knows what. He was Lothar the Magnificent, after all, and I imagine there were plenty of young women eager to find out just how magnificent he really was. I think Frau Neumann got lonely."

"She had a boyfriend."

Overmeier said, "I'm afraid, yes, she did, Herr Iversen. An instructor in history at a local gymnasium."

"And the boy knew about it and resented it, I take it?"

"Oh, I'm sure of it. I don't think he ever forgave her. He worshipped his father, who was Lothar the Magnificent, after all."

"Did Klaus have girlfriends when he got older?"

"Girlfriends? None that I can remember. For some reason, it was hard to imagine Klaus having a girlfriend, although I don't think he was a homosexual or anything like that. He played football in school, and had the usual interests of a boy his age."

"I see. Did you see Klaus after he grew up?"

"Not at all. When he was seventeen or eighteen, he applied for a job for Kruger's, which is where his father had gotten his start. He was interested in big cats, just like his father. Then later he switched to Hesse's. I remember his mother saying he wanted to travel. He lived in Africa, I think, Kenya or somewhere. I think he preferred it there. His mother said he traveled all over the world, that was part of his job. He helped capture and transport lions and tigers and other wild cats for zoos, but I'm not sure about that. But he never once came back to see his mother. At least not that I am aware of."

Iversen jotted a note. "What did he look like? Can you describe him for me, Herr Overmeier?"

"He was a broad-shouldered, rugged kid, that's all I can say. I didn't see him after he went to work for Hesse's."

Iversen said, "How about photographs? Do you know where I might find some pictures of him?"

"His mother might have had some photographs of him, but I don't know where those would be now."

"Did the adult Klaus look in any way like Lothar the Magnificent?"

"A circus poster won't help you, if that's what you're thinking. He took after his mother. That was clear even when he was a kid. He admired his father, but looked like his mother. That was one of the ironies. You should have been here a month ago, Herr Iversen."

"Oh?"

Overmeier looked surprised. "Why, Bette Neumann died. I thought you knew that?"

Iversen licked his lips. "No, I didn't. When was that?"

"In January, I believe it was."

Iversen made another note. "Did Klaus attend her funeral?"

"No. But afterward he was here in Munich. He cleaned out her house and took care of her estate. Was that young woman murdered in January?"

"Why yes, she was, as a matter of fact. Did you go to the Neumann funeral, Herr Overmeier?"

"Yes, I did. Bette Neumann spent her entire life in this neighborhood. She was a longtime customer, and I knew her likes and dislikes. I regarded her as a friend."

"I see. Were there other relatives who might have talked to him?"

Overmeier said, "Bette was in her early thirties when Klaus was born. By the time she died, her sister was dead, as well as her only nephew. So unless she gave her property to charity in her will, Klaus was her sole heir. He didn't deserve the house, but he got it just the same."

"Where did he go after he finished with the estate? Do you have any idea?"

Overmeier shook his head no. "I suppose he went back to Africa or wherever he was living, but I'm not sure anybody knew that for sure."

"Say, did a man from Berlin come looking for him after his mother died?"

Overmeier said, "Klaus's friend. Yes, he did."

"You can't remember his name, can you?"

"I'm not sure he even gave his name. He just popped in one morning wondering where he might find Herr Neumann. I said I had no idea where he was, but he might try Hesse's, which is where Klaus used to work. He said he'd already been there, so I said he might try Africa."

10

The Stohl Office Building was a glass-and-steel professional building in the southern outskirts of Munich. The sterile tone of the building was meant to establish a feeling of modernity, efficiency, and things scientific and logical, therefore dependable. To Hermann Iversen's analytical imagination, this cool, functional architecture translated as *all ye who would enter these portals, watch your wallet at all times.*

The statement began with the heavy glass door at the entrance: *I am a heavy, expensive, modern door, set in polished black marble that was imported from Italy; I am a dependable buffer against bitter cold and blazing heat; I will not chip; my hinges are designed to last—they will never rust or squeak.*

In the lobby, standing on pale, cream marble, Iversen looked up at the huge directory on the wall, which listed the occupants in sans serif lettering that was presumably in keeping with the clean, functional architecture; in this building were lodged the shamen of modernity: bone surgeons; brain surgeons; reconstructive surgeons; ophthalmologists; psychiatrists; accountants of one sort or another; civil lawyers; criminal lawyers; tax lawyers; architects; representatives of investment houses; engineering firms; computer and communications consultants; and the offices of international banks and firms whose business was unspecified.

The buzzardlike surgeons and criminal lawyers earned their living off pending disaster and so drove top-of-the-line Mercedes-Benzes. The investment counselors, bankers, and tax lawyers—

whom Iversen suspected dreamed of deutsche marks at night, waking up, sweating, to cry out for more—drove Mercedeses, too, although their models were probably not as fancy as those driven by the buzzards. The architects and engineers, having an intellectual bent, designed things, which had an element of pleasure, and so settled for Audis and Opels.

Iversen suspected that the psychiatrist Herr Doktor Rudolph Schumacher, a specialist in criminal psychology rather than the profitable neuroses of the rich, likely drove a Volkswagen, an expensive model, but still a Volkswagen. Schumacher had in the past provided expert testimony for both prosecutors and defendants, depending on who got to him first. But he had not achieved his professional reputation by tailoring his opinions to the needs of a client, as did some obvious frauds in the criminal psychology business; for this reason, he was respected by police and criminal lawyers, and his testimony meant something to judges.

Iversen tapped the elevator button with the up arrow, and the door obediently opened. His mind on Klaus Neumann, he tapped the button for the fourteenth floor and was propelled silently upward.

Hermann Iversen, having told what he had learned about Klaus Neumann to Herr Doktor Rudy Schumacher, waited while the tall, lean, elegantly handsome Schumacher kicked back in his leather swivel chair, staring at, but not seeing, a wall of books. Iversen was confident that Schumacher had actually read these books; they were not a form of interior decoration calculated to impress gullible clients.

As he thought, Schumacher stroked his close-cropped white beard. It was a fact much noted by Iversen's amused colleagues that Schumacher did, in a curious way, resemble the master himself, Sigmund Freud. But it was the consensus that the brilliant Schumacher was entitled to this affectation; he was a genuine intellectual who had forsaken the path of certain wealth to explore the swamp of human desire gone wrong. He was also coplike in two other key respects: He was interested in justice, which he felt was one of the touchstones of civilization, and he liked to solve puzzles.

Iversen, who had worked with Schumacher on numerous occasions in the past, waited. He did not mind this; Rudy Schumacher's opinion was worth waiting for. He remembered one of Schumacher's observations in the past, when they had waited together to testify at a trial. Schumacher had said life itself was an unsolvable puzzle; hence the human fascination with puzzles of all sorts. Puzzles were insistent and persistent; solve one and another immediately presented itself, demanding an answer. The ultimate puzzle, of course, was unanswerable, but never mind.

Finally, Schumacher said, "So, Hermann, you're asking me if it's possible that the death of Klaus Neumann's father might not have affected him more than most people might have imagined."

Iversen said, "Herr Overmeier told me Klaus appeared to change significantly after his father was killed. He was just entering adolescence."

"A volatile age, that's so," Schumacher said. "What you're suggesting is possible, yes, Herr Iversen. But of course almost anything's possible when we're dealing with the human brain, isn't it?"

"He taught his local sources how to trap tigers, and he saw to their transport to zoos all over the world. Think about that for a second."

Schumacher said, "A zoo is a form of jail, is that what you're thinking?"

"Right," Iversen said. "A zoo is a prison, as Herr Steinbach himself said. The animals there are doing time for having done nothing except be exotic and alive. That's perhaps a brutal way of putting it, but it's the truth, isn't it?"

Schumacher leaned back in his swivel chair, thinking. "So in fact Klaus Neumann earned his living jailing cats, putting them behind bars in zoos around the world."

Iversen said, "That's right. He was a kind of a bounty hunter."

"And you're suggesting that he might have done this to punish tigers because a tiger had killed Lothar the Magnificent?"

Iversen shrugged. "It makes a person wonder. But you're the psychiatrist, Herr Doktor, not me."

"The victims were painted like tigers and their throats were cut."

"One girl in Bhagalpur, India, a second in Padang on the west coast of Sumatra in Indonesia—both bordering tiger country, by the way—and the third one here in Munich last month, which coincides with Klaus Neumann's trip here to take care of his mother's estate."

"And it was a tiger that slashed Klaus's father's neck in the circus accident."

Iversen nodded. "Severed an artery in the center ring, and Lothar Neumann bled to death. A claw, a knife, a cut throat is a cut throat."

"You're thinking that Herr Neumann had a pathological need to avenge his father's death. His company's dissolution meant he could no longer imprison them, and you're asking yourself if he still had a need to punish cats."

"That's what I had in mind, something like that," Iversen said. "Tigers in particular, but maybe cats in general. And to punish women, owing to his long-standing resentment over his mother's affair."

Schumacher said, "You're thinking Neumann's obsession with revenge might somehow have taken on a sexual dimension. Human females have a sleek, smooth-muscled look about them."

"Yes," Iversen said, "Feline would describe it, don't you think? There's a certain catlike quality to many women if you think about it. Soft but volatile. Slinky."

"So you think Klaus Neumann might have started painting young women to look like tigers, after which he raped them and cut their throats as the tiger had slashed his father's throat."

Iversen said nothing. He sucked air between his two front teeth. "Nobody knows exactly how the human mind works. I understand that. And I realize I'm drawing conclusions as an amateur. I'm a detective, not a shrink."

Schumacher, thinking, pursed his lips. "We've studied the human brain and studied and studied it, Herr Iversen. We know the function of this part, or what that part does. We can operate on the brain and quite successfully in some cases. We can give it hits of electricity. We can flood it with chemicals. But if it's skewed in the wrong direction, for whatever reason, it can become a thicket of terror that nobody can understand, much less anticipate or control. It becomes an unfathomable darkness. In the case of a serial killer, we can only guess the reasons that trigger his madness." Schumacher thought for a moment. Then, he smiled. "It's easy to see how it was you became a detective, Herr Iversen."

"I do my job is all," Iversen said. "Someone painted my friend's niece and two other young women so they looked like tigers, then raped them and slit their throats. To bring the killer to justice before he does it again, I need to understand how he thinks. Why would he do something like that? He may be insane, but there must be a reason behind his madness."

The two men sat in silence for a while, thinking, then Iversen said, "Remember the poem by the Englishman, William Blake? *Tyger! Tyger! burning bright, In the forests of the night, What immortal hand or eye could frame thy fearful symmetry?* I woke up one night with that poem on my mind, and I've been thinking about it ever since. The killer fits the subject of Blake's poem quite well, doesn't he, Herr Doktor? A human tiger out there, stalking his victims."

Shumacher said, "Perhaps we all have tigers lurking deep within us, somewhere down there in the dark, uncharted regions of the brain, in the limbic or the R-Complex. *Tyger! Tyger! burning bright . . .*"

"*In the forests of the night.*" Iversen bit his lip.

"To find that tiger, you'll have to enter a truly dark and forbidding forest, Herr Iversen. It surely won't be easy."

Iversen sighed. "It never is."

11

He looked straight through the beggars as though they did not exist. He paid no attention to their clutching and pawing. Their sad eyes and pathetic infirmities and plaintive little cries had no effect whatsoever. He resolutely ignored them as he stepped from the cab and pushed his way through the milling horde of sweating brown bodies, sidestepping venders of snacks and trinkets, his eye always on the distant goal. All this meant he was a veteran of travel in India.

Experienced travelers gave no alms, lest they be overwhelmed by beggars jabbering at them, palms extended. Still, they were determined—as a point of honor and a test of his strength—to crack his will; they did their best, making spirited sallies at him, crowding around him, "Sahib, sahib, sahib!" They were ever hopeful that he would break and throw them a handful of coins in a futile effort to get rid of them. They might as well have been pleading to a stone or tree. The sphinx showed more emotion than the tall German.

First there was the business of getting a ticket, which was never an easy matter in India, even if you had the money to buy the most expensive ticket possible. There were too many passengers for the available trains; it had always been thus in India, and the German—traveling on a passport identifying him as Tomas Beck—had no doubt it would always be that way.

Beck had traveled through Chabra several times in the past. Although he suspected westerners all looked alike to most Indians, he passed on the sensible alternative for travelers with money—that is, of hiring someone to go through the odious drill of securing a ticket. He didn't want a professional stand-in to later tell the Indian police that yes, he had bought a ticket for a westerner at Chabra, a tall, blond westerner who wanted to go to Gorakhpur. Europeans might look the same to the average Indian, but a professional stand-in—having worked for all manner of Europeans—stood a chance of remembering their accents and personal tics.

The Indians did not believe in forming queues so that travelers could take turns confronting the inevitable bored and indifferent bureaucrat, who in Hindi, or lilting English, could tell them the train they wanted was delayed, full, under repair, or canceled indefinitely, or that the monsoons had washed out a stretch of the track or a bridge, or malcontents had ripped up the tracks, or any combination of the above.

In the middle of the throng in front of the third of twelve windows at Chabra station—nine of the windows were inexplicably closed—there stood a cow, relieving her bowels. As she did so, the cow chewed her cud solemnly, if not regally, as befitted her sacred status. The excrement had collected on the end of her tail where it had dried into a dun-colored lump, and she flipped the dried crud leisurely back and forth to swat flies. Beck supposed that these flies must have performed honorably in their last incarnation and so in this life were given sticky, sweaty India as a reward. This was fly heaven.

In spite of their need to press forward, the doughty travelers gave the cow plenty of room. To stand too close to her hindquarters was to risk getting tarred by the flipping tail.

In addition to the window with the cow, Windows 7 and 10 were also open. Beck, not wanting to deal with the cow, chose Window 7. He had gained nearly a meter in a half hour, when the clerk behind Window 7, without warning or explanation, abruptly closed the wooden door behind the metal grill. It was lunchtime, or break time, or a work slowdown, or something.

Upon realizing they'd been had, travelers in front of Window 7, looked about, wild-eyed.

Window 5 had opened.

Beck, being on the left of the throng in front of Window 7, had a head start over the other travelers, and so sprinted for Window 5 without a hint of hesitation or embarrassment. Being large and long-legged, he arrived near the front of the new throng.

As he waited for his turn at the window, pushing relentlessly forward, Beck supposed that while the British Raj had left the Indians with a civil service and a functional govenment, those assets could not prevent the people from multiplying like gerbils or squirrels. In Germany, where a civilized couple had a sensible one or two children, it was possible to enforce the ethic of cooperation; here, where people lived and died pressed against the flesh of their neighbors, surrounded by bodies, such a conceit was madness. In India, as in China or Indonesia, one learned to compete in order to survive; one pushed forward, patiently, but with determination.

When his turn came, Beck was shocked, if not stunned, to learn that not only was there a first-class seat available on a train that was scheduled to depart for Gorakhpur on time, but also the clerk at Window 5 could speak intelligible English, seemed alert, and had not run out of tickets. The clerk said the train would be leaving from Track D. All Beck had to do was find Track D and wait. Right, Beck thought. The more he traveled in India, the more paranoid and uncertain he became. At each point on an odyssey— the simplest trip was an odyssey in India—the traveler had to do a simple reality check: What can go wrong here? Failure to make repeated reality checks could mean spending a night in a filthy, dangerous hole.

Clutching his valise and ticket, Beck, exhausted, sweaty, and hungry, pushed his way through the beggars and panhandlers, and managed to claim a spot on the pavement by Track D, leaning against one of the filthy supports of the large overhang that extended from the terminal over the departure area.

The schedule board high above the several platforms comfirmed the ticket clerk's confident instructions. Track D was the correct point of departure for the train to Gorakhpur. The clerk's assertion that the train would actually leave on time turned out to be fantasy, but Beck was nevertheless delighted. He was going to make it. He was in the right place. He had a ticket. Word had spread, and so the beggars had given up on him.

At two o'clock, five hours after he had joined the crowd in front of ticket Window 7, the train to Gorakhpur—identified by cards placed above the doors—arrived on Track D as promised. Beck's spirits began to rise. Owing to a malfunction in the innards of the public-address system, the voice announcing arrivals and departures was unintelligible. But never mind. The correct train was sitting directly in front of him, being cleaned and serviced.

The last time Beck had bought tiger bones in Gorakhpur, he had paid a hundred dollars a pound, after which the Indian middleman had bragged that he had given a bag of lentils worth two dollars to the man who had actually killed the tiger. He said he had paid a second hunter in chickpeas. The middleman said he had loaned both hunters guns, so if they got caught by a game warden, they were the ones who had to stand trial, not him. Laughing, he said he told them that when they were being overpaid, they had to expect to take a chance.

Beck knew he would be forced to pay more this trip. Owing to pressure from conservationists, the cost of tiger parts was inflating relentlessly. He knew that the market was still there; the Chinese consumers had both the money and the desire. Still, Beck couldn't help but wonder how long the market could survive pressure from western conservationists.

On his last trip to Gorakhpur, he had arrived early in the morning, and the train had stalled just outside of town with the sun rising over a row of Indian males taking their morning shit. They had been unembarrassed about relieving themselves in such a manner, and were not bothered by the people peering down at them from the train. All animals move their bowels, after all. It had to be done. By lining up thus, it made it easier to collect the manure to spread it on the fields. When one could not afford commercial fertilizers, one used manure. Animal or human, it all worked.

What a country was India!

Tomas Beck waited, secure, half-drowsing, but keeping a watchful eye on the train in case it departed without warning. The man on the public-address system made another of his impossible, muffled announcements. But this time—for reasons that even he was at a loss to explain—Beck somehow comprehended what was being said: "Last call for Gorakhpur. Last call for Gorakhpur. The train for Gorakhpur is now departing on Track A. All passengers on board, please."

The German who had traveled from Chabra on a passport identifying him as Tomas Beck mopped his forehead with his handkerchief, glancing up at the single fan in his diminutive room. The room contained a single bed, an ancient bureau with a broken mirror, a threadbare oriental carpet on the floor. The flowered wallpaper, yellowed with age and brittle, was marred by bumps, bubbles, and scabs of peeling paper.

The first Indian, a tall, extraordinarily handsome Sikh in a white turban, started to address Beck, but Beck held his hand up. "Call me..." He glanced at the second Indian. "No names today, please."

The Sikh said, "Of course, as you wish, sahib."

Beck said, "What's in a name anyway? Business is the thing."

"Quite right, sahib."

Beck grinned. "On second thought, you may call me Otto, why not? I feel in an Otto mood. Today, I am Otto Klein."

"Perhaps in your last life you were Otto Klein," the second Indian said. The second Indian, a small man with a hawk nose and squinting brown eyes, was not a Sikh.

"Or in my next life, eh, Mohan?" Beck said. He had done business with Mohan before.

Mohan smiled. "Indeed," he said.

The Sikh opened the first suitcase. Inside, packed neatly, were eight football-sized bundles wrapped in newspaper. The Sikh removed the newspaper from a bundle, revealing a tiger skull. He held it in his hand, admiring it. He said, "You will observe, sahib, that this is a fresh skull. It is not dried out. We know that your friends like their skulls fresh. Here, see for yourself." He offered Beck the skull.

"You have the pelts, too?" Beck asked.

"We will sell the pelts to the Arabs, sahib. We have buyers in Arabia."

"I see." Beck turned the skull in his hand. "How much do you get for the pelts?"

Mohan quickly licked his lips. "The Arabs have more money than they know what to do with."

"If you sell me the skulls, what are in the heads of the pelts?"

"Plastic skulls, sahib," the Sikh said. "The Arabs are only interested in how it looks. They want the skin of a tiger with fierce eyes and great fangs. They know the eyes are made of glass."

Beck turned the skull in his hands. The two lower fangs fit neatly inside the upper two. Tigers were meat eaters, and the huge feline fangs had clearly evolved to rip meat. "And the fangs?"

Mohan said, "These are original as you can see, ah . . ."

"Otto," Beck said quickly.

"Yes, Otto."

Beck smiled.

The Sikh said, "The fangs on the pelts we sell to the Arabs are carved from elephant tusks. They look real enough, and the Arabs never know the difference. You need to understand that the Arabs are filthy, stupid pigs, sahib. Human jokes. If they didn't have oil, they would be nothing, and everybody knows it. Do you suppose anybody is really fooled by their arrogance?"

Beck looked amused. "What else do you have?"

The Sikh said, "We have noses and penises, sahib."

"And the noses on the pelts you sell the Arabs?"

"Fake as well, sahib. But there are Arabs who claim they can tell the difference, and insist on genuine noses, which is why I'm afraid we're forced to ask a premium for these."

"May I see them?"

"Certainly, sahib." The Sikh unsnapped one of the leather briefcases. Inside were preserved tiger noses, and the brownish, dried tiger penises. The penises—each about about twelve inches long, as wide as a man's finger—were coiled into six-inch circles.

Beck took a penis in his hand and examined its tip with a magnifying glass. The tip of a tiger penis was barbed. Beck was looking for barely visible V-shaped incisions that scam artists made in the glans of a bull's organ. When a surgically altered bull's penis was dried, these incisions curled up to form barbs similar to those on a tiger penis.

Mohan said, "It is genuine, rest assured. Do you really think we would try to fool you with fake pricks? sahib!"

Turning the penis, examining it, Beck said, "You may be able to fool an Arab with fake fangs and noses, but never a Chinese."

The Sikh looked shocked that Otto would suggest such a thing. "Please, don't insult us, sahib. We know our market very well. We know better than to try to fool a professional with a fake penis or nose."

Beck used the magnifying glass to examine a nose.

"There'll be many boy children born to the Chinese who hang that nose above their bed, sahib. Those are no-girl noses, guaranteed." Mohan found it hard to suppress a grin.

Beck laughed. "We can forgive them their conceits as long as they're willing to pay, right, Mohan."

Mohan smiled openly, displaying brown, rotting teeth. "It would perhaps be better if there weren't so many of them. But, like you say, as long as they're willing to pay."

"And your price to me today?"

The Sikh looked concerned, very grave. "I'm afraid we will have to charge you more this time, sahib."

"Oh?"

"There are fewer tigers and hunting is more difficult. You can understand. Besides, the British and Europeans and the Americans are becoming excited about the fate of the tiger. There was even a cover article in *Time* magazine. When that happens, the people here are after us. It is not like before, sahib."

"But without me to get them into the right hands, you just have bones and noses and penises."

"Please, sahib. You need to understand, the British is giving the government more money for game wardens. Before, it was all talk. But they appear serious this time, sahib, they truly do. Poachers risking prison are asking more for tigers. That's not unexpected, is it, sahib?"

12

Hong Kong was the principal port of entry for tiger bones and the parts of other endangered species destined for companies that made traditional medicine in mainland China, and most of these medicines passed through Hong Kong on their way to overseas Chinese communities throughout the world.

To get a fix on the problem through the eyes of the British colonial government, James Burlane had arranged for an interview with David Ames, an official of the British Foreign Service, who kept tabs on trade for the Hong Kong government and international environmental organizations.

Burlane had been to Hong Kong more than a dozen times beginning in 1970, when the British still had more than a quarter of a century remaining on their lease from the Chinese. Back then the girlie joints in the Wanchai district on Hong Kong Island were hopping with hormonal action—mainly Filipinas imported by the Hong Kong Chinese to entertain American soldiers in for rest and recreation from their ill-fated struggle in Vietnam.

There were of course many beautiful Chinese girls in Hong Kong, but Burlane found it difficult to believe that Chinese males selected their women for good looks. Even now, when he spotted a hot-looking girl at a distance, she almost inevitably turned out to be a Filipina. Also, Filipinas knew how to smile and laugh. When a mainland Chinese smiled—and the colony was bloated with refugees—it might mean they were embarrassed or confused, but not that they thought anything was funny. The startling dearth of good-looking Chinese girls in Hong Kong was a standing joke among western expats in Asia; the consensus was that attractiveness or good humor was irrelevant to a female running a sewing machine or painting Christmas tree ornaments in a sweatshop. Pinch-faced drudgery was all that was required.

The action in Wanchai was now lethargic and overpriced. The sex tourists went to Bangkok or Manila to play orifice roulette with AIDS. Hong Kong was not a city that appealed to those interested in history or culture; one went to the United Kingdom or Europe for that. A traveler interested in the ikons of pop culture went to America. But buyers, those curious people who somehow got their kicks from passionate consumption, went to Hong Kong for its many alleged good deals. In the United States, Burlane had seen women, presumably shopping mall addicts, with bumper stickers on their cars that read: I COULD SHOP TILL I DROP. In Hong Kong, he supposed, they almost surely would.

Burlane did not understand how anybody would spend one or two hundred dollars a night for a hotel room in order to save ten or twenty bucks on a video camera or boom box. It was palpably absurd. Yet the tourists, dry-mouthed from the expectation of bargains ahead, arrived every few minutes at the airport that stuck out into Kowloon Bay just east of the peninsula. Although it defied logic, it seemed to Burlane that, as the years passed, the Chinese, ever the eager sellers, had opened a shop for each new arrival. It amazed him that anybody made any money, but they obviously did.

In 1970, one traveled across Victoria harbor from Hong Kong island to Kowloon via the Star Ferry, which in the 1990s remained in service and which was still preferred by tourists and anybody not in a rush. Now the Chinese neckties working in Hong Kong's bustling financial market packed themselves in the modern underground that connected the island with the New Territories on the mainland.

The Chinese were fabled spitters, hawking up disgusting gobs of phlegm and nasal yuck and discharging them cheerfully wherever they were—in a café, on a sidewalk, or in a public park. When one felt like spitting, one spit.

Hong Kong, thanks to the tidy and determined Brits who ran the place, was clean and modern and well-kept. It worked. The handsome steel-and-glass skyscrapers in the Wanchai, Admiralty, and Central districts of Hong Kong took a backseat to no other city's on the planet. It was easy to understand why the comrades in Beijing, so eager to join the modern world, coveted such an Asian jewel. To them it was like a diamond necklace in a glass showcase. It sparkled and gleamed in the light, and they wanted it oh so dearly, never mind that they would likely screw it up.

Between Hong Kong Island and the New Territories on the Chinese mainland—also part of the colony—was Hong Kong Bay. The southernmost tip of the New Territories, facing Hong Kong island, was Kowloon, a peninsula—or a blunt tit of land— that was the shopping district so dear to the hearts of tourists. Kowloon, named for the nine small peaks to the north, literally meant Nine Dragons.

The bottommost heart of Kowloon was the Tsimshatsui district. The main north-south thoroughfare through the Tsimshatsui was called Nathan Road; Nathan Road formed a T with Salisbury Road, which ran along the bottom of the district. In 1970, the main shopping in Tsimshatsui had centered around Cameron Road, Granville Road, and Kimberly Road to the east of Nathan Road—opposite Kowloon Park on the west.

Now the commercial cancer of unending shops selling tape recorders, cameras, computers, jewelry, eyeglasses, binoculars, and boom boxes of every make and description had consumed the entire peninsula, and pushed out in all directions from its original center in Tsimshatsui.

In 1970, with China in the turmoil of the cultural revolution, Hong Kong harbor had been a colorful and romantic clutter of junks and sampans with an occasional rusting freighter awaiting goods that truly were made in Hong Kong, rather than goods made by mainland Chinese peasants but bearing a MADE IN HONG KONG label.

Now Beijing brazenly proclaimed that Hong Kong was its Wall Street, and Taiwan was its Silicon Valley. Gone were the junks and sampans that begged for a photographer from the *Na-*

tional Geographic magazine. The harbor had become transformed into a vast, incredible clutter of freighters and tankers waiting to service the superheated economy that was the new China.

But when he had visited the colony as an employee of the odious Company in Langley, Virginia, it had been a city of remarkable charm. As the years passed and it had come to be the chief connection to the outside world for the ambitious comrades running China, its soul had increasingly lodged in its securities bourse, the Hang Seng index.

Burlane had booked a room in the Royal Century in the heart of Wanchai. The Royal Century was a sterile cocoon so new that it wasn't yet listed in the guidebooks, the kind of hotel that popped up in Hong Kong like steel-and-glass mushrooms, intended for tourists who confused blandness with class. Burlane was there because it was the cheapest place on Hong Kong island where he could safely leave his computer, telephoto, and eavesdropping gear; that would be foolishness in a zoo like the Chung King Manor on the Kowloon side.

Out there, in Siberia, in India, Indo-China, and Indonesia, William Blake's mighty tiger roamed the forests of the night. The beautiful tiger was doomed, Burlane felt, not because it had lost its hunting skills or there was no more forest—although the forests were fast disappearing—but because of the human greed that was transforming Asia.

The Russians, poor bastards, had little to sell. If the Chinese were buying tigers, the Russians sold tigers. If the Chinese could make a profit selling tiger bones to people who believed they were good for one's joints—any of them—the Chinese bought the tigers from the Russians and anybody else who would sell.

Burlane knew that the conservationists who had hired him to track down the principal tiger smugglers believed the problem could be dealt with like a surgeon excising a simple skin cancer. Eliminate the principal smugglers and you saved the tiger—that was the logic. But the tiger trade, he knew, was more like a cancer of the lymphatic system—widespread and systemic. It was also cultural. The people believed in homeopathic medicine. It was virtually the only medicine they had. Take away their traditional cures and what did they have left?

And to the Chinese there was little difference between machines and striped beasts; they were both to be bought and sold. "You want tigah, mistah? We got tigah. How much you pay?"

Cameras?

Boom boxes?

Tigers?

James Burlane felt that if the Chinese could have gotten away with listing tigers as a commodity on the Hang Seng index, they would have. As he boarded the Star Ferry for the ride to Tsimshatsui, he composed a little poem:

> What, my friend, do you suppose
> Is the value of this tiger's nose?
> Here I have his awful claw,
> What's your offer for his mighty jaw?
> Ignore the ticking of that nagging clock,
> I have for sale a tiger's cock.
> Is your pee-pee less than fine?
> Take a sip of penis wine.
> Going once . . .
> Going twice . . .

James Burlane felt that to eat well, that is, interesting, varied food, was to live artfully. The most satisfying achievement was, whenever possible, to defeat the commercial food chain by gleaning wild food that was to be found right under the noses of the devoutly ignorant and to prepare it well; one of Burlane's heroes was Euell Gibbons, author of *Stalking the Wild Asparagus* and *Stalking the Blue-Eyed Scallop*. Burlane himself often made a salad of marinated milkweed buds that he thought was sublime, and his version of oysters Rockefeller, using pigweed instead of spinach, was fit for the gods.

Burlane thought Chinese food one of the best cuisines in the world, simple yet elegant, which is why he lugged a wok with him almost everywhere he went. With a few basic ingredients and elementary cooking skills, one could make a dish that would have pleased the most fastidious and demanding Chinese emperor of old. The food in southern China was based on three ingredients that had come to be nearly universally available in the West: fresh ginger, garlic, and green onions, or spring onions, as the Chinese called them.

But when Burlane was in Hong Kong, he did not eat Chinese food. Instead he headed straight for Chung King Manor on Nathan Street next to the Holiday Inn. Chung King Manor was a hive of spartan, cell-like rooms for hippie travelers and adventurous cheapskates—Burlane regarded himself as a little bit of both. The usual camera and boom box shops were to be found downstairs; the eateries run by Indians, Pakistanis, and Nepalis were upstairs in locations that were nearly impossible for the uninitiated to find.

In Burlane's opinion, the best cheap food in all of Hong Kong was to be found in these eateries. But getting to them—negotiating tortuous and confusing dirty stairwells, creaky, crowded elevators of uncertain maintenance, and cluttered, mysterious hallways—was an adventure in itself. Ordinarily first-timers were guided by one of the Pakistani or Nepalese touts posted downstairs. Burlane gladly accepted their services on the theory that Henry M. Stanley would have gotten lost trying to find a restaurant in the amazing Chung King Manor.

Some of Burlane's best Hong Kong memories were of eating Nepalese food and watching Hindi movies with Gurkha soldiers in Chung King Manor. He hoped most fervently that when the Chinese took over the colony in 1997 they would leave the Paks and Indians and Nepalis alone, but he had his doubts.

This time, Burlane was guided up the dark and dirty stairwells and down narrow halls, first left, then right, then left again, to a nondescript door with NEW DELHI RESTAURANT painted on it. Arriving nearly simultaneously, with his own guide, was the punctual gentlemen from the British Foreign Service, David Ames, who had been delighted when Burlane had suggested they meet here. Ames, a tall, middle-aged Welshman, was a handsome man with carefully trimmed salt-and-pepper hair and an empire moustache. He had once been posted in India and was also a fan of curries, dals, and chapati.

The New Delhi contained just sixteen chairs. Burlane and Ames, the only customers, settled in at a small table. The waiter, wearing leather sandals, white cotton trousers, and a long-sleeved white cotton shirt, was quickly upon them, menus in hand.

They studied the menus briefly and proceeded to order with abandon, having agreed that in view of the low price and extraordinary quality of the food, rank gluttony was in order. They ordered lamb korma, chicken biryani, fried fish stuffed with mint-and-coriander chutney, a lentil dal, curried vegetables, two dishes of yogurt to help quench the inevitable fire, and a plate of chapati, the unleavened Indian bread that Burlane found indescribably delicious.

To properly wash their feast down and to further douse the fire of chilies and spices, they ordered, at Ames's suggestion, bottles of Foster's, an Australian lager; the Welshman said this was a taste he had acquired in a tour of duty in Sydney.

The waiter brought them their bottles of Foster's. When he left to get their chapati, Ames said, "We've done our best to stop the trade in tiger bones, Major Khartoum, but as you know Hong Kong has remained a British colony only at the pleasure of the Chinese. If Beijing hadn't had a reason for Hong Kong to be officially British, the government would have ripped it off long ago, sod the Brits. When you Americans refused to do business with them for all those years, the Chinese simply stamped 'made in Hong Kong' on their trinkets and moved them through here or Macau."

Burlane opened his notebook and clicked open a ballpoint pen.

"You may remember when student protests were the fashion in the early seventies, and there was an obligatory riot against the Portuguese government in Macau. Well, the beneficent Uncle Mao sent the troops in to put the upstart malcontents in their place." Ames looked amused.

"A wonderful ideological spectacle," Burlane said. He poured a glassful of Foster's.

"But both sides can be a bit hypocritical, can't they, Major Khartoum? In more recent years, we've had the pleasure of watching Chris Patten establish democratic institutions in a city the Chinese have considered theirs all along." Ames tried some beer.

Burlane said, "An in-your-face gesture, the way the Chinese see it."

"Isn't this good stuff? The Aussies make good beer. One has to give them that. Previous to the lease running out, we never bothered to give the residents of Hong Kong the full democratic franchise. You need to remember, Major Khartoum, that the Chinese have never forgotten what the British did to them with the opium trade in the last century. I suppose it's difficult for one to blame them."

Burlane said, "Now we have the high-minded Americans and the loathsome British grandly telling them to lay off the tiger cock soup."

Ames grinned. "Well, that's just too much as far as they're concerned. The way they see it, they'll eat what they want without our advice or approval, thank you."

"Fuck the tigers."

Ames said, "They're other people's tigers, not theirs. We've done our best to stop the trade here in Hong Kong, but it's a losing battle."

The waiter arrived with a plate of hot chapatis, which both Burlane and Ames immediately began devouring.

Ames said, "Aren't these good with the beer? Mmm."

"They're delicious," Burlane said. He said, "TRAFFIC Network lists forty-one companies making patented traditional medicines in Hong Kong."

Ames grimaced. "How many in China?"

"Two-hundred-twenty odd."

Ames said, "The ones here in Hong Kong are fly-by-night operations. That forty-one figure might be up to sixty or seventy for all we know. We bust one here, another pops up there. The ones in China are huge, state-run enterprises. I'm afraid as long as the Chinese are buying traditional medicines made of animal parts, there will be Chinese who will be making those medicines. The trade openly flourishes both in China and in overseas Chinese communities. I bet you can buy ground tiger bones in San Francisco."

"That's what they tell me."

"For years the smugglers were based in Taiwan, but that changed somewhat after you Americans spanked their behinds with a trade embargo. But it really wasn't much of a spanking, was it?"

Burlane said, "Oh, I don't know. It was pretty good, I think. We told them we wouldn't buy anything made from animals— coral or shell jewelry, or shoes or handbags or whatever made out of snake, lizard, or crocodile skin, anything made of leather. They were running a ten-billion-dollar trade surplus with us. Now TRAFFIC Network lists only three traditional medicine companies in Taiwan. That has to be some kind of progress."

"True, but unless you address the problem of the medicines exported from mainland China, it's little more than an amusing exercise, rather like Don Quixote charging windmills."

"Not that you British haven't been tilting at windmills of your own. Trying to turn this place into a democracy at the last second."

Ames smiled weakly. "Touché, Major Khartoum."

Burlane, chewing on a chapati, said, "The world is full of windmills, Mr. Ames. I suppose we have to try. Never give up, fighting spirit. Stiff upper lip and all that."

Ames took another chapati himself. "Isn't that the truth? For years, the smugglers based in Taipei were the chief supplier of endangered species to the Chinese mainland. They had the necessary source or sources in Africa, India, Indonesia, and wherever."

"One or more than one buyer? I would like to tell you I plan on taking out the Mr. Big of the organization, but that would be hubris. First things first. I'd like to identify the individual who personally, physically buys the bones from local poachers, and put him out of business. After that, who knows?"

Ames motioned to the waiter and pointed at the diminishing plate of chapatis.

The waiter grinned. He appreciated westerners who liked chapatis.

Ames said, "Before the trade embargo, the tiger bones were apparently shipped to Taipei, where they were stored, and then sold to the manufacturers in China and Hong Kong or wherever."

Burlane made a note. "How were the bones smuggled? By ship? By plane? How?"

"On Taiwanese fishing vessels mainly, also on merchant vessels flying flags of convenience. To call them Taiwanese fishing boats is a misnomer. They're really Taiwanese smuggling boats. After the American trade embargo, Taipei halted the overt manufacturing of medicines using endangered species, but they simply drove the retail trade underground." Ames caught the waiter's attention and pointed at their empty bottles.

The waiter, grinning, went for more beer.

Burlane said, "By underground, I take it the merchants had to take the goods off their shelves and out of the display cases that faced the streets."

"That's right. Otherwise camera crews from western television stations might casually walk into shops and take embarrassing pictures at will. Such visits had happened, and contradicted the official Taipei line that they were doing everything to stop the trade. A lot of face had been lost because of television crews."

"Now customers in Taiwan have to know what to ask for and how?"

"We wouldn't want politicians in Taipei to forego their tiger cock soup, would we?"

The waiter arrived with more beer and a tray loaded with lamb korma, chicken biryani, lentil dal, and yogurt.

Burlane, helping himself to the dal, a staple of meals in south India, said, "But they did force the dealers in tiger bones and rhino horns to move their base?"

"Yes, they did, having removed the protection of the Taiwanese police."

Burlane smiled. "So a new Mr. Big moved in when the smuggling syndicate was pushed out of Taiwan. And he is?"

"We don't know," Ames said mildly.

"Mmm. Located where?"

"We don't know that either. As you must be aware, Major

Khartoum, this really is a Chinese city. It's a British colony in name only."

Burlane cocked his head. "In an overseas Chinese community somewhere?"

"Very likely."

"In Southeast Asia?"

"That would be a good bet. He very likely is engaged in more than one legitimate business, possibly in several overseas Chinese communities—possibly with connections to retail shops where the patent medicines are sold."

Burlane sampled the biryani, made savory by the use of fresh coriander. "Why didn't he simply move to the south China coast? Shanghai, say?"

"Because Beijing has been feeding the Americans an environmentalist line so it could get most favorable trading status from you Americans. Traditional medicine is a big part of Chinese life, and China is a large and complicated country. There just wasn't much Beijing could or would do about eliminating more than two-hundred manufacturers. But the government wasn't about to let the principal smuggler base his operations on Chinese soil."

"I see."

Ames concentrated for a moment on his lamb korma, loaded with nuts and raisins. He said, "What I'm telling you is based largely on informants in the Chinese community, and we always have to consider the possibility that we're deliberately being fed misinformation, but in this case, we think this story is probably accurate."

Burlane turned a page of his notebook, and made a quick scribble. "So where did the smuggler move? Hong Kong?"

Ames shook his head. "No. Just like Beijing, we can do something about a single organization of smugglers, but not the manufacturers. When the Chinese take over Hong Kong, *then* they'll base themselves here. The United States will never apply trade sanctions to China."

"Korea?"

"Not Korea. We don't think Macau or Singapore or Malaysia either. They all have too much to lose from trade sanctions."

"Where then?" Burlane tried the chicken biryani, a rice dish loaded with vegetables and given a substantial hit of spices.

Ames looked thoughtful. "CITES have a consultant who lives in the Philippines. If I were to bet money, I'd wager he's settled there because he suspects that's where the bones are warehoused for distribution to the manufacturers."

"Until Hong Kong is legally Chinese."

"Correct."

"The CITES consultant being Dr. Heinz Tepe."

"That's right. There have been a lot of Chinese immigrants to the Philippines in recent years, both legal and illegal, and the Chinese have come to dominate the Philippine economy. The Philippines is regarded as the most corrupt country in Southeast or East Asia, which is why international investors are wary about doing business there."

Burlane rolled his eyes. "I know. I know. Poor bastards."

Ames said, "Compared to the Filipinos, the Indonesians and Malaysians are Boy Scouts. The Filipinos'll sell anything to score a buck: justice, women, little boys, trees, animals, you name it. Major Khartoum. If I were trying to trace smuggled tiger bones, I would talk to someone in the seaman's union about Filipino sailors and Taiwanese fishing trawlers."

"The Taiwanese trawlers being owned by Chinese but run by Filipino sailors, I take it."

"That's right. Because Filipino sailors are cheaper. What you will learn might be an eye-opener." David Ames helped himself to some yogurt to cool the fire of the dal.

After days of depression, anxiety, and fervent prayer following the realization that she could not afford the prescribed heart medicine, Marta Fuentes went to a *hilot*, a faith healer.

The Philippines was famous for its many *hilots*. Most *hilots* were known for their skill in massage. Some were able to ease a child's fever by the laying on of hands and through prayer. The most famous *hilots*—receiving attention in the Manila newspapers and visited by tour groups of Europeans and Americans—were able to remove infected organs from a body without making an incision.

In Cebu, most *hilots* lived in Labangon, a poorer district in the eastern part of the city. The favorite *hilot* of the Fuentes family lived in Labangon. His name was Rey.

Marta went to Rey, and Rey closed his eyes and laid his right hand over Marta's heart. He earnestly enjoined her to feel the power of God, for He had the power to heal.

Marta was a believer and had faith. She did her best. She gave Rey a five-peso donation.

Still the pains did not stop.

13

James Burlane felt that human beings, what with their large heads and outsize cerebral cortexes—being smarter than their animal cousins—had evolved to walk, not run. He suspected that obsessive runners were largely dim bulbs who were somehow desperate to support the manufacturers of fashionable shoes and physicians who treated problems of the knees and feet.

Vigorous walkers tended to be those who wanted to see something of the world and get some healthy aerobic exercise at the same time. Also, one could walk in the country or the city, while running in the city was ostentatious if not downright, well . . . Burlane was willing to leave the running to antelopes and gazelles, which were built for it.

After his lunch with David Ames, Burlane called to arrange a late-afternoon meeting with Philip Cox, an officer of the British seaman's union in Hong Kong. He told Cox who he was and what he was after: the assholes who smuggled poached tigers for consumption by Chinese and Koreans with a fixation about homeopathic health. He was curious about Taiwanese fishing trawlers manned by Filipino sailors. Could Cox help?

Cox said sure. He'd help anyway he could. He sounded like a reasonable man, so Burlane, remembering his bone-chilling but memorable walk with the Russian wildlife official in Vladivostok, suggested they go for a walk while they talked. Was Cox up for something like that?

Cox consented quickly and with enthusiasm. Cox said he had

learned to love walking by exploring the nooks and crannies of port cities around the world before he settled down momentarily in Hong Kong to enjoy life with his Chinese wife and their young son. Indeed yes, they should walk.

He furthermore agreed with Burlane that walking wasn't good on the Kowloon side owing to the mind-numbing environment of endless, repetitive shops; the eternal peddling of identical goods was awful and opressive. While Hong Kong island had its share of radio, stereo, computer, and camera shops, these were—depending on the street—interspersed with an occasional noodle shop, girlie bar, food market, or restaurant.

They met the next morning in the lobby of the Royal Century. Cox turned out to be a good-humored, slightly built man with a weathered face and a ready smile showing teeth that could have been better, but never mind. He wore blue jeans, Reebok running shoes, and a dark blue nylon windbreaker over a pale brown, long-sleeved cotton shirt. He was from Liverpool originally and had a northern English accent that was somehow appropriate to a British sailor. Burlane knew without being told that when Cox got bored with the settled life in Hong Kong, he would put to sea again, if only occasionally.

They took a bus nearly to Causeway Bay with the idea of walking west on Hennessy Street, then east on Lockhart Road, then west again on Jaffee Road; this was a shuttle of nearly a mile if they went all the way to the Admiralty district that was located roughly in the commercial heart of Hong Kong island.

On the bus, Burlane learned that Cox too liked old-fashioned markets where one could browse and enjoy the color, texture, and odor of food unimpeded by plastic wrapping. The Liverpool of Cox's youth had had greengrocers and meat shops. Smell was one of the chief pleasures of food, although the anal-compulsive managers of American supermarkets were determined that not a hint of odor should be allowed in their domains. In addition, in the Hong Kong markets the Chinese sold live chickens and ducks that they kept in bamboo cages.

Burlane thought there was something to be said for having to wring an animal's neck and pluck its feathers before eating it. He wondered if there might not be children in the United States who were unaware that the animals they were consuming at Kentucky Fried Chicken or McDonald's had once coursed with the stuff of life. In addition to being antiodor, American supermarkets seemed equally determined to eliminate all hints of blood or mortality. No American supermaket would have a live animal on the premises; live animals went doo doo and smelled.

They decided that when they finished their walk, they might have an overpriced beer in a girlie bar, followed by an overpriced supper in a good Chinese restaurant, both courtesy of Burlane's conservationist employers.

They set forth down the crowded sidewalks at a brisk pace, dodging this way and that. Cox turned out to have a springy stride. The two eager walkers understood intuitively that the other enjoyed this immensely. Hong Kong was a city of buyers and sellers, not an industrial city, and it was by the water, so its air was not filled with lung-clogging pollutants. The sky was blue. The air was reasonably fresh. It was a great day and a good place for walking.

Burlane, pausing at a window that sold cheapie pirated videotapes of Sylvester Stallone, Charles Bronson, and Claude Van Damme action movies, said, "You know, I was in Vladivostok recently, and the place was swarming with Filipino sailors. A couple of years ago I was in Bombay, and I saw the same thing there. I see them here, too. They're everywhere, it seems. I'm curious, how many are there, exactly, and who they are they sailing for?"

Cox squatted on the sidewalk, examining the lowest titles in the window. "Filipino sailors?" He shook his head. "Estimates run from about fifty thousand on the short end to more than two hundred thousand at the top end. One hundred thirty thousand is the figure most often quoted. They're found mainly on ships bearing flags of convenience. For years, this meant ships were registered in Greece, Liberia, or Panama. More recently, owing to pressure by Lloyd's, it means Cypriot or Bahamian flags."

"Flags of convenience—meaning flags of countries that will register a ship with virtually no restrictions or inspections on provisions, safety, or communications equipment, reliable engines or anything else." Burlane straightened up from the window and continued down the sidewalk.

Following him, Cox said, "Correct."

Burlane said, "I knew the gist of the scam, but not the details."

Cox said, "I was talking to a colleague in Darwin the other day. He told me a Taiwanese vessel checked into the port that had been sent out of Taipei with no food aboard except rice. The Filipino crew had to catch fish along the way."

"Ooof!"

"The Australians wouldn't let them leave port until the ship was properly provisioned. Since sailors operate on the high seas under the flags of several nations, they have no political pull in any one country. Underpaid cops in Third World countries are famous for being corrupt. When sailors are underpaid, they do what they have to do to survive and support their families."

"Underpaid cops take bribes. Underpaid sailors smuggle."

"That's right. To understand, you have to understand the economics of training and manning vessels on the high seas. Tell me, Major Khartoum, have you recently noticed stories involving the deaths of Filipino sailors?"

Burlane stopped in front of the entrance to an indoor market. "I can remember two ships colliding in the Strait of Dardanelles, and a ship recently went down in the North Atlantic. Shall we take a look in here?"

"Sure, let's do it. And one went under off the coast of Japan a couple of weeks ago. The reason these events happen, Major Khartoum, is that those ships are unseaworthy pieces of manure manned by inexperienced Filipino sailors who don't know what they're doing, if I may be so blunt." He followed Burlane inside.

Burlane stopped before a long counter that featured mounds of snails, clams, oysters, and other crustaceans piled on ice. "Who are the officers? Would you look at this? Isn't this wonderful?"

Cox grinned. "It sure is. The officers are Greeks or Indians mostly, and a few Filipinos who can afford the forged documents saying they know what they're doing. Filipinos are willing to work for a couple of hundred dollars a month, whereas a British, Norwegian, or American seaman will cost a shipowner twenty-five hundred a month."

"I suppose you get what you pay for." Burlane proceeded to cruise a long counter of fish laid out on beds of shaved ice. These were whole fish, not fillets—unscaled, ungutted perch, sea bass, flounders, groupers, and several varieties of small, silvery fish that Burlane did not recognize. The sensible Chinese did not waste the heads, backbones, or fins. These all made good broth, and Americans who ate only fillets did not understand that the most succulent morsels were to be found along the spine at the top of the head.

Cox eyed the vista of fish as well. "The Philippines has no functional economy to speak of, so the government has to export labor to stay afloat. It's a truth they don't like to admit, but facts are facts. English is taught as a second or third language, after Tagalog and one of the regional languages—Illacano, Illongo, Chabacano, or Visayan, called Cebuano on the island of Cebu. The Filipino's ability to speak English enables the government to export domestic help, construction workers, sailors, nurses, and beautiful women for the sex trade. They can't produce jobs themselves, so they undercut labor in other countries. It's as simple as that."

Burlane proceeded to handsome bins of vegetables, various cabbages, and some greens that he'd never seen before. He towered over several tiny Chinese women who were examining the vegetables with intensity.

Cox, admiring the greens, said, "The Filipinos have established schools with fancy names—maritime academies and so on—I'll give them that. They go through the motions of training seamen, but if you have the money, they'll sell you whatever degree or certificate that's your heart's desire."

"An elaborate racket then," Burlane said. "No tomatoes, you notice that? The Chinese are not big tomato eaters."

Cox said, "Government-tolerated or even government-supported fraud is more like it. The schools work with employment agencies that charge the poor sods a fee to get a job—the fee being deducted from their salaries. Becoming a seaman is a way for desperate Filipinos to get past wary foreign immigration services so they can jump ship and work on land. They'll do whatever it takes to help support their families."

"I see. I like to throw a few chunks of tomato into stir-fried vegetables."

Cox said, "In order to get the experience they need for an international license, graduates of these maritime academies are forced to work free on interisland vessels. You have to understand, Major Khartoum, Filipino sailors don't smuggle because they're bad people. On the contrary, they're a wonderful, charming people with an intense loyalty to their families. They smuggle because they have to."

Burlane moved on past the vegetables, where placid ducks gazed out from behind their bamboo bars. He understood that domesticated animals, including ducks, were raised to be eaten, and it was in the natural order of things, yet he was still unsettled by the sight of a caged, bored duck. "The owners of the shipping lines working with the people who run the schools."

"Oh sure. The lack of experience of these graduates—from deckhands to boilerroom engineers—is the reason for the many horrific accidents in interisland boat traffic in the Philippines. Engines regularly conk out. Boats run into each other. Fires rage uncontrolled. It's a bloody horror. A person would have to be off his nut to ride one of those boats."

Burlane, squatting before the bored white duck, said, "That tells me about the motive for Filipino sailors to smuggle. Tell me about the Taiwanese fishing vessels they work on."

"Those boats poach in whatever water the Chinese captains think is profitable, never mind where. When the government in Taipei attempted to stop the hiring of Filipino sailors, the captains simply dumped the poor sods off at small offshore islands and picked them up again after their catch was unloaded.

"You say they'll fish whatever water looks profitable. Where is that exactly?" He stood and turned his back on the duck, and they went out into the street.

Cox shrugged. "Off the coast of Alaska, Canada, Korea, Russia, name it."

They were on the sidewalk now, and Burlane resumed his long

stride, dodging diminutive Chinese women who peered into the windows. "I read recently that Somalis grabbed a Taiwanese fishing vessel poaching off their coastline and demanded ten thousand dollars for their release. This was allegedly a payment for having to feed them for a week, mind, not a ransom."

Cox, laughing, skirted a spiffy Chinese necktie and his petite girlfriend, dressed in an immaculately tailored suit.

Burlane, thinking that the Hong Kong Chinese had somehow managed to out-Yuppie American Yuppies, said, "Somalia is just north of Kenya. Tell me, Philip, would Taiwanese fishing trawlers ever be in the smuggling business?"

Cox laughed even louder. "These are Taiwanese vessels manned by Filipinos, Major Khartoum. What do you think, for heaven's sake? Like smuggle the parts of poached tigers, I take it?"

"That's right. Tiger parts from India or Siberia, say, or rhino horns from Africa. The Chinese consider them aphrodisiacs, too."

Cox gave Burlane a wry grin. "Tell me. Do you think the Chinese captains and Filipino sailors could make money off tiger parts and rhino horns?"

This time it was Burlane's turn to laugh.

Cox said, "That answers your question, doesn't it, Major Khartoum? Girlie bar coming up. They have some hot-looking Filipinas in this one. Shall we have a quickie?"

Burlane raised an eyebrow.

Cox grinned. "I was thinking of a Foster's or Toohey."

"Sure, why not?" Burlane said.

14

■■■■As they talked, their breath came in frosty puffs.

The German calling himself Hans Kohl held on tight as the tiger poacher, Ivan Borolev, slammed the battered Toyota Land Cruiser into yet another pothole on the dirt road. A gusting wind blew blasts of snow powder across the vast clear-cut on either side of them, frozen white sea of stumps where once there had been forest. Ahead, where Borolev poached tigers, there was uncut forest, but Kohl was wondering if they would get there before Borolev destroyed the vehicle's suspension system or broke its axle.

The Land Cruiser had a heater, but it was broken, and Kohl, despite the fact that he was thoroughly bundled in long johns and layers of sweaters under his heavy wool coat, was cold to his bones.

Borolov, a thin-faced, ascetic-looking man who reminded Kohl of the Swedish actor Max von Sydow, was apparently determined to drive as recklessly and fast as he could. Also, he seemed oblivious to the cold as, wool-gloved hands gripping the steering wheel tightly, he charged over the frozen mud.

Bouncing in the passenger's seat, Kohl rechecked the map again, and swore softly in German. He could scarcely believe this so-called road was marked with an impressive red line on the map, as though it were an autobahn. *Sheisse!* The Russians truly were hopeless. There was something about the Slavs that Kohl would never understand. But they knew how to take the cold, as both

Napoléon and Hitler could attest. Kohl had had an uncle who had frozen to death at the seige of Leningrad, where the Russians, eating rat soup, had refused to yield.

It wouldn't be long before the Russians cut down all of their forests, Kohl knew. But nobody could talk to them, either about their forests or about their vanishing tigers. Before, when they were pursuing the Marxist brotherhood nonsense, all they could think about was showing the rest of the world how wonderful they were, so they stopped at nothing to develop. Now that they had a market economy, they thought of nothing but money, money, money. The result, in Kohl's opinion, was the same. But Siberia wasn't Kohl's country; it belonged to Russia. If they wanted to pollute their rivers and destroy their forests and kill all their animals, it was none of his business. Let them.

Beside him, Borolev was as always angling for more money for the tigers he poached. He said, "We delivered you the white tiger, didn't we? But the Siberian tiger has now got the attention of conservationists from the United States and Europe. You know how it is . . ."

Kohl cocked his head. "Oh?"

"They're paying for more game wardens. The more dangerous it is for us to poach, the more expensive it is for you. That's the way the world works. You know that, surely."

"How much more expensive?" Kohl licked his lips as the wind swirled another bank of powdery snow in front of them.

Borolev, momentarily taking his foot off the gas, shrugged. "Oh, I don't know. Make me an offer."

"Okay, suppose we give you five hundred U.S. dollars for each cat. No sense going through the drill of bargaining. That's prime rate."

Borolev rolled his eyes. "No, no, no. Please. Two thousand U.S. a cat, minimum."

Kohl closed his eyes. "When are you Russians ever going to learn how the market works? Without us to deliver tiger bones to the manufacturers of traditional medicines, you don't have any market."

"No?" The Toyota hit what amounted to a frozen ditch that cut across the so-called road at a right angle.

Kohl, gritting his teeth, held on. "No. Not in Korea. Not in Hong Kong. Not in Taiwan. Not in China. Not in Singapore or Malaysia. The gentlemen from Taiwan who used to buy your cats are no longer in the business. The manufacturers of the medicines remain, but the suppliers of animals and animal parts have changed."

"That's you."

"Correct. My employer now is the sole distributor of tiger bones to the manufacturers."

"How does he do that?"

Kohl said nothing.

Borolev, clenching his jaw, watched Kohl's face. "The Korean manufacturers, too?"

Kohl wished the Russian would pay attention to his driving. "There are only a handful of manufacturers in Korea. But yes, we supply the Koreans, too. Let me say it again: You either kill tigers and sell them to my employer, through me, or you go out of the poaching business. It's as simple as that."

"Okay then, fifteen hundred U.S. for each cat or no deal. It's just too dangerous to do it for anything less. Also, the fewer tigers there are, the harder it is to poach them. Did you ever think of that?"

Wham! The Toyota hit a rut hard.

"*Sheisse!*" Kohl cried. "We've thought about that, yes."

"There's a lot of territory out there, hundreds of miles of isolated forests and not very many cats. It's outrageously cold in the winter, and we have to buy vehicles and some means of communication so we can avoid the game wardens."

Kohl bounced in the seat, wondering how on earth the Toyota's suspension system was taking all this pounding. "Okay, I tell you what. You want to make big money? Maybe we can make a deal."

"Ah, good. I thought so." Borolev looked pleased.

"If we go by volume . . ."

Borolev, shifting gears, furrowed his brows. "By volume? What do you mean?"

"How many cats do you think you could kill in, say, six months?"

"Oh, I don't know . . ."

"Could you poach, say, fifty?"

Borolev straighted and actually slowed the vehicle. "Fifty?"

"Or even seventy-five?"

"What?" Borolev looked wide-eyed.

Kohl, hoping that the subject of money would permanently slow Borolev's driving, said, "Sure. We could work out a schedule of prices, based on how many tigers you're able to poach in the shortest amount of time."

"Schedule?"

"What if we set a time limit of one year and pay you on a sliding scale? The more cats you kill in one year, the more you earn for each cat."

Borolev looked interested. "Why don't you reach back for that thermos and pour us another cup of coffee?"

Kohl turned and retrieved the green thermos from the cardboard box behind the driver's seat. He poured them each another red plastic cup of coffee. It was incredibly strong as well as incredibly sweet.

Borolev slowed to accept his cup. "How much more for each cat? And starting at what?"

Maybe that was it. If they kept drinking coffee, Borolev would have to slow down or spill it all over his lap. Kohl said, "Those are fair enough questions. We would be willing to pay, say, seven hundred fifty dollars for the first ten tigers, a thousand for the next ten, fifteen hundred for the next ten, and so on. How much you make is up to you. If you could kill a hundred fifty or two hundred cats in a year, we'd buy them all."

"At the escalating rate." Borolev took a sip of coffee.

"That's right."

"That's a lot of tigers," Borolev said.

"We understand that."

"As the population thins, each tiger becomes more difficult to kill." Another gust of wind momentarily obscured Borolev's vision with powder snow; he slowed the Toyota.

Kohl said, "We understand that, too. That's a lot of money, top dollar, in fact, and a lot of risk on our part. We have to smuggle the bones and pelts and deliver them to the people who make the medicines. All illegal, and as you yourself said, the pressure to save the tigers is mounting. If we fool around with forty or fifty tigers here and there, we give the game wardens time to build their defenses. Even if they get more money in the next six months, it will take time to hire and train and deploy new game wardens, plus buy them new equipment. The only strategy that makes any sense is strike now, quickly, while they're still weak, and take all the tigers we can find."

"In the shortest period of time possible."

"That's right. The longer we wait, the greater the risk. To wait is foolishness."

"If we take two hundred in a year, there'll hardly be any tigers left." Borolev eyed Kohl over his cup of coffee.

Kohl, watching for the next pothole, deliberately avoided Borolev's gaze. He shrugged. "Maybe not in Siberia, but there'll be plenty left in India, and on the Malay Peninsula. No problem. If you wait, maybe they'll have the resources to put you poachers out of business entirely. You ever think of that?"

"And who would be my contact, should I agree to do this."

"Me. I'll make arrangments for secure communications. When you have a tiger, you call me, and I'll see to the details of butchering the body, and cleaning the bones, the transportation, everything."

Borolev bit his lip. "Two hundred tigers in one year. I don't know."

"Do you think you can do that?"

"I don't know. I'd have to hire some more poachers. We'd have to buy several new vehicles. Something with four-wheel drive. That's expensive."

Kohl said, "We know you'll have to invest in equipment to poach on this scale. That's why we're offering you top dollar, so you can buy what you need."

Borolev looked uncertain. "I suppose I could take a shot at it."

Kohl said quickly, "If you can kill two hundred fifty, we'd buy them all. To each according to his value, not according to his need. It's the capitalist way, Ivan. A new kind of world for you, eh?" His cup was empty. He wanted more coffee. He turned and grabbed the thermos again.

15

James Burlane and Dr. Vijay Sangrit had their talk as they strolled in a formal English garden on the side of a hill beneath the main Sangrit estate. The main house was a sprawling, multiwinged English country home of handsome stone with a slate roof that had been built by a wealthy British colonial official in the late nineteenth century to provide a comforting bit of England in what he regarded as barbarous India.

When the British were forced out of India in 1949, the Sangrits, a Brahmin family that had lived in the area for centuries and traced their lineage to the storied Guptas of old, took over the estate and resumed the traditional power they regarded as rightfully theirs. The newly independent India was a parliamentary democracy on the British model, but a parliamentary democracy with a difference. As the Indians saw it, the British had their lords and ladies and dukes and earls and the rest of it. Why shouldn't India have its classy Sangrits?

As a wealthy and privileged family, the Sangrits fulfilled duties and responsibilities to ensure that popular resentment against the perquisites of their status did not get out of hand. The Sangrit family was one of the largest backers of the Hindi film in Bombay that turned out some six hundred movies of adventure and romance each year. The Sangrit sons were expected to become producers when they were finished sowing their youthful wild oats.

As a young man, Vijay Sangrit had read history at Oxford, where he had been a cricket batsman of skill and reputation. He

rather overdid his stay in England, and, in the end, earned a doc-
toral degree. When he returned to India, he joined his older brothers in the movie industry, but his heart wasn't in it. His family,
seeing a public demonstration of responsibility as being in the
best interest of their family, that is, of maintaining their power, did
not discourage him. So Vijay was allowed to make an occasional,
money-losing "film," as opposed to a quickie, profitable "movie."
An artful "film" featured lingering shots, slow editing, and much
brooding; an escapist movie offered fast-paced romance and vio-
lence. Vijay's films were shown abroad in international film festi-
vals, their success bringing critical honor to the Sangrit family.

But tigers were Dr. Vijay Sangrit's thing; it was Vijay's preference to spend the better part of his time leading the Indian fight
to save the Bengal tiger.

Burlane thought the light-skinned Sangrit, dressed all in white
and wearing spotless British-marketed Reeboks, was a handsome
man. He was slender as a willow with long, elegant fingers. His
rather long black hair was parted on one side. He had a high forehead, a large, aquiline nose, and extraordinarily large brown eyes
that blazed with passion when he was on the subject of tigers.

The mustached Burlane wore khaki walking shorts, a sandy-
colored cotton shirt and a white cotton cricket hat to keep the ul-
traviolet rays off his vulnerable beak. Sangrit wore a nearly
identical hat, but his was Indian made; Burlane had bought his
Chinese-made version in Australia.

From the patio in the back of the house, where tables shaded
by colorful parasols flanked a small fountain, Burlane and Sangrit
could see the Olympic-size swimming pool a hundred yards below
them. Even at that distance, they could hear the Sangrit children
and their friends splashing and shrieking in the water.

Burlane had never seen anything quite like the English garden
between the patio and the large swimming pool below them.

A bush on the right, trimmed into a green ball, was matched
by an identical green ball fifty yards to the left. A green cone on
the right was balanced by a green cone on the left. In addition to
the balls and cones, the Sangrit family gardeners, given to geometry,
had carved matching triangles, rectangles, and cubes. They also

matched colors. A bush with yellow blossoms on the right had a yellow mate on the left. So it was with species of lavender and red blossoms.

Through this downhill landscape of mirrored color and shape ran a maze of immaculately trimmed green hedge, two meters high and quite thick. Identical gravel paths flanked the maze on either side, so that swimmers weren't required to negotiate the confusion of the puzzle.

Burlane said he wanted to challenge the maze.

Sangrit, who spoke British English with a modest hint of lilting Hindi accent, his voice rising and falling, said, "Of course, but you understand, Major Khartoum, I have the maze memorized, while for you, it will be a puzzle to be solved."

Burlane said, "That's why I'm here, to learn the territory from someone who knows."

"But of course. You're in the maze of the tiger poacher. Let's travel to the center, by all means."

"Straight into the mystery."

"It will certainly be confusing, I guarantee, Major Khartoum. Just when you think you have the path figured, you find yourself in the same place."

"Any advice before we start?"

Sangrit thought about that. "Pay attention. The hedge is very carefully trimmed and maintained. You might think the curves and corners are identical, but they're not. The way out of the maze lies in the details. Look for telltale anomalies."

"Good advice, I would think."

"Shall I have some cold beer sent on ahead? We can have it waiting in buckets of ice."

"I love beer. Certainly, dispatch the bearers of beer!" Burlane waved his hand grandly.

"Would you like imported British beer or some of my homemade variety?"

Burlane was impressed. Dr. Vijay Sangrit was his kind of man. He liked it that Sangrit had stayed in Britain to study history. He also admired Sangrit for having, on his own, undertaken the protection of the Bengal tiger. Now this: Here was a man who could import any kind of beer he pleased, and yet he made his own. Sangrit obviously understood that class wasn't simply what one owned, a critical fact in Burlane's opinion. Any asshole could simply buy beer. "You make your own beer? As the Australians say, 'Good on ya, mate!' Let's have some of that, by all means. Homemade beer is beer with soul."

Sangrit grinned. "Which do you prefer, Major Khartoum, lager or ale? I make both."

"Ale is good on a winter night with a fire crackling in the fireplace, but on a hot day like this nothing beats a cold lager—provided it's made with plenty of hops so it has some flavor."

Sangrit was pleased. "Impeccable logic, Major. I like my lager cold as well." Sangrit clapped his hands twice, and on the appearance of a uniformed manservant, gave his wishes in Hindi.

Burlane said, "I would have thought your years in England would have taught you to drink it cool rather than cold."

"No, no, Major Khartoum. I may have been educated in England, but I'm an Indian and have an independent mind. But given my choice, I agree with the Germans and you Americans on the matter of temperature and beer." Sangrit stepped down the path leading into the maze.

Following him, Burlane noted that it was impossible to mark the path, which was made of pale blue flagstones. He said, "I know it's fashionable to put down American lagers as being weak and sweet, but I, too, try to avoid groupthink, and besides, I'm an American. I don't see why we have to go around apologizing about everything. There's nothing like a large plastic glass of smooth, sweet beer and a hot dog with lots of sweet, bright yellow mustard at a baseball game."

"I like a man who shows pride in his culture, Major Khartoum. To my way of thinking, it's too easy to confuse the fashionable put-down of one's country with intelligence or taste. And how about your women. Do you prefer them light-skinned or dark?"

Burlane laughed. "That, too, depends on the circumstance. They both have their charms."

"Indeed they do. I know the Chinese regard us Indians as barbarians. They're always prattling on about their civilization being thousands of years old, and they constantly trot out the discovery of moveable type and the rest of it. At least you Europeans did something with it once your Herr Gutenberg tumbled onto the idea."

Burlane said, "After Gutenberg came cheap Bibles. Anybody could interpret God's word as he saw fit. No need to have a priest tell you how to think. That freed the human imagination from the bondage of the church. Not a bad step forward in my opinion."

They came to their first option in the hedge maze.

Burlane paused, then turned left.

Watching him, Sangrit said, "Those who believe the tiger is big medicine are willing to condone the casual elimination of the tiger, sod everybody who gets in their way. Their attitude is that Bengal tigers are our tigers, not theirs, so what do they care? They killed all of their own, and now they're after ours. And they call themselves civilized?" Sangrit laughed derisively. "They're barbarians."

Burlane strolled on, with Sangrit following close behind.

Sangrit said, "I'd think it would be embarrassing to be Chinese and have to admit a cultural fixation with hard dicks. If a juicy lady won't do the trick for their dysfunctional pee pees, I'm not sure what would. I told the people from the British Tiger Trust that they should fund research on cheap aphrodisiacs that they could market to the Chinese in lieu of tiger penis soup. They thought I was joking, but I was serious. That's what keeps the market going, you know, aged Chinese and Korean males worrying about their dickie-wicks, wee little things I hear, but apparently bigger than their brains, given their behavior."

They were at a hard right.

Burlane studied the turn. "Perhaps you Indians could sell them cheap editions of the *Kama Sutra*. A triple hit for you. Make some money on the books, turn them on, and save the tiger at the same time."

Sangrit grinned.

They came upon a dead end.

Burlane frowned. "Well, that's one turn I know is no good. We've been this way before."

"Do you think you can remember it now?" Sangrit said.

"I'll remember it. When I was a kid my parents and their friends played a card game called pinochle. My father was a good player because he memorized each card as it had been played. His memory used to infuriate my mother. The challenge is somewhat the same here."

Sangrit looked amused. "Cannabis seeds are a big ingredient of Chinese herbal medicine, by the way. They grind the seeds with a pestle and eat them to cure various ailments, but they don't smoke the buds. If they want an aphrodisiac they should loosen up and try the buds."

Burlane said, "In my experience a hit of pot in the presence of amiable company is a grand way of getting the hormones pumping."

"Ahh, you are a man of the world, aren't you, Major Khartoum? You don't hear of us Indians worrying about hard cocks."

Burlane laughed.

"Their problem is that the Chinese are too damn tense. They need to loosen up. Don't you agree?"

"The hippie word *uptight* covers the territory, I think. A momentarily fashionable word that was a useful addition to the English language, in my opinion. Too bad it's seldom used anymore."

They came to a corner.

"Right or left, Major Khartoum?"

Burlane knelt, studying the roots at the foot of the hedge. "Left here."

Sangrit said, "The cure for limp dicks was right under the noses of the Chinese all the time, presumably for thousands of years, and all they could figure to do with it was to grind the bloody seeds. How could they have failed to make that simple discovery? Is it because of some offhand comment by Confucius?"

"Makes a person wonder, I have to admit." The path was curving. They were walking in a circle now.

"We have about sixty percent of the world's tigers here in India, Major Khartoum. Maybe as many as four thousand, but that number seems high, I think. We have set up twenty-one game reserves to help protect them, but . . ." Sangrit sighed. "We are a poor country, Major Khartoum, and poor people do what they have to do to survive. We had sixty guards patrolling the Ranthambhore National Park in Rajasthan between 1989 and 1992, yet we know that at least eighteen tigers were poached. And you have to keep in mind that the reported kills are far fewer than the actual kills. The game wardens underreport the kills to make themselves look better. You take Nagarahole, for instance . . ."

"Nagarahole being?"

Another fork. Sangrit glanced at Burlane, awaiting Burlane's decision.

Burlane, again studying the roots, gestured right.

Sangrit, following Burlane to the right, said, "Nagarahole National Park. In the south. It's a two-hundred-fifty-square-mile reserve, which you'd think is generous enough. And for that, we have two-hundred-fifty guards." Sangrit pursed his lips.

"So far, so good."

"Then come the problems. Six thousand people live inside the park's borders, and it's surrounded by tens of thousands of villagers living in, say, another two hundred fifty villages. These are people who live on the very edge of existence, Major Khartoum. Each day is a struggle for food. An Arab will pay fifteen to twenty thousand for a good-looking pelt. But the bones are where the money is. Tiger bone will fetch more than five hundred U.S. dollars a pound! And a rich Chinese will pay four to five hundred U.S. dollars for a bowl of tiger penis soup."

"Ooof!" Another fork. Burlane, squatting for a quick glance at the roots of the hedge, confidently gestured to the left.

The curving path quickly doubled back to the right.

Sangrit said, "Of course the poachers don't get that much. The buyers are offering one hundred to three hundred U.S. dollars per corpse to Indians who're making a dollar a day if they're lucky. Of course, there's the inevitable middleman. The guy who actually pulls the trigger might get paid a bag of millet or lentils. The one who hires him might make a couple of hundred bucks. You can waggle your fingers and go tut-tut at us all you want, but the money is made by the smugglers, and they're not Indian."

"Who are they?"

"The Chinese are the main consumers, and the Chinese dominate the smuggling trade."

"Who deals with the local poachers? The guy with the hundred-dollar bills in his pockets. Not Chinese, I bet."

"The Chinese employ European or North Amerian buyers. The buyer gets a nick. And whoever it is who smuggles the bones to Asia. Owing to these thoughtful gentlemen, we think our tiger population may have dropped by as much as thirty-five to forty percent over the past five or six years."

"Thirty-five to forty percent! Ooof!" Another fork. Burlane looked chagrined. "We've been here before."

"You may be right. CITES is quite concerned over the decline. Their field consultant knows all the details, a German zoologist named Heinz Tepe. He's been here numerous times monitoring the decline of the tiger population. You should talk to him."

"Herr Doktor Tepe. He was in charge of the committee that hired me, and I certainly will be talking with him again."

Sangrit said, "We first became aware of the declining population in the early 1970s when Prime Minister Indira Gandhi took it up as a personal cause with Project Tiger." Sangrit bit his lip in frustration.

"What happened?"

"The predictable, I suppose. In retrospect we can see what happened. The Chinese slaughtered all their tigers. They had a stockpile of bones. But they started running low in the late 1980s, which is when the smuggling picked up."

"As it did in Korea."

"Yes, Korea as well," Sangrit said. "We should have been alert when we stumbled on the first bag of tiger bones, but we weren't. At the same time that game officials were exaggerating the numbers of tigers, the smuggling was increasing. A couple of years ago New Delhi police got eight-hundred-fifty pounds of tiger bones in one bust."

"How many tigers is that?"

Sangrit adjusted his cricket hat. "About forty-two. Out of curiosity, we dug up the tigers that had previously been buried at

Corbett National Park, and we found their bones were missing. It was then that we knew we were in deep trouble."

They came to a T, with paths going to the left and the right.

"Well, Major Khartoum?"

Burlane closed his eyes, listening to the shrieking of children in the pool. They were getting closer. He gestured to the left. "This path will take us to the pool and the cold beer," he said.

"You think so?"

Burlane laughed. "I hope so. I'm getting thirsty."

Sangrit smiled as they took the left path. He said, "You know, Major Khartoum, I loathe poachers, but perhaps for a different reason than the North Americans and Europeans who express such a grand love of the tiger. It's not that I believe you or they are outright hypocrites, mind, but . . ." He hesitated.

"But they put the burden of guilt on you and not on the Chinese and Korean consumers where it belongs."

"Correct. No market, no poachers. Where is the guilt to be assigned? On the poor wretches who shoot the tigers or the wealthy who consume the bones?"

The shrieking of children at the swimming pool was getting louder. "What have you heard about the smuggling route, Dr. Sangrit? Surely you must have heard rumors at least."

"For years the bones went straight to Taiwan, where they were distributed to the manufacturers of traditional medicines."

"In China mostly?"

"Correct. After the recent American pressure on Taiwan, the smuggler has apparently moved his business—at least temporarily. He'll no doubt resettle in Hong Kong after Beijing officially takes over."

"And he is?"

"We think a businessman who regularly does business with the Chinese. We don't know his identity for sure. He no doubt pays *tong* to a Chinese triad society to enforce his monopoly, but so does anybody who operates outside the law. If you smuggle anything in or out of China, you pay *tong* to a triad. That goes without saying." The offering of *tong,* sharing the goodies, was a way of life in Asia, an expected cost of doing business. High-minded westerners ordinarly understood it as a *bribe,* but that word insufficiently described the practice.

Burlane smiled. "So the smuggler was forced to move his base from Taiwan. To where?"

"We're told the Philippines is the current Asian port of entry. A temporary arrangement, as I said. And this is a rumor only, but it makes sense; the Philippines is notorious for its smuggling activities."

They stepped from the maze with the pool in front of them, surrounded by sparkling white tables and chairs. The tables, like those in the patio behind the house, were shaded by colorful parasols.

"Well, congratulations, Major Khartoum. I think you may have set a near-record for a first-timer."

Sangrit led the way to a shaded table near the edge of the pool, motioning to a manservant to deliver them their iced beer. As they took their seats, watching the children splashing in the water, he said, "There are more than seven thousand islands in the archipelago, and the Philippine Navy lacks the resources, and perhaps even the will, to monitor the coastal waters. And those patrol boats that they do have are commanded by, ah . . ."

"Crooks?"

"That may be too harsh a word. This is Asia, after all. The notion of public service is rather more elastic than in Europe or North America."

Burlane looked amused. "Patrol boats commanded by gentlemen amenable to the offering of proper *tong.* Will that suffice?"

Sangrit smiled. "You're familiar with Southeast Asia, Major Khartoum?"

"I've been there a couple of times."

"I thought so. Then you know that virtually one hundred percent of the sea traffic from Africa, the Middle East, and Europe passes through the Strait of Malacca that runs between Malaysia and Indonesia. It is the most heavily used sea-lane in the world; yet it is less than four kilometers wide in places."

Burlane waited while the uniformed manservant uncapped

Sangrit's homemade beer and poured them foaming mugs. The bottles had labels that read: VIJAY'S PRIVATE RESERVE.

Burlane, admiring the label and his host's imagination, said, "It's a regular funnel for seagoing vessels."

"You probably also know that because of Muslim pirates, neither the Indonesians nor the Malaysians effectively control the South China Sea east of the Strait of Malacca, along the northern coast of Borneo, if I have my geography right."

Burlane took a swig of beer. "Okay. Good stuff! Better than my own homemade swill. That's the direct route between the Strait of Malacca and Palawan and the Visayan Islands in the central Philippines and Mindanao below that."

Sangrit said, "In fact, we're told the Malaysians and Indonesians have largely given up trying to stop the traffic. The smuggling there is destined largely for Filipino ports, not theirs."

Burlane said, "I know those are considered some of the most dangerous waters in the world, real spooksville if you're trying to sail a yacht through there. And Zamboanga on Mindanao is famous for the smuggled goods in its public markets. Muslim country."

"Have you considered that route, Major Khartoum?" Sangrit raised an eyebrow.

Burlane said, "Yes, I have. So you Indians believe the smugglers are moving the parts of poached Bengal tigers out of, say, Calcutta, southeast through the Bay of Bengal and the Andaman Sea, then east through the Strait of Malacca."

"And from there due east through to the Philippines. Most likely in one of those so-called fishing trawlers flying a Taiwanese flag. That's the way we figure it, yes."

"Destined for where ultimately? Manila?"

Sangrit smiled. "Manila, perhaps. But we don't know, to be honest. As I said, I'm just giving you the scuttlebutt. But you might want to begin in Manila. They tell us the other bet is Cebu City, the chief port in the central Philippines."

"Cebu City?"

"There are lots of Chinese there, and more are being smuggled in every week if you believe the newspapers. Cebu City has become famous in recent years as an outpost of overseas Chinese, Major Khartoum. They dominate the economy there, and the wealthiest of them have business and financial ties to Taiwan and Hong Kong. But they've become spooked by the fact that their wives and children are the chief targets of kidnappers in Manila."

Burlane said, "Kidnapping Chinese is everyman's sport in Manila, Dr. Sangrit. The cops do it. The army does it. Fishmongers and cab drivers do it. They say if you're a Filipino living in Manila and haven't yet kidnapped a Chink, you're still a virgin."

Dr. Vijay Sangrit sampled his beer and said, "The Chinese are shrewd businessmen, you have to give them that. They're smart. They work hard. They're frugal. They help one another out. You should know that many people tried to break up the smuggling when it was based on Taiwan but failed. I admire you for trying, Major Khartoum, but it won't be easy."

16

Alexandr Kosov, a black-haired man in his early thirties, peered into the microscope with his piercing green eyes. He adjusted the focus.

Beside him, Oleg Karilov, the slow-talking chief of the Vladivostok forensics lab—a stooped man with a face of leathery folds—said, "See them?"

"I see them," Kosov said. What he saw were three long hairs, two white and one black. "What are they, besides hairs?"

Karilov, watching Kosov, said, "Cat hairs."

Kosov waited. He strongly suspected what would come next.

Karilov said, "Hairs from a Ussuri tiger."

Kosov adjusted the focus again in an attempt to see the hairs more clearly. "How do you know that?"

Karilov said, "They're longer, softer, and lighter than the hairs of any other known cat. They were evolved to protect the Ussuri tiger from these awful winters."

Kosov said, "Anything else? Could they have come from a white Ussuri tiger?"

"It's possible. But maybe not. An ordinary Ussuri tiger has white and black on it, too. But the odds are there would be some orange or dun hairs, too."

Kosov looked up from the microscope. "My bet is that the killer had been handling a white Ussuri tiger. Or the pelt of a white tiger. Why else would he have painted his victim like that?"

Karilov shrugged.

Kosov said, "I better call the German and let him know what we've found."

In the early hours of morning, Hermann Iversen lay awake, thinking. He could not sleep. Beside him, his wife lay sleeping, trusting, a comforting, lovely presence. When she had been young, she'd had a sexy, coltish walk that Iversen had admired greatly. Now, their daughter had that same walk.

Iversen got out of bed and wiped a hole in the frost on the glass so he could watch the snow falling softly on the street below.

With each passing year, Iversen's daughter Inga looked more and more like her mother. She, too, would make someone a good wife. She, too, would someday lie beside her husband, trusting, a comforting, lovely presence.

Some raging asshole had denied that pleasure to Erika Bauer and whoever it was who would have been her husband. Erika's perverse murderer had painted her like a tiger before he raped and murdered her.

A similar victim in Indonesia. One in India. Erika Bauer in Munich. More recently, a girl in Khaborovsk in Siberia.

Why?

Iversen remembered a poem by the Englishman William Blake:

> Tyger! Tyger! burning bright
> In the forests of the night,
> What immortal hand or eye
> Could frame thy fearful symmetry?

Somewhere in the tangled thicket of human desire, Iversen knew, lay motive. A reason why. There had to be. Even madmen acted out of logic. Or thought they did.

The phone rang.

Puzzled, Iversen grabbed it quickly before it woke his wife.

"I would like to speak to Herr Iversen, please." The male voice on the other end, speaking serviceable English with a Slavic accent, sounded apologetic.

"This is Iversen." What time was it? Iversen wondered.

The caller said, "I apologize for calling you this time at night, Herr Iversen, but we have a request from you, forwarded through Interpol. You asked to be notified immediately, day or night, if the tiger-killer struck."

Iversen was immediately alert. "That was my request, yes. And you are calling from?"

"Vladivostok."

"In Siberia."

"Yes, sir, on the Sea of Japan. I am Detective Lieutenant Alexandr Kosov."

"Thank you for calling, Lieutenant Kosov. What have you found?"

"Another victim, I'm afraid. A female in her early twenties painted like a tiger. Her body was found in a park. Her throat was cut. We haven't identified her yet. First Khabarovsk, now here."

"Thank you. Is there anything different or unusual about this one, Lieutenant?"

"Yes, sir, there is. This one has been painted with black stripes over a base of white instead of the black and orange of the previous victims. White Ussuri tigers are extremely rare, but they have been reported. They have no orange—just black stripes on white."

"Our killer is a real traveler."

"We found two white and one black tiger hairs on the body."

"Really?"

Kosov cleared his throat. "We've been hearing rumors that a poacher recently killed a rare white tiger near here."

Iversen said, "Really? Where 'near here'?"

"If the stories are true, in the Sikhote-Alin Range. Of course these hairs could have been from a regular tiger pelt, not a white tiger."

Iversen said, "Will you keep me posted if you learn anything more? Just call me here collect."

"Of course, of course, Lieutenant Iversen. We all want the same thing, which is to find the killer. Indonesian and Indian girls. A German girl. Two Siberian girls. They all deserve justice."

Iversen said his good-byes to the Russian cop and put down

the receiver. He returned to his spot by the window. He had come to regard life as a series of mysteries that constituted one large puzzle. When he was young and confident, he thought he knew everything. But the older he got, the more he was aware of how little he actually knew. The mystery of human motivation remained before him, ever elusive.

He had once read an interview in *Der Spiegel* with an author who said her fiction was always inside her; her daily chore was to plumb the depths of memory and experience for the shards and fragments that—fitted together in the form of an intellectual puzzle—took on meaning as a story. Pursuing these shards until they made sense more often than not required excruciating mental labor, concentration, and persistence; writing fiction was not an occupation for the fainthearted or dilettantes or quitters. Desire was required, if not obsession. At the time, Iversen had been amazed at how similar her description of her work was to his notion of his own. The answer to his quest—the identity of the killer who painted his victims like tigers—was down there in the murk of the human imagination, he knew:

> Tyger! Tyger! burning bright
> In the forests of the night

One victim in India, a second in Indonesia, a third in Munich, a fourth in Khabarovsk, and now this one; the killer had now struck twice in Siberia. The Russian cops had found three tiger hairs on the victim's body, two white and one black. Had these been from a Siberian tiger?

Was the killer returning to old haunts?

Iversen had run down every conceivable lead in Germany hoping to find a killing with an MO that was anything close to the tiger-girl murder. He had found none. He only had one suspect, Klaus Neumann. Neumann had a fascination with tigers and big cats. As an employee of Hesse's, he had bought cats in all the countries where girls had now been murdered. He was no great lover of his mother, and he had never been married. He had returned to Germany and was in Munich the night Erika Bauer had been murdered.

Was Neumann the murderer? It was time to tell Rolf and Karl Bauer all that he had learned and what he suspected about Neumann. Iversen thought he had enough circumstantial evidence to justify spending some of Rolf Bauer's medical clinic fortune. Going to Africa and then possibly on to Asia or Siberia would be expensive. He wanted to make it clear to both brothers that he only had circumstantial evidence and a hunch to go on, no more.

Outside the snow drifted silently onto the street, swirling softly by the yellow streetlight on the corner.

17

June 1996, Cebu City

▰▰▰▰ The long, narrow stage or ramp was located against a mirrored wall, and here Filipinas in, yawn, old-fashioned bikinis moved their bodies to recorded music in what was intended to be dancing. When one dancer finished her turn, she was joined by the next dancer for a tandem of lethargic gyration. The two dancers wiggled together for a few minutes before the first girl left to cadge ladies' drinks from the customers, who watched from small tables on the opposite side of the room.

The German who was calling himself Horst thought the girls could at least have worn string bikinis, or better still, take it all off, why pretend? Filipinas were primarily of Malayan ancestry, the same as the Thai girls, so their faces and figures were similar, but the Thais, Buddhists, were not restricted by the same religious inhibitions as were Catholic Filipinas. The girls in Bangkok or Chiang Mai or Phuket, knowing men wanted to see it all—to hell with silly-ass, old lady's bikinis—got right down to business. In addition they were skilled at doing tricks with cucumbers, Ping-Pong balls, and each other, if their guests were so inclined and the price was right.

The Thais were up front: Sex tourism turned a tidy buck. The Filipinos were torn between notions of propriety, forced upon them by one of their many invaders—the Spanish, with pious friars in tow—and coveting that same tidy buck. The love of a buck prevailed.

If a guest wanted to screw a dancer, all he had to do was pay management a five-hundred-peso "bar fine"—a little less than twenty bucks U.S.—and take her back to his room. There, for another five hundred pesos, he could buy a two-hour quickie—called a short time—or a thousand for an overnight, thorough debauch. If he weren't *tehik,* Cebuano for cheap, he might lay a tip on her for performing well.

Horst supposed that if a Filipina felt guilty about this, she could confess to her priest on Sunday, and the priest, if he was not after side action himself, could prescribe a proper penance, counting beads or whatever Catholics did, so that she could be forgiven.

There were many places in the United States and Europe where the girls danced with nothing on at all, but you couldn't bed them if you wanted—especially for what amounted to spare change. The dancers in Thailand could be sensational lays, but the Filipinas weren't bad either. And unlike the Thai girls, most Filipinas spoke some English, so you could tell them what you wanted without going through a stupid pantomime, which could be frustrating when both your hormones and imagination were surging. When one used English to tell a Filipina turn over, she turned over.

But bars with dancers and hostesses available for a bar fine were not just for foreigners, by any means. The Filipino males, in addition to their tradition of maintaining a *quierda,* or mistress, had their own places to score a quickie. In such an overpopulated, impoverished country, both sex and life were cheap.

The dancers in the bars for expats and foreign travelers mostly had one thing in mind, Horst knew, and that was to snag an Australian, North American, or European husband and get the hell out of the Philippines so that she would have a future—and she could send money back to help support her family. Young wives were a major export of the Philippines, whose government, in fact, was an institutional pimp of sorts—turning a blind eye to the export of so-called entertainers who were, in fact, prostitutes. And while foreigners were blamed for every ill imaginable, few politicians complained about the money the young women sent back home; fancy cars and mistresses cost money.

But Horst could not blame the girls. What attractive young woman wanted to spend her life in a country as hard up as this one?

When a newcomer came into Our Place or the Kentucky or Kukuc's Nest or the St. Moritz or Parker's on Mactan Island with an exceptional sweetie by his side, chest swelled with pride, the expat vets scoped her out to see if this union had a future. The cynical American expats even had a name for this private game. They called it Dumb Shit, and their unstated but critical questions were simple enough: Was the Filipina dressed in a classy outfit that she had obviously bought in the fanciest shop she could find? Or, if she was wearing jeans, were they expensive brand-name butt-moulders that nearly cut her in half at the crotch? Was she wearing an excessive number of gold bracelets, or chains around her neck? Did she smoke? Did she drink beer with her longnosed man? Did she hold hands or casually rest her hand on his thigh or the small of his back? Drinking and smoking by women, and public displays of physical affection, were all frowned upon in the Philippines.

If the answer to these questions was yes, the expats smiled to themselves. The foreigner flashing his trophy bride—who would surely cause his men friends back home to groan out loud—was in fact a Dumb Shit, a sucker squiring disaster in a B-cup bra.

Horst thought the business of buying overpriced ladies' drinks for a few minutes of chitchat was a monumental waste of time and resources. If you wanted a lay, which was the end object, after all, why not spend your pesos on the bar fine so you could take your lady out and do the dirty deed?

Horst watched the dancers for a few minutes, knowing immediately which one he wanted, a tallish, slender Filipina, maybe three or four inches over five feet tall, with large, brown, catlike eyes.

When the girl with catlike eyes finished dancing, Horst motioned for her to come sit beside him with the palm-down motion that Asians preferred.

When she sat beside him, he said, "You're very *guapa*. Would you like to come home with me?"

She grinned demurely. She was not there to play hard to get.

He said, "I've got a nice house in Beverly Hills. It's cool up there. I've got a view and plenty of CDs. We'll have fun. I've got Air Supply if you want, and Barry Manilow. Karen Carpenter, too." Horst hated the sophomoric romantic songs of Air Supply and Barry Manilow. He had originally liked Karen Carpenter's mellow voice, but in the Philippines she sang on tapes and on the radio so often that the very sound of her set his teeth on edge. In the Philippines, love songs were like a religion, promising heaven in the present, just as the Catholic church promised an everlasting life after death.

"Short time or all night?" she said.

"All night."

"Sure, why not? My name is Gloria."

"Horst," he said.

"You're very *guapo*, Horst."

Horst glanced at his watch. He said, "I'll pay the bar fine, then I have to go see a friend. You go outside in twenty minutes, and there'll be an air-con taxi waiting for you. We'll have a good time."

"Go outside in twenty minutes? Sure," she said.

Horst gave her a five-hundred-peso note for the bar fine, and left the Silver Dollar. He went next door and had himself a *lechon manok*—chicken barbecued Filipino style—and collected his Mercedes-Benz. When Gloria stepped onto the sidewalk, he opened the door on the passenger's side and whistled at her. "I figured to hell with the cab," he called.

She slipped onto the seat beside him, an exquisite, exotic beauty. "Beautiful car," she said.

Horst drove his bar fine up Jones Avenue, around the capitol building and through the district called Guadalupe, then higher up to what amounted to an American suburb, with ranch-style houses, along tidy streets high above the sprawl and squalor of Cebu City.

These hills—nicknamed Beverly Hills—had once been forested, but no more; every tree and twig had surrendered to provide charcoal for the tens of thousands of squatters who had moved in from the provinces, hoping to swap their bleak poverty for something better. There were people in the provinces who lived off ground corn or rice seasoned with sea salt, and *camotes*—sweet potatoes. Goiters, owing to the lack of iodine in the salt, were commonplace.

But up in the hills behind the city, the air was cooler, if only slightly cleaner; the lawns were watered and clipped; the shrubs were trimmed and maintained. Here, there were proper septic tanks for the sewage. And inside, people had regular stoves with ovens.

The higher Horst drove—and the fancier the surroundings—the friendlier Gloria became.

When Horst used a remote to open an electrically operated gate around his walled compound, Gloria's eyes widened. First the Mercedes. Then the electric garage door. Then the well-tended lawn with flowers, shrubs, and papaya trees. Now this: an American-style ranch home with a proper roof and windows.

And when they stepped inside, there came a rush of cool air! Horst had left the air conditioner running, something only the richest of the rich could afford to do in Cebu City. On top of that, the house was carpeted and had overstuffed imported furniture. He had a big-screen Sony, and a Sony CD sound system that must have cost thousands of dollars.

Horst showed her his fancy stove with an oven; he also had a microwave, a food processor, a blender—the works. And he turned on the tap at the sink.

She put her hand under it. Her eyes widened. "Hot water!"

"You like it?" he said.

"Oh, I love it," she said, and she was not lying.

He said, "It's uncivilized having to take cold showers all the time. Even in this climate."

He opened the refrigerator, which had a separate freezing compartment, complete with an ice maker. He grabbed a cold bottle of Beck's and led her to the bedroom. As they did, Gloria slipped her arm around his waist and gave him a squeeze. She was not there to study Goethe's poetry or Wagner's operas. And a bar fine did

not score a proper, that is, rich husband by being shy or uncoop-
erative. The way to a man's heart lay through his dick; all bar fines
knew that. No bar fine wanted to humiliate herself in front of her
peers by marrying a longnose who didn't own anything; how else
was success measured if not by expensive objects displayed for
others to envy?

They stepped into his bedroom, which had an Oriental rug
thrown over a hardwood floor. He had a stupid poster on the wall;
that would have to go. The door to the CR—the comfort room—
was open. The faucet handles were gold, as well as the handle to
the toilet. Okay!

"Now, I think I would like to see you naked, Gloria," he said
in a matter-of-fact tone of voice.

If Gloria was shocked at the abruptness of his request, she
didn't show it. If a man with all this money wanted to see her
naked, he got his wish. No problem. Without hesitation, she
started unbuttoning her blouse.

When her blouse and bra were off, he said, "You have very nice
totoys." He ran his hand across one of her breasts.

"Thank you," she said as she unzipped her skirt.

He motioned with his hand for her to turn.

"Nice *lobot,* too." He gave her rump a mild slap with the palm
of his hand.

She smiled. "I'm glad you like it."

"Hold out your wrists."

She did as she was told.

Horst retrieved a small box from a closet. He took two leather
wrist restraints from the box and strapped them on her wrists, one
at a time. "I'm not going to hurt you. I like costumes. We'll have
fun. You'll see."

Gloria licked her lips, not wanting to offend this fabulously
rich potential husband. She said nothing. A brand-new Mercedes
Benz. Hot water direct from the tap, and he had left the air conditioner running. Imagine!

Horst squatted and fastened leather restraints around her ankles. "Step in front of the mirror please."

A microwave and a big-screen Sony. And that sound system! Imagine the envy of her friends when they laid eyes on that. She stepped in front of the mirror.

With the click of a metal snap he fastened her wrists together and ran a green plastic line to the ceiling, ran it through a small pulley there, then fastened it to a hook on the wall.

"Spread your legs."

"Wider."

She spread them wider.

"Don't move."

Horst took two metal hooks and screwed them into little metal anchors set in the floor by her ankles. He quickly snapped her ankles to the hooks, then stood and pulled on the green line, stretching her wrists to the ceiling.

He momentarily massaged her *boto*, smiling as she squirmed and twisted her hips. Then, he stepped back to admire her. He said, "If you try to make noise, I'll have to shut you up." He held up a gag so that she could see it: a small ball fastened to a strap that fit around the victim's neck. "You see how this works?"

Gloria, for a moment forgetting cars, kitchen gadgets, and hot water, nodded yes.

While she watched—thus stretched from floor to ceiling—Horst opened the closet again and retrieved four white reflecting panels used by photographers. He carefully set them up around her, screwing the aluminum wing nuts into place on their tripods.

Gloria believed the prize of prizes was within her grasp: marriage to the German, and with it the Mercedes, the Sony big screen, the house high on Beverly Hills overlooking the sprawl of sweaty squatters in their bleak and dreary huts. She was determined to show him she was a good trouper, but hanging from her wrists was a tiring proposition.

Then he left the room briefly and returned with another cold beer, a painter's palette, several tubes of paint, and brushes.

Horst began by painting Gloria's slender body with a base coat of yellowish tan. He painted her face, her neck, her torso, her arms and legs, hands and feet.

Gloria watched herself being painted.

With the base coat in place, Horst began the chore of painting tiger stripes. He did not rush this.

Gloria had no idea how a man with Horst's wealth had been allowed to remain single, but she wanted to be the one who would sit beside this German in his air-conditioned Mercedes, with gold rings and necklaces, and watch lessers from behind the privacy of tinted windows. When he was finished with his kinky painting, she would show him how to throw a proper fuck, then she'd see. Then she'd have a better idea of her chances.

Horst painted on, stepping back occasionally to admire his work.

Gloria had been taken by the carpet and the fabulous CR. Now her eyes grew wide. "Are you going to paint me all over?"

"I think so," he said. "You'll be beautiful. You'll see. You know, in the movie *Goldfinger,* the villain killed a young women by painting her body with gold paint. The idea was that the paint somehow smothered her by not letting her skin breath. That was nonsense. This won't hurt you at all. It might tickle now and then, but that's about it."

"It looks sexy," she said. Watching herself in the mirror, she twisted her body for his pleasure. Gloria was determined not to complain. If Horst wanted, he could string her up and paint her like a tiger every night of the week, no problem. Better this than what the potbellied Swede had wanted her to do.

18

Risa Sanchez was raised on Katipunan Street in a working-class area of southwestern Cebu City known as Labangon. She was twenty-eight years old when Tigerman, as he was now being called, first struck in early June, the beginning of the rainy season in the central Visayas. The rain was a welcome relief from the brain-frying heat of April and May. Large-eyed, and with a remarkable figure, and a proud, erect carriage, Risa was an inch shy of being five feet tall.

Why the Tigerman had struck in Cebu after his global killing spree in such faraway places as India, Germany, and Russia, in addition to nearby Indonesia, was the subject of much speculation in Cebu's two tabloid-size newspapers, the *Sun-Star* and *The Freeman*, as well as the national newspapers published in Manila.

The larger question in the Philippines was: Would he strike again?

For Filipinas in Cebu, the question was: Will I be next?

Risa Sanchez's story was perhaps typical of a Filipina trying to fashion a future for herself, where a future—beyond household drudgery and a drunken, probably philandering husband—was hard to come by. Religion and love songs had much in common and for a good reason: They both promised relief from the dreary reality of the present.

Risa's father, Loloy, a broad, stocky Filipino, with an easy, genial smile, once had had money, but he had squandered it on mistresses and splashy parties, where he was known as a dancing fool.

This happy-go-lucky way of living was the fashion of men in the Visayas, where crops grew quickly and the fish were plentiful. In the Visayas, almost any occasion, from birthdays to wakes, called for a *lechon*—a suckling pig cooked slowly over charcoal—plus all the San Miguel the males could consume and then some.

If one wanted thrift and tightfisted sobriety, one went to Northern Luzon, where the Filipinos, working a hard, unproductive soil, were known for their penny-pinching ways.

As Loloy pushed seventy, he earned beer money by scouring the neighbor island of Bohol for carabao that he bought two at a time and ferried back to Cebu to be butchered for sale at Carbon market. Four of Loloy's five sons were butchers who toiled all night for eighty pesos—about three dollars U.S. A kilo of rice, good for two meals a day at best, cost nearly fifty cents.

Loloy's carabao business was torpedoed by one of his own sons, Leo, a carefree, irresponsible sort who ran off with the money his father needed to buy more carabao. Leo proceeded to blow the money on yet another mistress he could not afford. Leo had a wife, using the term generously—they were not legally married. The "wife" and her five children were now supported by Loloy.

Loloy and his wife Gemma, and Leo's wife and her children, and Risa, plus Loloy's four sons and their children—twenty-three offspring in all—lived in a family house on Katipunan Street. They would not have had the house if Loloy and Gemma had not been lucky enough to have produced two daughters who had married North Americans—one to a lumberjack near Kamloops, British Columbia, and one to an electrician in Southern Illinois. The house, a large, unpainted hive of crude rooms, was handsome by Labangon standards, containing as it did its own well, with an old-fashioned cast-iron hand pump. Contributions from the expatriate daughters built the house, and kept it maintained.

A lucky couple were Loloy and Gemma to have produced two daughters who had married North Americans.

As a girl, Risa earned money by selling *camotes*—fried in oil and sugar. Three pieces of *camotes* thus candied and skewered on a stick sold for two pesos, an affordable street treat along with fried bananas cooked the same way. Risa made fifty centavos for each stick she sold, selling as many as twelve to fifteen a day, which came to six or seven pesos—about thirty-five cents U.S. In Cebu, a construction worker laboring for twelve hours on a Chinese-built shopping mall might be paid seventy or eighty pesos a day. A pretty salesgirl in the completed shopping mall might earn eighty pesos a day.

Cebu was awash with children and young people. This was for two reasons. First, the Philippines lacked any sort of social security or retirement system. In old age, one depended on the generosity of one's grown children. Parents were unrelenting in their insistence on loyalty to the family, drilling filial piety into them from childhood. Also, the Catholic priests—for reasons that to critics seemed callous if not outrageous—were equally unrelenting in their insistence that continued reproduction was a required demonstration of loyalty to God. Catholics in North America and Europe ignored this cruel nonsense, but most Filipino Catholics did what they were told.

So it was that sensible Filipinos saved every peso to send their children to college, hoping against hope that they would have a future. An investment in their children's future was an investment in their own security. Thus thousands of young people from all over the Visayan Islands flocked to Cebu, a city chock-full of "colleges" and "universities" and "institutes" of one sort or another.

Students entered these schools at age sixteen. Education was regarded as a ticket to employment, not as a good in itself in the western sense. One became an engineer or a seaman or a nurse, that is, something that could conceivably score a job on the labor market outside of the Philippines. There was no work at home, and there likely never would be. Everybody knew that, although few would publicly admit it.

In Cebu, employers routinely added "pleasing personality" to job requirements and Filipinas under five foot tall—the majority—were, for no apparent reason, not considered for employment. "Pleasing personality" was often demonstrated to employers on a couch or floor, in a manner storied of Hollywood.

Risa's family could not afford to send her to a diploma mill,

and Risa, being just four-eleven, was thus disqualified from even making it to the pleasing personality couch, even though she had a broad, infectious smile and a deep-throated laugh. This lack of a college degree disqualified her from what was regarded as a splendid job—a hundred pesos a day assembling Timex watches on Mactan Island, a task, some cynics claimed, that could be done by a trained chimpanzee.

She had tried to emulate her sisters and score a North American or European husband by going to the swimming pool of a resort hotel in Talisay. There, when she was seventeen, she met and fell in love with a German physician twenty years her senior, but after several years of romance, that fell through.

Still, having learned serviceable English from the German, she had pluck and kept trying. She sold *camotes* to spring for the five-peso round-trip on a crowded jeepney to Talisay, where she had met the German. At the swimming pool, she lounged around in her bikini with her friend, who had a job as a cashier in a Cebu bar, and drank a five-peso orange soda. Although she was cute in the extreme, she was not amenable to a quickie, audition lay, and time passed with no North American or European husband in sight. Her sisters-in-law claimed she was too picky. Perhaps she was. As she passed her mid-twenties, Risa suspected she was too old. To be twenty-eight and unmarried in the Philippines was to be an old maid. But she did not want to marry a Filipino. She wanted to marry a North American or European so she could have a future.

Risa wanted to be a photographer or an artist. But a camera was out of the question, and such photographers and artists as existed in the Philippines were in Manila, and, usually, related to someone. Almost everything in the Philippines depended on who you were related to, certainly any profession that could remotely be called artistic. All the movie stars in Manila were related to someone, powerful monied families, politicians—senators or mayors or provincial governors. Politicians were without exception rich, owing to a Filipino tradition that the public treasury was for them and their relatives and friends to loot.

When they sacked the Philippine treasury, the larcenous President Ferdinand Marcos and his wife Imelda were assumed by foreign observers to be anomalous. In fact, any change in administrations—as all Filipinos knew from long and bitter experience—merely signaled a change in looters. A politician who did not loot was regarded with not a little suspicion: He or she was either a fool or a fraud or both. The North American and European notion of a politician riding a white horse of service and responsibility was unknown.

A camera aside, Risa Sanchez could not afford the simplest pad and pencil for sketching, much less watercolors and acrylics, and all the brushes and gear that went with that. To a Filipina like Risa aspirations to be an artist were nonproductive foolishness, pie-in-the-sky fantasy.

Which is, why, week after week, month after month, she scoured the job ads looking for anything that would get her out of her house and away from the watchful eye of her demanding mother.

19

The big story in Manila when James Burlane arrived at the combat zone of serial thieves and hustlers that was officially the international airport was the search for the serial killer who painted his victims like tigers. The murderer had made an appearance in the Philippines two weeks earlier, murdering a dancer in a Cebu City nightclub.

The painted Filipina had been found on nearby Mactan Island with her throat cut. Mactan Island, site of Cebu's airport, was the place where Chief Lapu-Lapu—his name now given to a delicious fish—had sent the Portuguese explorer Ferdinand Magellan to his heavenly reward. It was also the island where the CITES consultant, Heinz Tepe, lived.

This was the killer's sixth victim, and officials of the Philippine National Police and the National Bureau of Investigation had announced they were working with international authorities, and they would not quit until they ran the killer to ground. Manila's lively national newspapers were calling the killer Tigerman, and the chief of the Department of Tourism warned that unless Tigerman was brought to justice, the country's tourism industry stood to suffer.

Burlane thought that was remarkably unlikely, because few female tourists had reason to go to the Philippines. Tourism in the Philippines depended on males who went there for sex and little else, and with each passing year fewer tourists were willing to risk their lives and wallets even at the airport.

When Burlane was in the Philippines, he regularly read two

newspapers, *Today,* published by the talented, if eccentric Teodoro "Teddyboy" Locsin, a Harvard-educated Filipino who had helped write the speech President Corazon Aquino read before a joint session of Congress in 1986, and the firebrand nationalist newspaper, the *Philippine Daily Inquirer.* Few newspapers in the Philippines were above what the Filipinos called "envelopmental" journalism, in which payoffs and bribes were routinely and casually extended to reporters and editors; the "truth" was an elusive if not impossible concept in the Philippines. But, in Burlane's opinion, *Today* and the *Inquirer* were the most trustworthy, or at least the best edited.

He scanned the front pages of *Today* and the *Inquirer* as he sat down to enjoy coffee and breakfast in the restaurant of the Carlton Hotel in Pasay City, one of the new sex-and-sin locations now that Manila Mayor Alfredo Lim had shut down the notorious sex district of Ermita. Metropolitan Manila was a hodgepodge of municipities; the purpose of these numerous city halls, Burlane assumed, was to ensure the maximum number of crooked mayors and on-the-take police departments.

Before Burlane turned to the editorial pages of *Today* to see what deserving target was the object of Locsin's erudite scorn, he studied once more the fax he had received in India from Ara Schott, who had subcribed to a clipping service of Asian newspapers. The fax was an item from a column in the *Inquirer* by the accept-no-horseshit-and-take-no-prisoners columnist Ramon Tuflo, who covered police and military affairs.

The column stated that people in the Chinese-Filipino community were currently reporting the availability of the nose, claws, and penis of a Siberian white tiger. The claws were going for two thousand dollars each, and the sellers were holding out for a thousand dollars for the nose, and a cool five thousand for the penis. The purchase of the latter, Burlane presumed, was for the Chinese who had everything.

The Philippine National Bureau of Investigation, modeled after the American Federal Bureau of Investigation, quoted allegations from CITES that the Philippines was a suspected distribution point for smuggled body parts of endangered species destined for the manufacturers of traditional medicine in China. Tuflo said the government, under pressure from North America and Europe, was investigating this report.

Burlane wondered if the allegations by CITES might not have been based on his own reports from Hong Kong and India. If he was the ultimate source of the leak, he wished Heinz Tepe and the eager bureaucrats in Geneva would curb their enthusiasm until he got to the bottom of the rumor.

Burlane had decided to talk to the author of the item before he proceeded south to Cebu to talk to Tepe. He phoned the *Inquirer* city desk and was told that he could find Mon Tuflo having breakfast at the Sorriente Hotel a block off United Nations Avenue in Ermita. A *balikbayan* friend of Tuflo's was visiting from the United States and was staying at the Sorriente. *Balikbayans* were Filipinos who lived overseas.

B urlane took a cab to the Sorriente, an economy hotel half a dozen blocks from the American Embassy. He had a good idea what Tuflo looked like because the *Inquirer* ran his picture together with his column. He found Tuflo immediately, having a cup of coffee alone in the small café on the ground floor.

Tuflo, a handsome, virile Filipino with a lean face and piercing brown eyes, wore black slacks and a short-sleeved yellow shirt, open at the throat and revealing a substantial gold chain.

Burlane, wondering where Tuflo's friend was, introduced himself. "Your city desk said I could find you here, Mr. Tuflo. My name is Major M. Sidarius Khartoum. I was wondering if I might cadge a few minutes of your time." Burlane gave Tuflo a business card: Major M. Sidarius Khartoum, Mixed Enterprises. The card gave an American telephone number.

Tuflo, eyeing him over his cup of coffee, read the card. "I've only got a few minutes. I'm waiting for my friend to make some phone calls from his room." He looked at the card again. "If I call this number, who will I get?"

"My associate in Montgomery County, Maryland. We keep in touch. He'll patch the caller through to me, wherever I am."

"And Mixed Enterprises is?"

"A private company," Burlane said. "We accept international assignments of one sort or another."

"I see. And this time you're working for?"

"The Convention on International Trade in Endangered Species that you mentioned in one of your recent columns. CITES."

Tuflo shook his hand. "Sure. We can talk. Why not? As long as you're friend and not foe."

Burlane grinned. "I understand your caution. You've even got the gunfighter's table."

"Oh?"

"The corner table so nobody's at your back. But what I don't understand is how come you're still alive."

Tuflo pulled an automatic pistol from his trouser pocket, then put it back and took another sip of coffee. Obviously he had decided Burlane meant him no physical harm.

Burlane said, "I thought you must pack something, the way you spear those crooks. I read your column every time I'm in the Philippines." Then, grinning mischievously, he said, "By the way, what happened to your cranky pal, Mr. Henares? I haven't found his column, last couple of passes through town." The columnist Hilarion M. Henares, a graduate of MIT, was a Filipino nationalist who, in a column called "Make My Day," had once regularly called Americans pinheads, assholes, and worse. Bullshit artists, shitheads, bastards, sons of bitches, and all manner of other straightforward perjoratives. Down-to-earth expletives routinely made it into print in the Philippines; this unshackled their writers and made Filipino newspapers more honest and fun to read than America's sanitized pap.

Tuflo laughed. "Larry has become a national affairs advisor to the president. They're both Panganisians, you know."

"Hilarious, I always called him, but he was fun to read nevertheless." Burlane handed him the faxed clip. "I was wondering if you know where I could most likely find the people peddling tiger bones to manufacturers of Chinese traditional medicines."

Tuflo read the clip, considered the question. "I don't know for sure. Maybe Zamboanga, but Cebu City more likely because of all the Chinese there. Zamboanga is Muslim country."

"Why didn't you include that in your column?"

"About Zamboanga and Cebu?"

Burlane nodded.

Tuflo said, "Because I didn't get that from the NBI or PNP." The NBI stood for the National Bureau of Investigation, PNP was the Philippine National Police. "I got it somewhere else, and I have no idea whether it's true or not. The only reason my NBI source leaked the tiger bit is that Malacanyang wants western conservationists to think the government is concerned about the traffic and is doing something about it." Malacanyang was the presidential palace. Tuflo said, "Malacanyang doesn't want to suffer the same fate as Taiwan. We run a three-billion-dollar trade surplus with the Americans, and the president's people know the *Inquirer* is read regularly at the American Embassy."

"Fair enough," Burlane said. "Do you think Malacanyang really cares about stopping the smuggling?"

Tuflo grinned. "The government is hard-pressed to stop jaywalking. What do you think?"

"So the leak was done with a wink."

"The smugglers know the government has to make a public show. No harm done."

Burlane said, "What if the NBI and the PNP really did try to get to the bottom of the smuggling? What would happen then?"

Tuflo looked amazed that Burlane could be so stupid. "You mean, what would happen if someone went down to Cebu and asked honest-to-God real questions?"

"Right," Burlane said.

"The smugglers would lay *tong* on him to report there was nothing to the rumor, or they'd have him whacked to discourage such foolishness. You know, Major Khartoum, what you're proposing to do truly isn't healthy. If there is a Mr. Big in Cebu, he's no doubt paying hush money to the PNP and Filipino judges, and he won't like western investigators asking questions."

"I don't suppose he will."

"Do you know how much it costs to get somebody whacked in the Philippines, Major Khartoum?"

Burlane shrugged.

"There are *barangays* where you can get somebody killed for two hundred pesos. But most places it would cost four or five thousand." That was roughly ten to two hundred dollars.

Burlane looked amazed. "The Philippines has to be one of the last places in the world where you can get a bargain like that. But surely whacking an NBI investigator would cost more."

Tuflo grinned. "You could get an NBI or PNP investigator whacked for ten thousand pesos, more or less. But you'd have to bargain pretty hard."

Burlane laughed. "But if somebody doesn't ask real questions, the tigers are history. At least that's what they tell me."

"I agree. It isn't good to kill all the tigers."

Burlane said, "A cop in Hong Kong and an Indian wildlife official both believe the main smuggler of tiger bones has moved his headquarters from Taiwan to the Philippines."

Tuflo raised an eyebrow. "Say, Major Khartoum, maybe you can do me a favor sometime down the line. If you don't get whacked, and if you do bump into anything that might make an item for my column, why then . . ."

"I'll get right on the horn," Burlane said quickly. "You scratch mine, I scratch yours."

Tuflo glanced at a large Filipino coming through the door from the hotel. "Well, I see that my friend's finished with his calls. You can come visit me at the *Inquirer* if you like. Feel free."

Burlane rose from his chair and extended his hand. "Thank you, Mr. Tuflo. It's been a pleasure."

"No problem. Anytime." That said, the chief nemesis of crooked cops and soldiers in the Philippines—accept-no-shit Mon Tuflo—rose to meet his friend.

Finally, in desperation, Marta Fuentes went to one of the Chinese herbalists doing business out of a tiny store not two blocks from Carbon Market. This establishment, recommended to Marta by a friend, was flanked on one side by a hardware store and on the other by a pawn shop. Its name was Chen's, and it was run by Mr. Chen himself, the grandson of the original proprietor. A tiny, sincere man in his early seventies, Chen stocked many condiments and ingredients the city's substantial Chinese population could not find in Cebu City's western-style grocery stories—special pepper sauces, cooking wines, soy sauces, and vinegars, also certain vegetables popular with the Chinese. That and peanut oil. Corn oil was good, but peanut oil was traditional in Chinese cooking.

In addition, Chen maintained a modest stock of traditional Chinese medicines.

Chen listened with sympathy as Marta Fuentes told him of her problems.

Chen said, "Well, we have several medicines that might be of help, Mrs. Fuentes. All of them are marketed by a firm on Mactan Island, Chua's."

Marta looked around at the clutter of Chinese goods on the shelves of the shop. "They market food, too, don't they?"

"Yes, they do. They make a good Hoisin sauce and a first-rate oyster sauce. They sell several medicines that are good for the heart. One of these is *Chua's Restorative Tablets,* containing *Niu Xi* or *Ox Knee,* which helps lower your blood pressure. Another medicine that can reduce your blood pressure is *Eucommia Bark,* called *Du Zhong* in Chinese."

"Also made by Chua's."

Chen nodded. "Chua's also sells its *Special Heart Pills* made from the roots of milk vetch, called *Huang Qi* in Mandarin. This widens the vessels of your heart."

"I see," she said. "And which would you recommend?"

"I would think a combination of *Du Zhong* and *Huang Qi.*" Chen set a bottle of each on the counter. Marta Fuentes asked the prices: The daily dose of the two medicines cost just one sixth that of the western prescription.

"And if I were to take just one of the two?"

"I would take the *Huang Qi.*"

Marta Fuentes said, "Sold."

20

Hermann Iversen had never been to Africa before, but he was aware, both from interviewing Herr Steinbach at Hesse's and from reading numerous magazine articles, that the Kenyan coast both north and south of Mombasa was a favorite of beach-loving Germans. Iversen suspected that people who had lived their lives in the tropics most likely wanted to see the snow and ice of northern climes, but the Germans, having all the cold wind and ice they could handle in the winter, thank you, wanted the beach.

After a brief stopover in Nairobi, Iversen's Lufthansa flight arrived at Mombasa's airport shortly after dark. Retrieving his baggage and checking through customs, he walked to the nearby bus station to choose from the several companies making the run to town. The stars were bright and there was a full moon; on the way into town he could see mud huts nestled among trees and greenery.

Mombasa was located on an island in the mouth of the harbor; the bus passed over a causeway on the west end of the island that also provided the city's rail link. The bus passed the train station and proceeded down Haile Selassie Road, and Iversen was pleased to see the many fine examples of nineteenth-century colonial architecture—sprawling old homes with verandas, shuttered windows, and decorative lattice. At the same time, he was startled by the Muslim influence; he had always associated Kenya with safaris and Mount Kilimanjaro, not Islam and mosques.

Iversen was exhausted from his long ride and in no mood for bargain hunting. The bus passed New Chetna Restaurant on the right, and after crossing Shibu Road a half-block later, Iversen spotted something called the Continental Guesthouse on the left and got off the bus.

There were no single rooms in the Continental Guesthouse, but he was able to get a clean double with its own bath and breakfast for about eight bucks U.S. It was nearly ten o'clock by the time he stashed his belongings. He went back outside, to stretch his legs and get something to eat.

The marine air was balmy and fresh as he walked back to the New Chetna Restaurant, which to his surprise and delight, turned out to be run by Hindus and to feature vegetarian food from South India. Iversen had himself a hopping hot vegetable curry cooked with coconut milk, and a less fiery dal made with lentils—these served with plenty of chapati and a nice pot of tea.

That night, as Iversen slipped into bed, he remembered the meeting with Karl and Rolf Bauer when he had outlined what he had learned about Klaus Neumann. He had told Rolf that he couldn't yet prove it, but he was certain Neumann was the killer. He had found no other suspects worth pursuing.

The determined Rolf, still angry and depressed over the loss of his daughter, had said he wanted justice for Erika; he had more than enough money, and Iversen shouldn't be afraid to spend a little of it to run Neumann to ground.

The next morning, Iversen would begin with the man Orel Steinbach had recommended, the engineer Reiner Weithoff, who lived at Mamba Village.

The next morning, rested and ready, Hermann Iversen asked the desk clerk, a dark-skinned Hindu, where he would find Mamba Village.

The clerk, in his lilting English, said, "Mamba Village. A very, very nice place, indeed, sir. Very expensive. And many, many Europeans, sir, English and Germans. And it is very near here, too. They raise crocodiles there, and there is a golf course. Just above

Nyali Beach, sir, a lovely beach, and they hire boys to keep it clear of seaweed. It is just north of here, maybe five kilometers. Very easy to get to, sir."

"How do I get there?"

"You can either take a cab, sir, or you can catch a bus just outside. It will cost you five Kenyan shillings for the ride. Very cheap. You are now on Haile Selassie. The bus will go to the end of the street, which is Diga Road, where it will go left, then straight ahead until it becomes Gamal Abdel Nasser Road. You will cross a bridge, and there will be forest as you ride out. The Europeans have homes in there and on the hill that goes down to the beach. It is very, very exclusive, sir. Quite impressive."

Iversen caught an olive-colored bus for the ride north across the bridge and up the highway north of Mombasa. The highway was flanked on either side by enormous, sprawling trees with thick trunks and high canopies, and when Iversen got out at the Mamba Village sign, he could see monkeys peering down at him through the foliage.

Steinbach had said Reiner Weithoff lived in the second house after the entrance, an easy walk and simple enough to find. He was right, Weithoff's large modern house of European architecture was cement with a blue-tiled roof, and lush, flowered, immaculately manicured grounds.

He asked a uniformed African guard if Mr. Weithoff was in and the guard said yes, and waved him ahead. He strolled toward the house on a curving sidewalk that was surrounded on either side by well-tended beds of flowers. To one side, on a roofed concrete slab, were a Toyota Land Cruiser and a Mercedes-Benz.

As he drew near the house, he saw a man watching him from a wide veranda that faced the flowered grounds. The man was sitting in one of several white chairs around a white table. He had a tall glass of lemonade and a bowlful of salted peanuts that had been cooked with their skins on. He had been reading a book, which he put down at Iversen's approach.

"Good morning. Herr Weithoff?" Iversen said in German.

"It's me," Weithoff said. "Come on up and have some lemonade and peanuts."

Iversen said, "Certainly, sounds good." As his host motioned to the houseboy who appeared from the side door that he would like another lemonade, Iversen showed Weithoff his badge.

Weithoff read it and leaned back in his chair. "From Munich! You've come a long way, I must say, Herr Iversen. Do take a seat, please. And you're here because . . . ?"

Iversen sat. "Because of a young woman who was recently murdered in Munich."

"Really?"

"She had been painted like a tiger. You may have read about the murder in the papers. The same killer has now apparently murdered six young women: one in Indonesia; one in India; the girl in Germany; two girls in Siberia, and one in the Philippines. I talked to the man who used to own Hesse's, and he told me about Klaus Neumann."

Weithoff's eyes widened. "You think Klaus Neumann is some kind of a serial killer?"

"No, no, no. I didn't say that. He has an interest in tigers. We want to talk to just about anybody we can find who knows about tigers. Neumann happens to be one of them. What was that saying out of Miguel Cervantes's novel? Birds of a feather flock together. If we think there may be a murderer in a flock, we talk to each bird separately."

"I see," Weithoff said. "Klaus knew his big cats all right. He brought many a lion through Mombasa, and not a few leopards."

"You know him then?"

Weithoff waited while the houseboy delivered another round of lemonades. "Oh, yes, I know him. Or knew him. But I don't know where he is now. He disappeared. I don't know of anybody in the expat community who has seen him lately."

Iversen took a sip of lemonade and helped himself to some peanuts. "You don't know where he went, do you?"

"Klaus? No, he kept his business pretty much to himself."

"I see. Maybe I can find him through his current job. You don't know what he's doing for a living now, do you?"

Weithoff said, "No, but I bet it has something to do with cats. Klaus had a thing about cats."

"Loved his cats, eh? Say, this is good lemonade! The peanuts, too."

"Drink all you want. The lemons and labor are both cheap. The peanuts, too. Klaus loved cats. Or hated them. It was hard to tell. But if you had a question about a cat anywhere on the planet, no matter how exotic or rare, Klaus knew the answer."

"Mmm."

A wizened little monkey hopped up on the porch. He looked up, examining the two men with furrowed eyebrows.

Weithoff said, "This is my little friend Berndt. When I have peanuts, he expects his share. It's only fair. Berndt keeps me company. He never complains. Just give him a peanut now and then and he's happy." Weithoff gave Berndt a peanut. "His girlfriend will show up in a few minutes, you watch."

Berndt took the peanut and looked up at Iversen, who gave him a peanut as well.

"Maybe Klaus is in India," Weithoff said.

"India?"

"He thought lions were essentially boring. Tigers were the thing. It's my bet he pushed off for India, or maybe Cambodia or somewhere."

"Ahh," Iversen said.

Weithoff laughed. "He's probably selling tiger bones now. I wouldn't put it past him."

"Tiger bones?" Iversen sat up.

Weithoff, seeing that both lemonade glasses were empty, waved for another round. "Sure. I remember him saying once that there was a fortune to be made poaching tigers. He said the Arabs pay top dollar for their pelts, and the Chinese and Koreans think tiger bones gives them stiff cocks." Weithoff looked amused.

Iversen, chewing on a peanut, said, "The quest for the big erection."

"I've read I don't know how many articles on the evils of poaching, but I can't remember one where people addressed the evils of the clients who are ultimately buying. Why is that, do you suppose?"

Iversen shrugged his shoulders.

Weithoff said, "Because there is money to be made in China, or at least that's what people think, Herr Iversen, and nobody wants to be left out. Thou shalt not offend potential buyers of your products. Big money is sucking up to the Chinese, tigers and rhinos be damned."

Berndt sat by Iversen's feet looking up with curious eyes. Iversen gave him another peanut. "You're saying as long as people are willing to buy, the Africans and Indians don't have the luxury of worrying about endangered species."

"That's succinctly put," Weithoff said. "Say, how would you like to have lunch? I've trained my cook to prepare proper schnitzel."

"Well sure. I'd like that."

"I've got a refrigerator full of beer. Lemonade tastes good, but after a while it's just so much citrus and sugar. We'll have a nice lunch and then take a nap. Africans believe in naps, a civilized taste."

"You have a beautiful place, Herr Weithoff."

A second monkey joined Berndt.

"Here she is. She has decided it's okay to join us. This is Berndt's friend Anna," Weithoff said. "She likes her peanuts, too."

Iversen gave Anna a peanut.

Weithoff grinned, "I don't mind sharing peanuts with Berndt and Anna, they know better than to become a nuisance or I put them on the run. I live here because of the beaches and the women. White sand as far as you can see. Nyali Beach is just over the hill. Palm trees. Cheap rum. All the cannabis you can smoke. And African women are wonderful."

"I was told you're an engineer."

"I build game lodges and resort hotels. And roads, electrical generators, and sewage systems. It is all paid for by tourist dollars. Unfortunately, the Kenyans don't have a lot to export except palm oil, but just about everybody in the tropics is trying to sell palm oil. The Nigerians have palm oil. Zaire has palm oil. Everybody has palm oil."

Iversen said nothing. Anna sat by one of his feet and Berndt by the other and they looked up at him, as though studying him.

"You know it's crazy to live in Germany, no offense. The taxes and all that rain and cold wind and snow and having to put up with the feminist crap the women're learning from America." Weithoff furrowed his brow in consternation.

The houseboy arrived with a tray containing another bowl of peanuts, two cold bottles of Beck's beer, and two mugs. He set them on the table and quietly retreated with the empty lemonade glasses.

Weithoff, pouring himself a beer, suddenly brightened. "Now I remember the last time I saw Neumann!"

"When was that?"

"I don't know, five or six months ago. Something like that. He came back to pick up some stuff that he left in storage with me. His main interest was his circus poster. He'd never part with that for long."

"Was it a poster promoting a June 1957 performance of the Captain Prince–Cox's International Circus?" Anna, pursing her mouth, reached timidly up and put a tiny hand on Iversen's thigh.

"I think that was it. In Hamburg. Klaus's father used to be a tiger trainer, and that poster promoted his final performance, when he got killed by a tiger. It was handsomely mounted and he showed it to everybody. His father was billed as Lothar the Magnificent. He was the circus's featured performer on the poster. Klaus would never leave that poster behind, never. Now I remember! Of course! The Philippines!"

Anna, growing more bold, tugged at a loop on Iversen's trousers.

Weithoff said, "Anna!"

Anna removed her hand.

Iversen said, "What about the Philippines?"

Weithoff said, "Klaus always had stories to tell about his travels. The Philippines was one of his favorite places. Just as I like African girls, Klaus likes Asians—especially Thai girls and Filipinas. But he said there's getting to be too much AIDS in Thailand for his taste. He likes beaches and scuba diving, and most people speak a little English in the Philippines. I remember him saying Filipinas were easy to come by and cheap, and there was a substantial community of expat Germans there, just like here. When he came back for his poster, he was telling these stories. I think he may have recently been there."

Iversen cocked his head. "Did he say where exactly?"

Weithoff, trying to remember, frowned.

Iversen held out a forefinger to Anna and she grasped it solemnly. He said, "They don't have tigers in the Philippines, do they?"

Weithoff shook his head no. "They have them in Malaysia and Indonesia, but not the Philippines."

Iversen thought for a moment, then said, "Tell me, you're a veteran expat, if I could narrow his location in the Philippines to one city, say, where would I most likely find him, do you suppose? Where would I start?"

Weithoff took another drink of beer. "Klaus?" He thought a moment. "You've lived all your life in Germany, I take it."

"*Ja.* I've traveled. My wife and I like to take our holidays on Costa del Sol in Spain, and we went to Florida once."

Weithoff bunched his face. "Fair enough. But it's not the same. Two or three weeks or a month or two is going for a swim. You have to take a bath to understand the nature of the water."

"Oh?" Berndt now joined Anna. He wanted a finger to hold also, so Iversen spread his hand. Anna took the thumb. Berndt got the little finger.

"Listen, Herr Iversen, whether we like it or not, western and northern Europeans and North Americans and Australians have a fundamentally different way of looking at the world than people here in Africa or in Asia. You can have local friends here, yes, but you inevitably think on different wavelengths. Western educations don't entirely remove the gulf. Westerners need expat bars as a refuge from the pressure of constantly dealing with the foreign. By foreign, I mean an entirely different way of thinking."

"Psychic relief." Iversen tried to retrieve his hand, but Berndt and Anna would have none of it.

Weithoff said, "Shoo, shoo, you two. You're making a nuisance of yourselves."

Berndt and Anna, looking sore, reluctantly retreated to the rail of the veranda.

Weithoff said, "In a place like this, and I suspect in the Philippines as well, expat bars are pockets of civilization, as we understand the term. The drinkers are refugees from the craziness they have to deal with every day. If they don't occasionally talk to somebody who understands them, they tend to go mad. Expat bars exist for the same reason that people form ethnic and racial neighborhoods, Herr Iversen. Nobody forces people to live with their own kind."

"They prefer it."

Weithoff nodded. "And let me add that a good expat bar is intellectually far, far more interesting than any place back home. When a German returns to Germany after years of living in Africa or Asia, he'll have to fight the boredom of the comfortable and predictable. There's an element of danger living in the Third World that's missing back home."

"So you're saying that if Klaus Neumann is living in the Philippines, I first locate the city where he lives, then find the expat bars and hang out there."

"That's what I would do. They're watering holes for westerners. Be patient. Just talk. And wait. If he's there, you'll eventually find him. That's what I told the other guy who came here looking for Neumann." To Berndt and Anna, he said, "Oh, okay, you can come back, but keep your hands to yourself."

Berndt and Anna, responding as though they were fluent in German, hopped off the rail and came forward for more peanuts.

"The other guy? A German?"

Weithoff, feeding Berndt and Anna, nodded yes. "A middle-aged guy, blond hair."

"Can you remember his name?"

Weithoff thought for a moment then shook his head. "Sorry."

Iversen, scooping up some peanuts for the monkeys, said, "From where in Germany?"

"Can't remember that either."

"Berlin?" Iversen asked.

"Maybe. He wasn't from southern Germany. From Berlin maybe, or farther north."

"Did he say why he was looking for Neumann? If he flew all

the way to Africa from Germany, he must surely have had a reason." Iversen fed Berndt and Anna, who obviously wanted to tug at him again, but didn't.

Weithoff said, "Oh, yes. He had a reason. He said he collected circus posters. He was interested in Klaus's poster."

"Of the Hamburg performance?"

"That's right. He said he had a collection that covered the entire period of the circus's existence, a ten-year stretch starting in 1947, I think it was. He had all the posters, autographed by the featured performer, except the one promoting what turned out to be the circus's final performance. He spent several weeks here, hanging out in the expat community. Maybe he learned the name of a specific city in the Philippines. You should talk to him. Save yourself some work."

"You don't remember even his first name?"

Weithoff said, "It was Fritz, Franz, or something like that. Should I order our lunch now? I'll have the cook fix us a nice salad, too. They grow wonderful tomatoes here, and the avocados are very nice."

Iversen, feeling good, said, "Sure. Some schnitzel and a salad sounds wonderful."

"And some more beer," Weithoff said.

Iversen grinned. "That goes without saying."

Weithoff suddenly looked triumphant. "It was the island of Cebu. It just came to me. How about that?"

"What came to you? Where Neumann went?"

"Yes. I remember Klaus saying Cebu had a city he liked, with plenty of Germans to talk to and a first-rate beach with good diving in coral reefs. He said there were enough Germans there that they marketed fairly decent sausages—originally made by a German-speaking Swiss. He said the beer was good and cheap. And he said the Cebuana women were hands down the best in the country. Sweet little beauties, he said. Too bad I couldn't remember that when the poster collector was here. I could have saved him some trouble."

21

Heinrich thought *bankas* were beautiful; he had to give the Filipinos that. The sleek craft, everyman's boat, were long and slender with graceful, upward curving bows. He liked the ones with sails the best. Profiled on the horizon, single sail furled, they were lovely.

By European standards, the V-shaped hulls—made of marine plywood and supported by outriggers on either side—were little more than canoes. This simplicity made them easy to make. The two spars that held the outriggers were laminated. They were designed like narrow leaf springs, thicker in the middle—where they crossed the narrow hull—and thinner at the ends, where they fastened onto the outriggers. This was so they could withstand the swells without snapping, but they looked like fragile wings, and Heinrich could not imagine that they would last through a real storm. Still, it was a simple, clever design, he had to admit. And, having little drag, they knifed swiftly through the water.

They were also called pump boats because the smaller ones, used by fishermen, were—in addition to a single sail—equipped with American Briggs and Stratton pump engines that were also used to move water from one rice paddy or fish pond to the next. The frugal Filipinos rode the wind as much as possible, but when they were becalmed or were overtaken by a storm, they turned on their trusty Briggs and Stratton, *pop-pop-pop*, and headed for shore or into the wind, depending on the circumstances. The usual pump boat, used by a single fisherman, was about twenty feet long.

But this *banka,* nearly thirty-five-feet long, was propelled by a diesel engine, one of the many used diesels the make-do Filipinos imported from Japan and installed in the homemade jeepneys that they used in lieu of a mass transportation system. Jeepneys provided jobs for jeepney makers, and Filipinos didn't like the idea of one bus driver taking the place of up to six jeepney jockeys—never mind the insane traffic that choked their streets.

Just as they decorated their homemade jeepneys with chrome and Day-Glo oranges, greens, and yellows, the resourceful Filipinos felt compelled to do a real number on the boats in which they roamed far from their island in search of the ever-diminishing population of fish.

This big *banka* rented by Heinrich's chief Filipino assistant, Dodong Gutierrez, was pale green with a red mouth and evil-looking white shark's teeth painted on the bow beneath the graceful prow. It was stable, Heinrich conceded, and yes, he knew that the islands of the Pacific were settled by adventurous Micronesians and Polynesians in boats like this, but still, Heinrich was a German, and couldn't help but wonder if a boat with a proper hull and keel might not be more seaworthy.

Now, Heinrich, watching the rise and fall of the outriggers, wondered why on earth the spars that held them in place did not snap. He felt the very act of surviving in the Philippines was a form of adventure, much less taking a trip like this, which he had done only on the advice of his employer.

Heinrich had been told it was bad policy not to personally oversee the transfer of the bones from trawler to port, just as prudence demanded that he weigh and mark the bones before they were loaded onto the trawler in the Indian Ocean. If Heinrich did not see to such chores personally, how would he know how many bones were stolen and peddled on the side? The concept of trust, when money was involved, was western foolishness, and these were Filipinos. Filipinos might be a happy and charming lot, swilling San Miguel and calling him their friend—trying to tell him that he was just like their brother—but Heinrich should remember that Filipinos regarded the mangoes on their neighbor's tree as their mangoes as well. And mangoes belonging to a Chinese or westerner, well . . .

But Heinrich's Filipino companions—Gutierrez and four helpers—a merry little band, smoked and laughed, jabbering in Cebuano. They were equipped with Armalite automatic assault rifles, a commercial version of the American M-16, plus napalm hand grenades and two wire-guided missiles. Most of the Tagalog-language movies shot by studios in Manila featured grimacing cops, soldiers, and crooks shooting one another, *rat-a-tat-tat*, or blowing each other up, *ka-boom, ka-boom*. This profitable mayhem was broken only by an occasional, if less profitable romance or comedy. Heinrich's escorts looked as comfortable with their deadly arsenal as soccer players carrying the ball on the way to the park on a Saturday afternoon.

Gutierrez had dispensed with such foolishness as running lights, and the *banka* now slid confidently forward through total blackness—the curved prow of the slender hull going *whap, whap, whap* against the waves. If Gutierrez or his companions were hesitant about the darkness or the weather or the vessel's course, they didn't show it.

Heinrich wondered what they were talking about— certainly it wasn't about politics or history because they didn't read. They were talking about him, he supposed. He had been told to remember that Cebu was only superficially a city. It was really a large village, as most Third World cities were, and, as in villages the world over, people gossiped.

For a while, Heinrich could see lights on what he was told was the southern tip of the island of Negros, which lay between Bohol and Panay. When those lights disappeared, Gutierrez pushed on into the void. He lacked navigational gear, and a cloud cover blanked out the stars, but, when asked, he said confidently that they were on course proceeding due west, toward Palawan on the edge of the South China Sea.

They entered a fog bank, and plunged cheerfully on. Finally, dead ahead, Heinrich saw the profile of the Taiwanese fishing trawler. This was their rendezvous. Even in fog! Heinrich was amazed at Gutierrez's navigational skills. His escorts could see the surprised look on his face and were amused that he had been worried. They lived from day to day, if not hour to hour, and Heinrich wondered if they worried about anything, ever—the loss of face being a critical exception.

Gutierrez, obviously pleased at having demonstrated his prowess as a pilot, said, "See, we're here. No problem."

"I was wondering."

Gutierrez laughed. He cut the diesel and drifted alongside the waiting trawler.

A rope ladder was thrown over the stern of the trawler, and Heinrich and his Filipino companions took turns climbing aboard, taking their Armalites, their rocket launchers, and their napalm hand grenades with them. On deck, Heinrich squatted a couple of times to work the cramps from his legs and shook hands with the mustached Mohan Goel, the narrow-faced, dark-skinned Indian captain whom he had last seen in Calcutta two weeks earlier.

"Have a good trip?" Heinrich asked.

"It was no problem," Goel said in lilting, Hindi-accented English. "We circled north to avoid pirates out of Borneo, but we had good weather and met no one. A couple of hours ago, we saw what might have been a Filipino patrol boat, but lost it. I think it was one of those used boats they recently bought from the Koreans."

"I suppose we should get on with it, then," Heinrich said.

"I don't see why not. Bong?" Bong Lopez, Goel's first mate, went below.

A few minutes later, Lopez emerged with the first of several locked, tagged canvas valises that he flopped on the deck at Heinrich's feet.

As Heinrich kneeled to begin checking the contents of the valises, he heard the sound of a marine engine somewhere out there in the murk.

They all did.

Heinrich looked up at Goel. "What is it?"

"Maybe the Filipino patrol boat," Goel said.

Heinrich's employer had said Heinrich should not worry

about the appearance of a Filipino patrol boat. The commanders of these vessels, in effect publicly licensed bandits, would only be seeking *tong* before allowing Heinrich and his people to continue on their way. There was nothing wrong with giving *tong* to people whose regular cooperation was required, customs officials, say, but in the case of Filipino patrol boats—in fact chance extortionists supported by diesel bought at taxpayers' expense—direct action was the best policy; this was in order to discourage such bothersome demands in the future.

Gutierrez looked at Heinrich. "Well?"

Heinrich said, "We'll never have to deal with them again, so we won't pay *tong*. Better they be taught a lesson."

Goel said, "Good policy. Such greed!" He shook his head in disgust.

Heinrich said to Gutierrez, "Okay, do what you have to do, Dodong, but be careful none of our people gets hurt."

Gutierrez grinned. "Us? Get hurt? You don't have to worry about that. The rockets aren't good if we can't see them." Looking at Goel, he made his decision. He said, "We'll need the top removed from the forward hold, and then you should get your people below."

Goel said, "Do as he says, Bong. Do it now."

Lopez did as he was told, quickly ripping off the canvas cover lashed over the forward hold.

Gutierrez said, "We'll be using napalm, so we have to be careful. When I whistle once, start your engine. When I yell 'Now!' you should goose your engine full throttle to get clear of the heat. Just listen for the whistle and the yell, and it should be safe enough."

"I start my engine when you whistle, and go all ahead full when you yell 'Now!' "

"That's it," Gutierrez said.

Heinrich grinned. "I made them practice."

"The efficient German, good for you," Goel said.

Heinrich and Goel each grabbed a valise full of tiger bones and led the way down into the main cabin.

Gutierrez and his mates jumped into the open forward hold, Armalites and napalm grenades at the ready.

As the Filipino patrol boat slowed, preparing to board the trawler on the side opposite the pump boat, Gutierrez whistled.

Mohan Goel started his engines as the napalm grenades looped outward.

Gutierrez yelled, "Now!"

The Korean-made vessel burst into flames . . . as the trawler shot forward, engine roaring.

Gutierrez and his companions, laughing, scrambled onto the deck and had fun firing their assault rifles full automatic into the inferno and the screaming Filipino sailors, who were into the water with their bodies on fire.

The patrol boat exploded as the fire reached its fuel tanks. As it slid under the waves, Gutierrez and his associates gleefully wasted the swimming survivors with short bursts of their Armalites. This was a far bigger kick than watching the pretend action in the Tagalog-language movies. The adrenaline rush was something else. Being a hero had nothing to do with the sport. The slaughter was the thing. And besides, the burning sailors in the water were neither their relatives nor their friends.

Later, to celebrate the successful sinking of the Filipino patrol boat, and the receiving of another load of tiger bones, Heinrich sprang for a proper blowout—this on the advice of his employer, who said a flagrant gesture was necessary to maintain morale among Dodong Gutierrez and his crew.

Under such circumstances, the Filipinos would regard a party as mandatory. What was the fun of toasting a presumptuous patrol boat with napalm if one couldn't enjoy retelling the story later with much food and booze?

Heinrich had been told that when the shipments of bones started arriving in number from Siberia, the Filipinos, remembering this celebration, would be eager to help. If Heinrich did not treat them to their fun, they would feel cheated. Good food and some show-off whiskey was cheap public relations compared to the profit they were making. They needed a dependable crew when they started stockpiling bones.

The six of them—Heinrich, Dodong Gutierrez, and their four helpers—threw their bash in a room rented in the Chinese restaurant in Cebu's newest shopping mall, Chua's. Heinrich made sure there was plenty of San Miguel at this feed, of course. He bought two large *lechons*—suckling pigs slowly turned over a charcoal pit until their skin was the color of rich mahogany. This crisp skin, and the layer of fat just beneath it, was mandatory for Filipino parties. A child's first birthday demanded *lechon,* even if the family had to go hungry to save enough money to buy it. A party was measured by how many *lechons* there were, the more the better.

In addition to the *lechons*—so the crew members would have leftovers for their families—Heinrich also ordered lavish tureens of *kinilaw,* which was raw *tangigue*—Spanish mackerel—marinated in *kalamansi* juice—*kalamansi* being a marble-size kumquat the color of a lime. The juice tasted halfway between that of an orange and a lemon, and was superior to lemon, in Heinrich's opinion. *Kinilaw* also contained chunks of tomato and onion, and often, as in this case, coconut water.

Finally, Heinrich took the additional show-off step of springing for all the Johnnie Walker Black Label that Gutierrez and his band might desire. Johnnie Walker was more expensive than other Scotches, so it had to be the best. It was an okay boss who sprang for Johnnie Walker Black. None of that Red Label for Heinrich's crew.

Gutierrez and his friends knew how to have a good time, Heinrich had to give them that. Laughing, munching on fatty hunks of *lechon* skin, they reenacted the ambush. They lobbed pretend napalm grenades across the table, and fired pretend Armalite assault rifles at the survivors in the water. Giggling with unbridled glee, they referred to the screaming, burning sailors as *lechons.*

Nobody at the party felt in the least bit sorry for the roasted Filipino sailors they had slaughtered. The captain of the patrol boat, perhaps not a fourth as clever as he thought he was, had simply chosen the wrong smugglers to rip off. He had made a mistake, an oopsie; it was simple as that. Life was so hard in the Philippines that it bordered on being a zero-sum game. Where there were winners, there were losers. The captain, by his foolish miscalculation, demonstrated that he was a loser.

The families of the dead sailors had to be satisfied with back-page items in the Manila dailies about a missing patrol boat, and solemn assurances by the navy—all nonsense—that a vigorous attempt would be made to find out what had happened, and, if foul play was involved, to prosecute the guilty.

Dodong Gutierrez and his hardy crew were clearly winners, and so got to eat as much *lechon* and *kinilaw* as they wanted, washing it down with great slugs of Johnnie Walker Black, the best of the best. Hey, life couldn't get much better than that!

22

The Portuguese navigator and explorer Ferdinand Magellan—in a foolish if not outright stupid display of bravado—was killed on Mactan Island by Chief Lapu-Lapu, or at least by one of Chief Lapu-Lapu's men, on 27 April 1521. Mactan, connected to Cebu Island by a half-mile-long bridge, was now home to Lapu-Lapu City, founded by Augustinian monks in 1730, and the site of the international airport that served Cebu and its major metropolis, Cebu City.

More recently Mactan had become the site of a booming "export processing zone" where the Philippine government, in an effort to reduce its trade deficit, gave tax breaks to light industries selling abroad. The makers of Timex watches were among the many firms that established production facilities in the zone.

In addition to the airport and export processing zone, Mactan was home to several overpriced beach resorts, a couple of them the near-exclusive domain of Japanese tour groups; the rest were popular with visiting Germans and a few Australians bearing foreign currency. Such beaches as were left for Filipinos were small, overcrowded, and swarming with flies, litter, and food vendors. The beaches were all on the eastern, or seaward side of the island, opposite from the airport, and the land surrounding them—at least the land near the private beaches—was obtainable only at a premium, and was mostly Chinese-owned.

Chinese loan sharks known as six-fivers obtained the land by charging the eager Filipinos six dollars for every five loaned—

with the borrower's land as collateral. Little by little, the Chinese six-fivers had sucked up nearly every square foot of real estate in and near Cebu City and on Mactan Island.

The CITES tiger consultant, Dr. Heinz Tepe, had built what appeared to be an imitation Swiss chalet a hundred meters from the exclusive Tambuli Beach Resort. A wealthy Filipino might have to sacrifice a month's pay for one night's rent at Tambuli; a poor Filipino might have to yield a full year's earnings.

The two-story house, with a steeply pitched roof and gabled windows, was surrounded on three sides by a high cement wall that blocked out the view of the ubiquitous Filipino shacks and *nipa* huts on the interior of the island. The solid look of the house suggested real walls, that is, double-paneled and insulated, which meant air-conditioning was mandatory; ordinarily, houses in Cebu or Mactan were single-wall construction with fans and glass louvers to take advantage of sea breezes. This fact alone was an eyeopener, because such electricity as there was on this part of the island was provided by private generator.

In order that Herr Tepe might have an unobstructed view of the ocean and Olango Island a quarter of a mile offshore, the estate was protected by a moat on the seaward side, the bottom of which was a tangle and snarl of barbed wire. Perhaps Uncle Remus's Brer Rabbit preferred the briar patch, but the barbed wire on the bottom of Tepe's moat was just impossible.

As Burlane drew near Tepe's estate, he could hear the buzzing of air conditioners, but no telltale drone of electrical generators. This meant that Tepe had resorted to the expensive solution of putting the generator in a soundproofed underground chamber; in fact, two generators were required for twenty-four-hour service; generators had to be rested occasionally, and a backup was needed in case one went down.

Burlane, amazed at the layout enjoyed by the CITES field representative, told the beefy, uniformed guard at a heavy iron gate in the wall who he was. The guard checked with an intercom. After receiving an affirmative reply from Herr Tepe himself, he ushered Burlane through the gate and down a flagstone path through a recently mown lawn to the massive front door of the house.

He was met by Heinz Tepe with a beautiful woman by his side, at least twenty years Tepe's junior. This stunner had to be Lily Tepe, who had so impressed the Russians when she accompanied her husband to Siberia.

Lily Tepe had gorgeous silken hair, hanging in a jet-black sheen to the small of her back. But it was not her hair that was her most dramatic or memorable attribute. Burlane remembered a wonderful line by the travel writer Paul Theroux who claimed the bra was the most superfluous item in Asia. Well, Lily was an exception to this. Her breasts were large without being Partons. To properly display their remarkable size and exquisite form, she wore a black T-shirt that was a size and a half too small, with CEBU written on it in Day-Glo orange. She ommitted a bra in order that other women and her male admirers might know—to their envy or frustration—that these were genuine bouncie-bounce, real-deal tits. The black T-shirt concealed the color of their aureoles but the insolent nipples poked out like pencil erasers.

Her jeans, like her T-shirt, were far too small—to render without ambiguity the clean lines of her nice rump and elegant hips. She had pale skin, highly prized in the Philippines, and her face was dominated by outsize Asian eyes and a nearly aquiline nose, suggesting that the nose she had been born with had likely been surgically altered. And when she smiled, as she did now, she possessed a faultless set of the whitest of white teeth.

And she's rich, too, Andrei Bure. A businesswoman. Lily Tepe wore large gold earrings, and a handsome gold chain around her neck. When she extended her hand to Burlane, gold bracelets rattled on her delicate wrists. Her manner suggested she was familiar with money.

She said, "Major Khartoum! I'm Lily Tepe. I'm so pleased to meet you. We've been wondering when you'd finally get around to visiting us."

Shaking Burlane's hand, Tepe said, "So good to see you again, Major." Tepe wore khaki walking shorts, plastic sandals that fit between his big and middle toes—the kind Americans call thongs and Filipinos call slippers—and a tan-colored cotton shirt with tabs that buttoned over the pockets. Burlane estimated him to be in his early fifties, although he had the kind of face that Burlane found difficult to assign an age. He had a largish nose, a high, broad forehead, and rather heavy eyebrows. His hair, no doubt once blond, was now sandy colored. He had intelligent blue eyes and an agreeable way about him, and appeared fit and vigorous.

But to Burlane, Tepe didn't look like the kind of man who would land a beauty like Lily. For one thing, he knew, the Chinese ordinarily wanted their daughters to marry Chinese men. The foolish Western notion of romance had nothing to do with marriage; the point of marriage was an alliance of families. This strengthened one's *quanxi*, or useful circle of friends and relatives and connections. Those within one's *quanxi* enjoyed reciprocal good will; those outside could expect none. This was the Chinese way, and its application had caused much resentment in Malaysia, Indonesia, and the Philippines where the Chinese had established themselves as money lenders and middlemen.

Good-looking Malayan Filipinas often married western men in hopes of being whisked off to North America or Europe, but tall Chinese beauties married rich, powerful Chinese men—the better to advance the fortunes of their families—not German academics who studied the decline of the tiger.

Tepe said, "I'm very pleased to meet you, Major Khartoum. The CITES people said you'd likely come calling."

Burlane, eyeing the grounds, said, "This is quite a place you've got here, Herr Tepe."

Tepe smiled. "I'm glad you like it. Would you like some beer? I've got some good German beer in the refrigerator?"

"Sure, but a San Miguel will do for me. I think there's a case to be made that it's one of the best cheap beers in the world. I'll save the Beck's for when I go to Berlin or Düsseldorf."

Lily waved to a uniformed maid, a little Filipina looker, who stood eyeing Burlane. "Two San Miguels, Den Den." To Burlane, Lily said, "I'm afraid I'm going to have to leave you in a few minutes. I have an appointment with my hairdresser in Cebu City this afternoon."

Den Den went for the beer.

Burlane, momentarily watching Den Den's rump move to and

fro, said, "Andrei Bure in Siberia said you were a businesswoman, Mrs. Tepe. What is your business, if I might ask?"

"My family makes and sells food products to overseas Chinese communities. We have a factory here on Mactan Island."

"In the export processing zone?"

"That's right. I'm in charge of the export end of it."

"Chinese food products?"

Lily smiled warmly, flashing white teeth. "Let's see, what all do we sell? Various kinds of cooking wines and vinegars for one thing: Chinkiang vinegar, red vinegar, and rice vinegar, and Mei-kuei-lu wine, Moutai wine, and Shaohsing wine. We sell shrimp and sesame paste and fish sauce, Asian chili sauce, yellow and black bean sauces, Hoisin and oyster sauce, and several kinds of soy sauces."

"Really? I lug a wok around with me. I like to cook fish with yellow bean sauce. The black bean sauce is a bit salty for my taste."

Lily gave him a curious look. "You like to cook, really?"

Burlane grinned. "My wok has turned as black as midnight. I put it in a plastic bag when I travel. They say I'm not a bad cook for a longnose. What's the brand name?"

"Chua's."

Burlane grinned. "Ahh, Chua's is a good brand indeed. I've used it many times. You sell it in the United States, too. I've bought Chua's in Portland's Chinatown."

"We sell in overseas Chinese communities all over the world."

"Any relation to the Chuas who own the shopping malls? I've seen them here and in Taipei and Hong Kong."

Lily smiled. "And Singapore. Yes, those belong to my family."

"Well, I'm impressed."

"A hard-working family," Tepe said.

Den Den arrived with a tray of frosty bottles of San Miguel and equally frosty mugs. She poured a mug each for Burlane and Tepe.

Lily, glancing at her watch, said, "I really should change before I go, and I think the driver must be ready by now. I do hope to see you again, Major Khartoum. Make sure Heinz gets your number so we can call you for dinner."

Tepe said, "Or maybe we can hire a plane to fly us down to

Moalboal. There are some nice beaches there, and good diving in the coral."

"Sure, that might be fun," Burlane said, watching the extraordinary Lily disappear deeper into the house.

Tepe said, "I've enjoyed reading the reports of your preliminary investigation. Rassileva and Bure are first-rate game officials, and I know Dr. Sangrit very well indeed. The Indians are lucky to have him as their chief tiger man. If we had more people like him, the future of the tiger would be guaranteed, I assure you. He's smart and dedicated, and he's not about to quit." Tepe pulled at his nose, thinking. "Plus that he's independently wealthy. He doesn't have to depend on grants for survival."

Burlane said, "Both the Russians and Dr. Sangrit said you collect things having to do with tigers. I was naturally curious."

Tepe laughed. "They're right about that. I've been nuts about tigers since I was a kid."

"Do you keep your tiger collection here on Mactan, or back in Germany?"

Tepe looked surprised. "Why here, of course! Why do you suppose I've gone to such lengths to secure this place? I know it must look like a bunker from outside, but inside it's cool and secure, and I've got all the modern conveniences. Hot and cold running water even."

"I saw the solar panels outside. You're going to show me your collection, of course."

Tepe laughed. "Major Khartoum, whatever made you think I'd let you go without seeing my collection? It's taken me a lifetime to assemble it. Come with me. We can talk in the tiger room."

23

James Burlane followed Dr. Heinz Tepe through a heavy, carved wooden door secured by multiple, heavy locks and stepped into what he regarded as one of the most extraordinary private collections of anything that he'd ever seen. Burlane had known a couple of stamp collectors, a coin collector, a man who collected paperback novels with lurid covers, a woman who collected old bottles, and one—his own mother—who collected ceramic cows. He did not understand the fascination of collecting, although he admired the collection of paperbacks. But Heinz Tepe was the all-time champ.

Tepe's collection room was about twenty feet wide by sixty feet long, and there wasn't an inch of the walls that did not contain tigerana—either shelves of objects, or pictures, or other memorabilia. For Tepe to call this a "room" was being excessively modest, Burlane thought; it might have qualified as an exhibition hall in a substantial museum.

A handsome black-and-white tiger head and two tiger pelts of classic orange, black, and white coloring were mounted to the right of the door as they entered the room.

Tepe, seeing that Burlane's attention was drawn immediately to the head and two pelts, said, "I hasten to explain that the heads and pelts were confiscated from poachers."

Burlane stepped close to the head and ran his hand over the long, soft fur. "This one was shot in Siberia, I take it."

"Yes, it is. It's the most valuable by far. The one on the right is a Bengal tiger shot in northern India near the Nepalese border. The one on the left was taken in Burma. The Arabs buy most of the pelts, but I suppose you know that already."

"What happened to the rest of the pelt of the Siberian tiger?"

"Ordinarily, an intact pelt would be the most valuable, if it was marketed to the Saudis or a rich Kuwaiti or Iranian. But in the case of a white tiger, the claws may have been marketed separately to the Chinese at a premium price."

"Big medicine. I see. Out of curiosity, how did you come by the head?"

"A Russian game warden who had confiscated it from a poacher gave it to me out of appreciation for a CITES grant I had approved for him, plus I laid a little extra on him, I have to admit. When I saw it, I just had to have it. It's worth a small fortune."

"I bet." Burlane wanted to ask Tepe the name of the game warden, but thought better of it. "For an Arab to display a tiger pelt on the wall of his den is rather like ghetto kids who think they're only something when they're wearing expensive Nike athletic shoes. Is that the logic?"

"Something like that," Tepe said.

Young people in American urban slums had been known to kill one another for their stupid shoes. Burlane couldn't imagine a more bizarre motive for murder than to covet shoes with a Nike swoosh. He also wondered about the mentality of someone, even a zoologist who was a field researcher for CITES, who collected tiger memorabilia on a scale this nutty.

Burlane moved deeper into the room. Tepe's collection was nothing short of amazing. He had gathered photographs of European sportsmen posing beside the carcasses of tigers in India and Malaysia and Indonesia. Burlane studied the faces from the past, a day when, he supposed, people assumed there would never be an end to the tiger. The tiger hunters in the photographs ran to bearded, mustached males in macho-men poses; some held pith helmets; some wore suspenders and proper neckties. Surrounded by exotic brown-skinned Asians, some wearing tubans, they posed stiffly for the photographers. They were adventurous gentlemen of empire, public schoolboys in the service of Her Majesty's Government; they had been posted in the land of bloody wogs and looked the part, that is, like characters out of Rudyard Kipling's fiction. The photographs that did not wind up in Tepe's collection were no doubt still on the walls of English country manors, evidence that great-grandfather so-and-so had indeed gone to India or Malaysia in the service of Queen Victoria and had successfully bagged a tiger.

In addition to photographs of great white hunters, Tepe, his eye ever on the myth of the tiger, had copies of the old Exxon ad instructing drivers to PUT A TIGER IN YOUR TANK. He had a photograph of Tony the Tiger touting the benefits of sugar-frosted cornflakes. This was, he understood, a version of the ancient notion of sympathetic medicine that obviously accounted for the Chinese and Korean belief in the powers of tiger bones. Burlane told himself he'd have to check out what the author of *The Golden Bough,* Sir James George Frazer, had to say on the matter. There, he suspected, lay the key to stopping the trade in poached tigers, not trade sanctions or game wardens.

Burlane stepped up to a shelf of tiger balm and other products packaged in handsomely decorated tins and boxes, all featuring snarling tigers, leaping tigers, and Chinese characters that he couldn't read. One that did have some English words on it, in addition to Chinese—presumably intended for the Hong Kong or San Francisco markets—was a can of capsules featuring the obligatory snarling tiger leaping over the words LILLIES FOR THE EMPRESS.

Burlane examined a stiff loop the size of his little finger that was hung on a wooden peg. "What is this?" Burlane inquired, although he thought he knew the answer.

Tepe pursed his lips. "That's the most profitable part of a poached tiger, Major Khartoum. That's a dried penis, as I bet you suspected."

"May I handle it?"

Tepe laughed. "Of course. It won't bite."

Burlane picked up the dried penis and put it over his forefinger and took a close look.

Tepe said, "The Chinese turn it into a concoction they call tiger penis wine, or they make a soup out of it. Either way, it's said to be an aphrodisiac in the extreme."

Burlane put the dried penis back in its place beside a small pint-size bottle of amber fluid. The bottle was a flagrant imitation of Johnnie Walker scotch, except that it had Chinese characters on the black label.

Burlane tapped the bottle with his finger. "Tiger penis wine?"

"Correct," Tepe said.

"One would have thought the Chinese could have thought of their own bottle design. Is it really made of tiger penises do you think, or is it a rip-off like the bottle?"

Tepe picked up the bottle and examined the Chinese characters on the label. "Difficult to say. There are wealthy Chinese who claim to be experts on tiger penis wine, the same as Europeans who know their Bordeaux or Burgundies."

Burlane made a sour face. "If I had a hundred bucks for every self-proclaimed connoisseur of wine who could pass a blind test between jug wine and expensive swill, I'd be a millionaire."

"I agree. There must be a lot of bogus tiger's penis wine on the market. But this is truly supposed to be genuine." Tepe handed the bottle to Burlane.

Burlane held it up to the light and studied it, squinting his eyes. "The logic is identical to the properties ascribed to soup number five, I take it."

"Soup number five?" Tepe looked puzzled.

"It's the Filipino version of a soup with aphrodisiac qualities, but it's made from a bull's cock. A proper soup number five contains slices of penis and chunks of testicles, along with more pedestrian ingredients such as tomatoes, green peas, and chunks of potato. The idea is that the hormones of the bull—it can also be made from a carabao's dork or a stallion's honker—somehow collect in the cock and balls and when you eat them, you get a concentrated shot. Same logic with the tiger penis?" Burlane flipped the circled penis in a circle around his forefinger.

"The same," Tepe said.

"Too bad the Chinese couldn't settle on being mere raging bulls or crazed stallions rather than tigers. Or how about dogs? He picked a black object off a shelf and held it up. He knew what this was, too. "And this is?"

"That's a tiger's nose. I suppose you've already learned about the belief there."

"If you hang it above your bed when you screw, your wife will deliver a male baby."

"Correct. The price of tiger noses shot up dramatically when Bejing instituted its policy of only one child per family. The Chinese want male babies."

Burlane moved on. Tepe even collected jerseys from the Princeton Tigers, Clemson Tigers, Auburn Tigers, LSU Tigers, Missouri Tigers, Cincinnati Bengals, and the Detroit Tigers. He said, "I'm curious, Herr Tepe. How did you begin this collection? What was your first item?"

Tepe laughed. "Everybody asks that question. Over here. Look." Tepe pointed to an autographed circus poster featuring a tiger trainer named Lothar Neumann, dubbed Lothar the Magnificent. "When I was a youngster in Hamburg, I was a member of a soccer team that won a youth league championship, and as a reward we were taken to see a performance of Captain Prince–Cox's International Circus. We had the best seats in the house, right in front of the center ring. A few minutes before he entered the cage with his tigers, Lothar Neumann autographed my poster for me. A few minutes later, less than five meters in front of us, a tiger tore open his throat and severed an artery."

"My God!" Burlane looked closer, examining the face of Lothar Neumann. "Did he survive?"

Tepe shook his head. "He bled to death while we watched. His blood literally squirted every which way. It was horrific, and the sight of it affected me for the rest of my life. I'll never forget it. To answer your question, that's when I began my tiger collection."

"Beginning with this autographed poster."

"That's right. That was also the last performance of Captain Prince–Cox's International Circus, which was on the verge of bankruptcy anyway. There are only two known autographed posters known to exist. Mine and his son's."

"That's some story." Then, Burlane added, "What's all this worth, if you don't mind my asking?"

Tepe smiled. "I certainly don't mind you asking, Major Khartoum. It's a natural enough question."

Burlane laughed. "But you're not going to give me an answer."

"It's worth a lot. That much is obvious. But I don't like to put a figure on it in deutsche marks or dollars. A specific number, if it got out, would almost certainly attract attention. Also, I should tell you that most of it was bought by Lily. She wanted us to have something to do together, a shared-interest sort of thing. And once she got into it, I couldn't stop her. She loves to go on shopping trips, and this collection was just made to order. Now she never comes back without something to add to the collection, and some of her finds are amazing, they really are."

Burlane surveyed the room with awe. "But surely would-be thieves must suspect you have something in here of value. The Filipinos are a curious people. When they see a locked door, they want to know what's on the other side. Your household help will inevitably speculate, that can't be helped. And speculation travels fast in the Philippines."

Tepe said, "They no doubt suspect I have something of value, but the Filipino notion of security is labor intensive. They believe a security guard equals security, but the truth is the security guards in this country are half asleep or thieves themselves. Filipinos also like their fences with shards of glass at the top, but any moron can scale a fence and cover the broken glass with something. But if someone wants to get into my collection, he'll be in for some rude surprises. If he's determined enough to negotiate the barbed wire at the bottom of my moat, he'll have to deal with high-voltage electricity that he won't be able to spot, followed by sirens that can be heard from here to Manila. I've got my own underground generators, so he can't cut my electricity. And finally he'll have to be wearing a gas mask."

Burlane's eyes widened. "A gas mask."

"Not any old gas mask. It will have to have the proper filter that he'll probably be unable to obtain even if he knows what he's up against." Tepe gestured to the ceiling. "You think those nozzles are solely for fire protection?"

Burlane glanced at the fire nozzles. He counted sixteen of them spaced evenly on the ceiling.

Tepe said, "Protection that lethal would be frowned upon in the West, I know, but here, well . . ."

"Here justice is for sale."

"To put it baldly," Tepe said. "If you have enough money in the Philippines, you're above the law. It's as simple as that. To satisfy your curiosity, yes, Major Khartoum, my wife's money paid for all this. You may have passed one of the Chua shopping malls on your way out."

"Why yes, I did, as a matter of fact." Burlane thought he had detected a wistful look in Tepe's eyes. Was it possible that—despite his beautiful wife and handsome setup on Mactan—the German suffered from some form of disaffection or angst? Tepe was no doubt doing his best to suppress his melancholia, but it was there.

Burlane was not surprised by this. Life in a place like the Philippines—having to be constantly on the alert for hustlers, scam artists, and thieves—had to be a grinding ordeal after a while. Burlane suspected that some foreigners could handle the stress of having to live defensively while others couldn't. Also, cross-cultural marriages had their special problems under the best of circumstances. Was a mutual interest in a tiger collection enough marital glue? Perhaps it was.

But Burlane still wondered if Tepe might not long for the courtesy, manners, and discipline of his native Germany—if not the casual availability of good cheese, sauerkraut, and dill pickles.

Burlane could see just how it was that Tepe had come to fall in love with Lily Chua in Hong Kong. Lily's physical attraction was obvious, plus she was rich. But Lily's attraction to Tepe was more obscure. Tepe was educated and successful in his way, but a powerful Chinese family like the Chuas did not put a premium on intellectuals. By nature, intellectuals, nurtured by western individualism, were freethinkers. What the Chinese wanted almost uniformly, was money and power.

Tepe said, "Would you like to have a beer on the lawn? We can watch the pump boats. They're beautiful, and there's a breeze coming off the water."

James Burlane and Heinz Tepe sat in handsome rattan chairs by a rattan table on a concrete pad protected from the tropical sun by a thatched roof set on four bamboo poles. There were indeed pump boats on the water, riding the wind with their traditional sails, and Burlane thought they were, in fact, grand. Also lovely in the distance was Olango Island.

Burlane, pouring himself another mug of San Miguel, said, "Dr. Sangrit thinks the smugglers may have shifted their base temporarily to Cebu after the United States hit Taiwan with trade sanctions on all products made from animals. Did you know that when you moved here?"

Tepe shook his head. "I moved here well before the United States hit Taiwan with trade sanctions. Lily's family bought this property a few years back before we met. In fact, I met and fell in love with her when she was on a shopping trip in Hong Kong. We have a membership in Tambuli if we want to use the beach. Cebu is convenient to the tiger country where I do my research. What better place to live?"

That was true; Indonesia lay to the southeast of Cebu; the Malay and Indochina Peninsulas and the Indian subcontinent were to the west and northwest, and Siberia was to the northeast. Tepe said, "Flying back and forth from Europe gets to be too much—both tiring and expensive. This is a nice central location, and I like it here."

"Sun, sand, cheap beer, and a beautiful wife, not a bad deal."

They sat in silence for a moment. Then Tepe said, "Do you think you can really do anything about the tiger smuggling?"

"When I started, I thought maybe so or I wouldn't have taken the job."

"And what do you think now?"

Burlane said, "I think that with more than two hundred twenty manufacturers of traditional medicines in China and another forty in Hong Kong, the Chinese will find a way to smuggle tiger bones. Whether the smuggler has his headquarters on Taiwan, Hong Kong, or somewhere else doesn't make a whole lot of difference, although I agree with David Ames: Once the Chinese take over Hong Kong, that will almost certainly be their base."

Tepe grimaced in agreement. "Although I agreed with the decision to hire you, I'd think stopping the smuggling will be an impossible chore for an outsider."

Burlane said, "As far as I can see, the only way to stem the tiger poaching even temporarily is to go for the buyers, who are apparently westerners, North Americans or Europeans."

Tepe bunched his face in agreement. "Where do you propose to find these buyers?"

Burlane shrugged. "Here, maybe."

"On Mactan?" Tepe blinked.

Burlane shook his head. "Cebu, although Mactan can't be ruled out."

"Cebu?"

"Why not Cebu?" Burlane said. "Mr. Big doesn't need triad enforcers here for it to be his headquarters. Cebu City has a high population of Chinese, remember. The Chinese have the money here, witness the prosperity of your wife's family. Also Cebu's an ideal location for moving tiger bones to the manufacturers in China and Hong Kong. And cops and courts are for sale, so buyers don't have to worry about investigators from conservation organizations."

"I've heard that theory," Tepe said. "I know Dr. Sangrit believes it. It might be true, you know. I may have inadvertently managed to settle one island away from Mr. Big in the tiger trade." Tepe rolled his eyes, and gave Burlane a lopsided grin. "Talk about irony!"

Burlane raised an eyebrow. "A worrisome possibility?"

Tepe shook his head. "I'm not going to lose any sleep over it. If the smugglers are based in Cebu, they would be foolish to do anything to me, wouldn't they? That would tip off tiger conservationists everywhere, and they would never quit until they found out who did it."

"From the traders' standpoint, it would be better to leave you alone."

"That way they know where I am and what I'm up to. Or think they do. What better way to deflect attention than to have your headquarters right under the nose of the CITES representative? At any rate, we shouldn't overlook the possibility, and the two of us should certainly work together."

"That goes without saying," Burlane said.

"They don't have any idea that you're here, so you have that advantage, Major Khartoum. If you will pass along any tips you might get, I'll do the same. I want to get these bastards, Major Khartoum. I want them real, real badly." Tepe's face turned hard.

"You and me both," Burlane said, thinking of Heinz Tepe's amazing collection of tigerana. "Have you ever read *The Golden Bough*, Herr Doktor?"

Tepe looked puzzled. *"The Golden Bough?"*

"Written in the last century by an Englishman, Sir James George Frazer. He was an anthropologist, a superb one. Interested in myths, magic, and religion."

"Frazer? Sir James Frazer?" Tepe thought for a moment. "No, I haven't," Tepe said.

Burlane thought it was a weakness of many academics that they were poorly read in other disciplines. Here was a man working to stop the poaching of tigers who had no idea who Sir James George Frazer was. He likely knew who Karl Jung was and perhaps Joseph Campbell, but not the master himself. This was dismaying, but Burlane did his best to conceal his disappointment. The trick of scholars trying to comprehend the forests of the night, was not to focus obsessively on each tree, but to see how all the trees made sense when put together.

Burlane said, "I think it's just possible that Sir James may hold the key to ending the tiger trade. The solution may be considered illiberal and impolite to the people who are currently paying our bills. Certainly there would be howls of protest from many quarters."

In the end, Burlane knew, it all depended on how serious the conservationists and people in charge of wildlife trusts were about saving the tiger. Did they really want to save the tiger, or were they content with their research grants, their travel money, their conventions in fancy hotels, their interviews on television, and their self-righteous opinions quoted in news magazines? It was entirely possible that many conservationists put their egos before the wildlife they presumed to care so passionately about, and did not really want satisfying controversies brought to a successful conclusion.

The awesome power of the research grant was not to be underestimated. Burlane remembered that in the 1970s, scientists sacked the public pocket for grants by claiming the planet was headed for another Ice Age; in the future everybody would be wearing long johns; suddenly, when money started running low for that boring conclusion, yawn, the reverse was held to be true: due to the depletion of the ozone layer, global warming was on the way, threatening coastal cities with water from melted ice caps. Thus sayeth computer models—although temperature records, strangely, didn't yield any noticeable change.

Burlane decided he would tell Heinz Tepe no more about Sir James George Frazer. If Tepe were a genuine intellectual, as opposed to a grant-grabbing academic hustler, he'd be moved to find out for himself.

24

In Cebu, Burlane, wondering if some traditional Chinese medicines might be found in the public market, set out to do some pen-and-ink quick sketches. As he did, curious Filipinos crowded around him, staring over his shoulder. Some called "Hey, Joe!" Others called, "Joe, Joe!" Or "What are you doing, Joe?"

While Burlane got used to the "Hey, Joe!" drill, he could never get used to little kids calling "Hey, man!" to him like they had seen punks do in American movies. When someone called "Hey, my friend," Burlane walked faster, changing directions if possible. He did the same thing in Latin America whenever someone called, "Hey, mi amigo!" Mi amigo. Right.

Burlane never carried a wallet in the Third World. Instead, he wore a multipocketed photographer's vest so he could move his money about in a form of shell game: Guess which pocket it's in, asshole. Burlane had disciplined himself so that when a Filipino yelled "Hey, my friend," he suppressed the urge to check the pocket where he kept his money; to do that would lead his would-be "friend," possibly a pickpocket or razor artist, straight to the prize.

He was not a Filipino. He was an outsider, an exotic, an object of curiosity. Burlane felt there was surely no culture on the planet where people so casually and routinely asked personal questions as in the Philippines.

Burlane did his best to ignore these intrusions, but he understood that Filipinos didn't share his western sense of privacy. They openly stared at him. No, stared wasn't the word; they gawked, mouths agape. They pointed at him. They asked him who he was and where he was from. They asked him if he was married. Was he looking for a wife? What was his job? How much money did he make? What did he think of the Philippines?

"Where are you going?" they asked. This was a favorite question, and they never seemed to tire of asking it: Where are you going? Where are you going? Where are you going?

He wanted to say, "I'm going to hell, no doubt," but he didn't. Some even asked, "What are you doing, Joe?" Burlane felt this was the most amazing question of all. When he was simply walking down the street or stopped at a crosswalk, did they think he was baking a cake or flying an airplane? What a question! He wondered if they might not mean by that, "What are you doing here, in this awful place?"

Filipinos knew from watching American movies and television programs that Burlane possessed an odd sense of values. They knew they could treat him as a passing spectacle, indifferent to his feelings, and he would do nothing. He had been raised to believe that not to be courteous was to be boorish, and the concept of boorishness was foreign to them.

Courtesy, as taught by Burlane's mother, was based on the idea of reciprocity; I treat you in a civil manner, and you respect me in return—a rephrasing of the biblical golden rule, which the philosopher Emmanuel Kant had deduced was a form of elementary moral logic. It didn't take dieties with exotic powers or an omniscient single God, cap G, to deduce that reciprocal courtesy was the best way of doing business.

Burlane knew from previous trips to the Philippines that what appeared to be politeness there, was in fact largely based on fear, rather than reciprocity; if you offended somebody in the Philippines, causing them to lose face, you could get hurt. To get sore at the intrusive, moronic questions might cause a loss of face, and the consequences of a Filipino losing face in public, especially a male, were unpredictable. The word *amok*, to lurch into a murderous frenzy or go completely wild, found its way into the English language from Tagalog. Filipinos did not readily warm to the imputation of error; the aggrieved might run amok on the spot, or he might retreat, nursing his wounded pride, but bent on revenge. A few days after the real or imagined offense, a hired goon might step from the shadows and break the offender's head open with a lead pipe or knife him from behind.

Likewise, the reciprocal concept of trust was extended only to relatives or one's circle of friends in the Philippines—one's *barkada.* Only fools and inexperienced westerners trusted strangers. A customer was someone to screw if possible, not someone to please.

Burlane was regarded precisely like a monkey in a zoo, so, just as monkeys largely ignored people staring at them, he ignored the Filipinos who gathered around him asking their barbarous questions; he stared right through them as though they didn't exist. He was the dispassionate, blue-eyed, western iceman; they were suppressed passion, tinder waiting to ignite.

He quickly sketched one pile of fruit and a counter heaped with fish, then moved quickly on, doing his best not to get pissed.

One person who watched him, but at a respectful distance, was a pretty young Filipina.

When Burlane caught her eye, inviting her to ask him a question if she wanted, she said, "Why don't you use a camera like other foreigners? If you had a camera, you could go snap, snap, and move on."

Burlane ripped off a drawing of a handsome pile of fish and signed it. He gave it to her.

"Is this for me?" She was pleased.

"Sure."

"Why, it's beautiful."

"Thank you," he said. "And your name is?"

"Teresita Sanchez," she said. "But people call me Risa. I've always been interested in art."

"And your medium?"

Risa grinned shyly. "I don't have one really. I wanted to be a photographer, but I never had the money for a camera."

Burlane said, "Photography can be a wonderful art. Photographers can be artists, of course. You can manipulate light and shutter speed. But ordinarily a photograph is to art what nonfiction is to fiction. Do you understand what I mean?"

Risa shook her head.

"When I sketch, I select the details that are suggestive, dramatic, or memorable, and let the viewer fill in the rest."

Risa held up her drawing of fish, admiring it. "I'll put this on my wall."

Burlane said, "Did you ever think about the difference between watching a movie and reading a novel? Anybody can watch a movie. People who read novels like to immerse themselves in the interior world of imagination. Each reader imagines a sentence just a little differently, so a novel is the same yet different for however many people read it. Reading fiction is an act of creativity. If I didn't have people peering over my shoulder and jabbering at me—not you, Risa—I'd do the market in watercolors."

"You do watercolors, too?"

"I try. But watercolors are more difficult than quick sketches. To do a proper watercolor, you start with white space and work your way through ever darker colors, layer by opaque layer. An accident can be valuable, but errors are irreversible, just like life itself. To do a watercolor, I need peace and quiet so I can concentrate."

"You'd have to go to the provinces to find much in the way of peace and quiet here, I'm afraid."

Burlane folded his drawing pad and put away his pen. "I'm losing my light today anyway. Say, do you think tomorrow you could show me some interesting places to sketch? By interesting, I mean places where real people live, not official sights intended for tourist guidebooks."

"Really?"

"Sure. You pick the subjects. Among other things, I'm curious about traditional Chinese medicine. If you know of any, I'd like to see some places where the Chinese buy their ingredients."

25

The next morning, James Burlane and Risa Sanchez toured the small Chinese shops near Carbon Market and found none that stocked medicines claiming to contain tiger bone. Burlane didn't believe for a second that the proprietors didn't have them, only that they were off-limits to longnoses; western conservationists were on the prowl in Asian cities, and the American boycott of Taiwanese animal products was no secret.

At one of these establishments, Chen's, a middle-aged Filipina was buying heart medicine made from milk vetch. In his research of traditional medicine, Burlane had learned that western clinical research of *Astragalus,* the Latin name for milk vetch, showed that it was an effective medicine for relieving blood pressure and hypertension. It did this by widening the blood vessels. Moreover, mice injected with milk vetch gained weight and had greater endurance.

Frustrated western athletes had been accusing the Chinese of using all manner of exotic performance-enhancing drugs. Burlane wondered if it might not be plain old milk vetch.

Later, as Burlane and Risa walked down Colon Street on their way to the Pasil fish market, Burlane saw passengers being pulled in large, two-wheeled carts. These were called *cartenillas,* he knew. The heat was searing and the drivers, called *pocheros,* casually whipped the small, skinny horses, with sore-ridden, calloused backs, with the same mindless repetition as jeepney and taxi drivers honked their horns. Drivers had horns, so they honked. *Pocheros* had whips, so they whipped.

The undersize horses looked dreadful. Their bones poked out. They were both underfed and overworked. Their backs were raw from the whipping. They were forced to go at a constant trot, *clip-clop, clip-clop,* dodging in and out of traffic.

When they did get a chance to rest, the diminutive horses stood pathetically, heads drooping from exhaustion, mouths foaming and drooling.

Burlane, internally seething, regarded the drivers as barbarous, reprehensible, if not outright monsters. If Filipinos agreed with him, they did not show it. Cruelty, he supposed, was a part of their lives. Lucky it was the horses that were being so mercilessly whipped—and not them.

Burlane said, casually, doing his best to suppress his rage, "What do you think of the *cartenillas?*"

"I never ride them," she said. "I don't like the whipping."

Burlane felt relieved. "Good woman," he said. "I wonder how the drivers would like to be treated that way? Whipped all day. Made to trot in this heat."

Burlane remembered reading that Douglas MacArthur's wife had hated the *cartenillas* in Manila and was always pestering her husband to force the Filipinos to get rid of them. Whipping the poor animals like that? She was enraged. Burlane was never an admirer of MacArthur especially; he felt the business of retaking the Philippines in World War II was a costly exercise to appease MacArthur's ego, resulting in pointless loss of blood and treasure—not to mention the unnecessary sacking of Manila—but he didn't think MacArthur's wife had been all bad.

"They've always had them here," Risa said. "There have been efforts to get rid of them because of the traffic, but people say they're good for tourists. Tourists like to take pictures of them."

Burlane ground his teeth together. "Horses may be animals, but they surely have feelings, same as us. These horses are earning money for the driver's family. It's uncivilized that they aren't respected for that much, at least." He remembered seeing a documentary about Thais who trained monkeys to retrieve coconuts for them. The monkeys there, at least, were treated as honored members of the family.

Risa looked at the strange, long-haired, mustached man that was Sid Khartoum. She said, "I bet you don't like zoos either."

"Nope. Animal prisons. And I don't like shows with trained animals. They can talk to me all they want about how much animals love it, but I bet most animals would prefer to be free. It's possible that race horses love to run and compete, I'll give them that. But I'll pass on dogs that walk on their hind feet or monkeys that play basketball."

But Burlane did not mention to Risa the real reason he suspected the *pocheros* on Colon Street whipped their horses so enthusiastically. This was Asia. Here, power over anything, even a dumb, suffering beast, was a power to be exercised. Here, dogs were not kept as pets in the western sense, as something to be petted or taken for a playful romp. Their job was to warn of strangers in the night, possible thieves; in the daytime, they made do. Like the pathetic beasts pulling the *cartenillas,* the dogs were underfed, many of them to the point of starvation, and their ribs poked out. They were scab-ridden, and afflicted with fleas and the mange. In central Luzon, if the family got hungry enough, they ate their dogs.

They watched as a European man rode by in a *cartenilla.*

Burlane said, "I couldn't do that. I'll pass on that tourism attraction, thanks."

Risa said, "That's no tourist."

"No?"

"That would have been my new boss if I'd gotten the job in his camera shop."

"You interviewed for a job with him?"

Risa nodded. "He said he'd get in touch if I had the job. He hasn't called."

"Too bad."

"I didn't really expect to get it anyway. His name is Klaus Something. He drives a Mercedes and lives in a house on Beverly Hills."

"Oh? How do you know that?"

"You think this is a city, but it isn't. It's a village."

"Ah, gossip, then!"

Risa laughed. "The cousin of my neighbor works as a *yaya* for a Chinese family in Beverly Hills. She was talking to the *yaya* who works for the family next door, when he drove by in his Mercedes and parked it two doors down."

"A *yaya* being?"

"What the British call a nanny. She takes care of their kids. A rich Chinese family would be humiliated if they didn't have a Filipina to take care of their kids. If they're rich enough they have a *yaya* for each kid."

Burlane looked puzzled. "Well, how did the *yaya* next door know the German was opening a camera shop?"

Risa looked amused. "Easy, she learned it from the *yaya* who works three doors over. The *yayas* up there don't have very much to do. The laundry and household chores are done by maids. So they visit one another and gossip while the kids play together. You foreigners think you have privacy just because you live behind a wall." She arched an eyebrow.

Burlane still didn't understand. "But how did the *yaya* three doors over know he was opening a camera shop? Did he tell her?"

"She learned it from her cousin who works for a company that supplies all the camera shops in Cebu. When a foreigner opens a shop everybody knows it. The first thing the *yayas* and maids in the neighborhood want to know is whether he's married or not. You never can tell."

Burlane said, "Ah, yes. Of course." Unmarried foreigners represented a ticket to a good life, Burlane knew. Their curiosity was understandable. An unmarried foreigner was a potential trophy husband.

Risa said, "He seemed like a nice man."

"Well, what's the answer to the main question?"

"The main question?"

"Is he married?"

Risa gave Burlane a playful punch on the shoulder. "Oh, you. No, he's not married."

James Burlane watched as the *cartenilla* bearing the German named Klaus disappeared into the crush of traffic on Colon Street.

26

The next day James Burlane began hanging out in the expat bars in Cebu on the theory that these were cultural watering holes for westerners. The Russian game warden Andrei Bure had told him watering holes were prime places for a hunter to wait. If the buyer of poached tigers were in Cebu, he would arrive with protective coloring: he would lie about his past and talk a good game. But it was through talk that Burlane, exercising his built-in bullshit detector, would eventually discern the identity of his quarry.

The two German-run expat hangouts in Cebu City were Kukuc's Nest on Gorodo Avenue, and the St. Moritz Hotel, just down the street. But plenty of Germans hung out at the other two expat bars in town—Our Place, in the downtown area, that featured schnitzel, German sausages, and *fleisse kasse,* and the Missouri Bar, uptown near Fuente Circle.

As his own protective coloring, Burlane, sticking with his nom de guerre of Major M. Sidarius Khartoum, told people that he was an international buyer. For a two percent knick, he bought things from the Third World, Asia and Africa for small firms in North America and Europe. To earn his two percent, he dealt directly with the makers and arranged the details of shipping and customs regulations. He said he bought jeans from Bangladesh, carved ducks from Indonesia, baskets from central Luzon, shell jewelry from Cebu, rattan furniture from Palawan. Whatever. In fact, years earlier, Burlane had done exactly that as a cover for his employment by the Company in Langley, Virginia. Back then, the Chinese, although paranoid about outsiders, were not nearly so picky about someone who could help them gain access to an American market that was attempting to freeze them out.

Neither Our Place, Kukuc's Nest, nor the Missouri Bar were girlie bars. The St. Moritz, which was also popular with Germans, offered dancers available for a bar fine, but the dancers apparently so liked working at the St. Moritz that the joke among its foreign customers was they were the oldest bar fines in town.

In a proper, nongirlie expat bar, the western customers spent most of their time complaining about how ruined things were back home and about the apalling lack of civilization in whatever country they were currently holed up. This meant the usual collection of retired servicemen, ex–Peace Corps volunteers, merchant seamen, fugitives, drifters, oddballs, and eccentrics of every imaginable description, and insecure tellers of all manner of tall tales. If Burlane had a nickel for every loudmouth who claimed to have once worked for the CIA, he'd have been a millionaire.

In Cebu City, the foreign males included a smattering of sex tourists and middle-aged men fresh off the plane with their hearts thumping in expectation of meeting their pen pals—would-be Filipina brides who had placed ads in one of several magazines published in Southern California and Las Vegas. In these magazines, winsome Filipinas allowed as how they would be interested in meeting an American man, older man okay.

The American expats bitched mostly about man-hating feminist zealots back home. As they saw it, the zealots—led by a coterie of battle-axes and butch lesbians—had declared war on all males, overrunning and ridiculing sensible women everywhere. Ensconced in the fortress of academia, the man-haters flat invented dubious if not outright impossible statistics, and this nonsense—portraying males as an inherently savage and evil gender, the forever enemy of all women—was passed along largely unchallenged by the mass media, which thrived on charges and countercharges and unchallenged hyperbole.

American expats, ordinarily white males, were the primary ranters about these female nutballs; they didn't care much for lawyers either, whom they regarded as impossible-to-control, greedy bloodsuckers who leeched off everyone. When the occasional African-American expat showed up, he was regarded as an American first, Black man second; men whom Burlane suspected were racists back home set aside their prejudices on distant shores.

Swedes and Germans were enraged about taxes, which also made the Canadians sore as hell; refugees from British Columbia claimed they worked for the first nine months for the government. But few expats were such colorful malcontents as the hard-drinking Australians. The chief complaint of the Australians, who were given to calling people cunts and wankers—a wanker being a chronic masturbator—was what they regarded as the pernicious public policy that supported abjectly lazy Aboriginals. If the Australian expats were to be believed, the population of good-for-nothing Abos and recent immigrants contained excessive numbers of cunts and wankers. And what's more, the odious government in Sydney insisted on piling more and more taxes on their beer to finance the giveaway. The wankers!

Burlane had hung out in enough Asian expat bars to have the prejudices pretty much down pat: To a man—female expats were rare to nonexistent—they all thought Arabs were flagrant pricks. Few who had traveled in boring, overpriced Japan ever wanted to go back again; they felt the Japanese were unembarrassed racists who really wanted foreigners to stay the hell away. Another place to avoid was China, where a screw-the-longnose attitude was the order of the day.

At the opposite end, the expat talkers had a love-hate relationship with the Philippines. They felt that the rapacious, corrupt culture—apparently endemic to the Pacific Islands if the travel writer Paul Theroux was accurate—doomed the Philippines to eternal poverty. But the Filipinos were the most likeable, fun people in all Asia. Filipinos genuinely knew how to have fun, and were capable of great peals of laughter, even outright guffaws. They were the best singers, dancers, actors, and actresses in all of Asia.

And then there were the women, the wonderful, delightful Filipinas. . . . If an expat got his hands on a good one, he really had something. Oy!

Burlane drank San Miguel at Our Place, which had gorgeous architecture, high ceilings and listless fans out of old movies; its Spanish windows overlooked Palaez Street, which was crowded with sexy college girls on their way to and from the University of San Carlos. He hung out with German expats and played an occasional game of darts at Kukuc's Nest, a nice little bar with an open-air courtyard. At the Missouri Bar, a sour-smelling, cavelike hole-in-the-wall, he bullshitted with expats and travelers, and watched CNN or baseball on the bar television.

Along the way, Burlane met, among other possible buyers of poached tigers, Peter, a German ship's captain, and Rolf, also from Germany, an expert in seaweeds who was a professor at the University of San Carlos. Otto had settled down in Cebu with a Filipina and ran a bakery that marketed German bread to upscale restaurants and export shops. Berndt was a German who ran a camera shop. Steig, a large-bellied motorcycle-riding Swedish housepainter, had retired to Cebu. Don was an Australian rancher who, fed up with the wankers Down Under, had chucked it in to live on a sailboat. Several young Canadians were dive jocks at Moalboal; the Canadians were forever coming and going, smoking pot and getting laid. Stan, an American, had settled in with a Filipina and was making quality furniture with power equipment, something nearly unhearded of in the labor-intensive Philippines. Nigel was a complaining Englishman who peddled soybean meat additives. Tony, a retired Irish construction superintendent, was a teller of tall tales. Rudy was a German social worker retired on a disability that he didn't specify and that wasn't obvious. Barry ran a crab cannery on Bangtayan island that supplied crabs to a famous chain of seafood restaurants on the American east coast.

A second Barry, a quiet man with a wry smile, wore his hair in a substantial ponytail. He had a sweatband around his forehead and rumbled around Cebu on a vintage Harley-Davidson. This Barry, a good-looking, rugged man, had once been a boxer and occasionally disappeared to work on oil rigs. Or so he said. Burlane didn't care what he had done in the past. He had landed in the Philippines and now had a wife, a house, and four kids.

Almost all of these expats had the time to travel, and could do it virtually unnoticed, but none of them gave a hint of anything that had to do with tigers, hunting, or traditional Chinese medicine. But Burlane was patient. His quarry might not be an overt tiger nut or reveal a history of dealing with tigers or studying them, at least in public. In this case, the tiger's stripes would be a web of lies.

Then one lazy, sweltering afternoon, with the air conditioner stalled because of an electrical blackout—called a brownout in the Philippines—a German named Fritz Steiner showed up in the Missouri Bar. Steiner said he was looking for a man named Klaus Neumann, who used to supervise the capture and shipment of tigers for Hesse's, a Munich firm that supplied animals to zoos.

This got Burlane's attention.

Tigers?

Yes, Steiner said. Had anybody heard of Klaus Neumann or know of his whereabouts?

27

Dodong Gutierrez carried the pistol in a plastic Gaisano shopping bag.

The desk clerk at the McSherry Pension on Palaez Street was busy pretending to be busy—she was reading a Tagalog movie magazine—and did not bother to look up when Gutierrez asked her in Tagalog if Fritz Steiner was in.

"Ho oh," she said. This meant yes.

"*Unsang numeroha na?*" What number is that?

Still not looking up, she said, "*Dos cien y siete.*"

"*Salamet.*"

Gutierrez, grateful for the clerk's obsession with movies, moved quickly to the stairwell. If he waited for the elevator, she might check the clock to see how much more of her boredom she had to endure, and Gutierrez didn't want to be seen.

The second floor. Not bad. There were metal fire escapes in the McSherry. If something went wrong, he could quickly escape. He moved quickly up the stairs, and down the hall to number 207.

He knocked quietly on the door.

Fritz Steiner opened it. On the television behind him, an earnest Charles Bronson talked to a pretty young girl. "What is it?" he asked.

"I would like to talk, quietly please," Gutierrez said. He pulled the pistol out of the bag.

Steiner, his eye on the pistol, stepped back. He said, "I don't keep large amounts of cash."

Gutierrez stepped inside, closing the door behind him. "I'm not interested in cash, although I'll take what you've got."

Steiner licked his lips.

Gutierrez said, "You've been asking about a man named Klaus Neumann. Why is that?"

"I'm a collector, I . . ."

Behind him, someone knocked on the door. A man's voice said, "Herr Steiner?"

Gutierrez cooly shot Fritz Steiner in the heart. Quickly, he grabbed Steiner's wallet, yanked open the window, and was gone down the fire escape into the darkness. He'd had rotten luck, but at least the clerk hadn't seen his face.

James Burlane knocked again on the door of Fritz Steiner's room. Still no answer. "Herr Steiner?" he said again. Burlane could hear voices on a television set.

Without looking up from her magazine, the desk clerk had said Steiner was in his room, and he had a Filipino visitor.

"Herr Steiner?"

No answer.

He heard gunfire on the television set.

Burlane looked around. Screw it, he thought. He retrieved his lock picks from his pocket and began working on the door. The lock, old-fashioned and crude, wasn't much of an obstacle to someone trained by the best instructors the Company had to offer.

In a couple of minutes, Burlane had it mastered and opened the door.

Inside, Fritz Steiner was on the floor. Burlane knelt beside the corpse, as, on the television set, Charles Bronson did the same.

Burlane stood and punched off the set.

Quickly, he rummaged through Steiner's room. He found nothing of interest in the bureau drawers, only socks, underwear, and folded shirts. There was nothing in the closet except clothes.

In the nightstand, he found a special edition of a collector's magazine featuring circus posters. In a corner by the nightstand, he found a large plastic tube. He popped the lid off the tube and retrieved a poster. He unrolled it and discovered that it promoted the 12 June 1957 performance in Hamburg of Captain Prince–Cox's International Circus. The poster, autographed by Lothar the Magnificent, appeared identical to the one Burlane had seen in Heinz Tepe's collection. This was the poster that had sparked Tepe's obsession with tigers. Tepe had said there were only two known autographed copies of this poster, his and one belonging to Lothar Neumann's son, although it was possible that this signature was forged.

In the Missouri Bar, Herr Steiner had said Klaus Neumann once worked for Hesse's, a Munich firm that provided animals to zoos.

Was Klaus Neumann Lothar's son? Had to be.

Was this poster genuine or a facsimile? Could be either. Burlane was no expert on circus posters, and it would take an expert to examine Lothar Neumann's signature.

Should he show the poster to Heinz Tepe?

Andre Bure knew how to hunt tigers. Post some bait, he had said. Burlane decided he should bow to authority. He would use the poster as bait for his tiger man. He would talk the owners of the Missouri Bar into hanging the poster in the bar and see what happened. After all, University of Missouri fielded the tigers. A poster featuring a tiger trainer and tigers was surely in order.

Post some bait. The collector's magazine was good bait, too. He would leave the magazine in Steiner's room, knowing that hungry Filipino reporters would report it in the newspapers.

Klaus Neumann would surely read that.

So would Heinz Tepe.

Having thus made his decision and not wanting to deal with the unpredictable Filipino police, Burlane followed the murderer's path out the window and down the fire escape.

28

■■■■■Hermann Iversen was shocked at the clarity of the connection with Karl Bauer. He had somehow expected a Cebu-to-Munich connection to sound like a link with the moon, but no. Bauer sounded like someone talking from across the city.

"Was I right?" Iversen asked.

"You were indeed. I think you're closing in, Hermann. Good work."

"When I read in the papers that Steiner had a collector's magazine featuring circus posters, I knew it was the same man who was asking questions in Munich and Mombasa. Had to be."

Bauer said, "The Berlin police ran down his sister, and I talked to her on the telephone. Easy duty."

"And what did you find out?"

"That Fritz Steiner was an investment manager in a brokerage firm. He had a complete collection of posters, one for each performance of Captain Prince–Cox's International Circus. Each of these posters was autographed by the featured performer, which makes them extra valuable. The circus's final performance, in Hamburg, on 12 June 1957, featured a tiger trainer named Lothar Neumann, who you know all about. Steiner had that poster, too, but Neumann's signature was forged. He told his sister there were known to be two such autographed posters, one belonging to Lothar's son Klaus, and a second to a collector he didn't identify. On the off chance that more than two autographed posters existed, he recently ran an ad in a collector's magazine offering fifty thousand deutsche marks for the one he wanted."

"Really?" Iversen asked. "Did he get an answer?"

"No, but he recently took a month-long trip to Africa looking for a man he thinks owns an original."

"A *month*? How much is that poster supposed to be worth?"

"Steiner's sister says that depends on how badly a collector wants it. If you're someone like Steiner, and you're one poster shy of a complete collection, it could be worth upwards of a quarter of a million deutsche marks."

"A quarter of a million deutsche marks. *Sheisse!*"

"That's not all, Hermann. She told me that her brother returned from Africa pumped with excitement. He immediately extended his leave, saying he had found out that Klaus Neumann now lives in the Philippines."

"In Cebu City?"

"Yes."

"Did you ask his sister if he'd go so far as to steal Klaus's poster and replace it with his if Klaus refused to part with his copy?"

"She said she wouldn't put it past him. He was down to that one autographed poster for a complete collection, and he was determined to have it, no matter what the cost."

"Did she say how her brother learned that Klaus was in Cebu?"

"She said he followed the advice of a German engineer and hung out in expat bars in Mombasa."

"That would be Reiner Weithoff, the same engineer I talked to. Have you ever seen one of those documentaries where the animals are gathered around a watering hole? Weithoff says expat bars are watering holes for expats both in the literal and figurative sense."

"How did I do, Hermann? Not bad work for a man with arthritic ankles. I can still talk to people on the telephone." Karl Bauer sounded pleased.

"Our poster collector may have saved us some time. Too bad it cost him his life."

Bauer said, "I think you're closing in on your man, Hermann. I've been keeping Rolf posted on your progress. He says stay with it. Don't give up."

Iversen said, "That's one thing you and Rolf don't have to worry about, Karl. Klaus Neumann is here in Cebu. I'll find him, and I'll watch him. Eventually, I'll get a photograph of him for our witness and a tissue sample for a DNA test. If they both match, we've got our man."

29

Hermann Iversen knew his prospective landlords, two young Chinese-Filipinos, had jacked up his rent the moment they set eyes on him. In the Philippines there was a special, ascending scale of prices for everything: the cheapest rates were reserved for relatives; friends—one's *barkada*—were charged a fraction more; members of the Chinese-Filipino minority routinely jacked up the price to the dominant Malay Filipinos; the standard price—if that term had any meaning—was that charged to strangers who came from the same island. This was followed by a casual rip-off of Filipinos who spoke another language and so were countrymen in name only; then the freebie grand gouge—a Filipino embarrassed himself if he did not put the maximum screw to foreigners.

As the dismayed Iversen had learned quickly, all prices, costs, and rates were negotiable, except to outsiders.

In the end, Iversen was forced to pay ten thousand pesos a week rent—nearly four hundred U.S. dollars, absurd by local standards—for a single room in the business complex across the street from the Missouri Bar on Mango Avenue. This robbery was being paid by German taxpayers, but Iversen was still annoyed, especially when the thieves, all smiles, had made a big fuss about giving him a special deal because they really liked Germans. Germans were their special friends, they said; one even went so far as to claim that he had a German who was just like his brother. Right! No wonder the Filipinos couldn't get foreigners to invest in their economy.

The American Sid Khartoum, who had found Fritz Steiner's body in the McSherry pension, had placed a poster on the wall of the Missouri Bar featuring the 12 June 1957 Hamburg performance of Captain Prince–Cox's International Circus—the last performance of Klaus Neumann's father, Lothar the Magnificent. Iversen didn't think Khartoum had murdered Fritz Steiner, but two serious questions remained:

Why had he lifted Steiner's poster?

Why had he chosen to display it on the walls of the Missouri Bar?

Iversen couldn't figure Khartoum out. He didn't think Khartoum was a buyer for goods made in Asia, but that wasn't impossible. He had told the bar owner he wanted to hang it there because of the Missouri Tigers.

Was Khartoum also after Klaus Neumann?

Did he also collect posters?

Had he posted the poster in the Missouri Bar as a form of bait?

For the moment, Iversen decided to just watch the American; later he would confront him directly and get some answers.

For the time being, Iversen would shoot pictures of the customers of the Missouri Bar through the open window of his overpriced room. There would likely come a time when Klaus Neumann, curious about the poster, would go inside to check it out. Then Iversen would take his picture for the woman who had briefly seen the killer of Rolf Bauer's daughter.

30

■■■■■Heinz and Lily Tepe had chosen to eat their supper outside, on the covered patio, so they could enjoy the gentle breeze
coming off the water and watch the graceful boats in the distance.
Den Den, their Filipina helper, was placing ceramic bowls and
plates of Chinese food on a revolving lazy Susan in the center of
the table. While Lily looked as cheerful as a bird, her husband
looked rather less upbeat. In fact, he looked downright dour.

Lily took a sip of Chinese tea. "Don't look so down, darling,
things are going well. You and Klaus did very well on your trips
to Siberia. First he scored the white tiger, and now you work this
new arrangement with the Russian poacher."

Heinz licked his lips. He started to say something, then closed
his mouth. After a second, he said, "We'll see how it works out."

Lily said, "Where Klaus doesn't have contacts, you do. And he
knows his cats and how to hunt them, you said so yourself. When
Klaus finds a local who is willing to try his hand at hunting cats,
he can show him the tricks of the trade." She surveyed the spread,
and seized a deep-fried shrimp with her chopsticks. This was a
quick, agile move; the chopsticks dove for the morsel neat as a
bird's beak. "After all that Communist foolishness, the Russians
are desperate for capital. They'll sell anything they can lay their
hands on, including tigers. There's no reason why we shouldn't
have a long and fruitful relationship with the former comrades."

Heinz bit his lower lip, then dipped out a ladleful of corn and
asparagus soup that had chunks of chicken breast floating in it.

Lily said, "But in all honesty, I must tell you I don't like this business of Klaus having Dodong Gutierrez kill Steiner. Why did he do that?" She took another shrimp.

"Steiner was asking questions, and Klaus didn't like it."

Lily clenched her jaw. "Questions about tiger poaching?"

"No, questions about Klaus."

"Is Klaus worried about something we don't know about?" Lily furrowed her pretty brow.

Heinz shrugged. "Not that I know of."

She narrowed her eyes. "Then why? Surely, Klaus was more specific than that. After all, he was ordering Gutierrez to murder someone."

Heinz sighed. "We've been through this before, Lily. All Dodong knows is that Steiner was asking questions Klaus didn't like. Dodong respects Klaus for the balls he displayed when they had to sink the Filipino patrol boat. When Klaus said he wanted the German whacked, Dodong whacked him, no questions asked."

Lily frowned. She took a loud slurp of soup. "Well, the American Major Khartoum is asking questions, too, and we've left him alone. You said no need to worry." She paused, looking thoughtful. "I don't like this foolishness, not one bit." She sucked up a noodle with such ferocity that the end of the noodle whipped her on the lip on its way into her mouth. "Did Klaus ask Gutierrez to search Steiner's belongings?" She dabbed at her mouth with a napkin.

"No. Dodong started to anyway. You know Filipinos. But he was interrupted and had to leave by the fire escape."

Lily sucked up another noodle. As the noodle disappeared into her mouth like an eager eel, she said, "Now Klaus doesn't show for our monthly meeting. Why is that, do you suppose? He's always very punctual."

"I really don't know. I don't have any idea."

"I don't have to tell you this is not good. If Klaus is not telling us something we should know, we will have to find out. This could be dangerous."

"I'm sure Klaus is just spooked is all. I don't know what else to say."

Lily smacked her lips with satisfaction at the taste of a stuffed crab's claw. "It truly is best to have the two of you working together. Just one of you wouldn't do. This way, Klaus works the field where he is very, very good, and you keep an eye on the conservationists. You don't think Khartoum suspects you, do you? You're with CITES. You're his boss, for heaven's sake. He reports to you."

"If the thought hadn't occurred to him, he wouldn't be a professional, would he?"

Lily poured herself some more tea. "I think you should let him continue poking around. Eventually he'll get restless, and when he does, you can come up with something that will lead him elsewhere. It's all nonsense anyway, dispatching a solo investigator to Asia. A waste of money." She waited for Tepe to say something; when he did not, she said, "Good that Klaus opened a photo shop. He needed something to explain his tiger money. You should try some of that fish, darling. The yellow bean sauce is delicious."

Heinz tried a piece of the fish and ate it without joy.

Lily speared what appeared to be a black egg and laid it on her husband's plate.

Heinz leaned to examine the egg. "And this is?"

"A boiled egg that's been soaked in salty mud for a hundred days. They're delicious. Try one, I insist."

Heinz picked up the egg with his fingers and gave it a tentative bite.

"Did you call Klaus to remind him of our meeting tonight?"

Heinz, examining the egg, put it down. "I've tried calling him for two days now. All I get is his answering machine."

Lily thought about that. "Mmm. You have a key to his house don't you? If he still doesn't answer the phone in the morning, I think you should drive up there and take a look around. We can't overlook the possibility that he's holding something back on us. That could be dangerous."

Heinz nodded.

"We have to be careful," Lily said. She turned and shouted an instruction to Den Den who waited at a respectful distance. Then she turned to Tepe and said, "Incidentally, I've bought new freez-

ers for our hoard of tiger bones. We've got one of those machines
that sucks the air out of a plastic bag so the bones will keep almost
indefinitely. How many years do you think it will take you?"

Heinz hesitated. "To put the tigers under?"

"In Siberia, yes. How long?"

Heinz licked his lips. "The officials in Vladivostok and
Khabarovsk say they've got two or three hundred left, something
like that. Maybe as many as four hundred."

"But the truth is they don't know for sure. Isn't that right?"

Heinz blinked. "No, they don't. But if Borolev is able to deliver a hundred-fifty or two hundred cats in one year, that truly
ought to go a long way toward sending them under for good."

"Do you think he'll be able to do that?"

"Borolev's a professional poacher."

"Ah, good. When the population thins out and the hunting becomes more difficult, Klaus can show him a few tricks he might
not have thought of. Isn't that what you said? You said Klaus
knows the tiger country there almost as well as Borolev."

"Klaus knows how to kill tigers."

"Didn't you say he really likes it?"

Heinz nodded.

"And Borolev wants the money."

"Borolev lusts for the money." Heinz compressed his lips.

"Well, good. This way it's clean for him. Working for us, he
can go for broke in one year and work the market for all it's worth.
If he can kill a couple of hundred cats in a year and get out clean,
he's got it made." Lily slurped another noodle and smiled. "He can
then buy himself a legitimate business and settle down as a rich
man. For him, it's less risky than remaining a poacher over the long
haul. Smart thinking on his part."

Heinz gazed out over the water toward Olango Island with a
faraway look in his eyes.

Den Den arrived with a cold bottle of liebfraumilch and two
wine glasses. She poured a half glass each for Lily and Tepe, then
quietly disappeared.

Lily said, "If people want bones from the Siberian tiger after
they're officially extinct, they'll come to us and pay our price. To

get rich is now officially glorious in China. What will all those new millionaires in South China do to show off their money, after their new Mercedes-Benz and beach villas and the rest of it? If they want a bowl of tiger penis soup from the extinct Siberian tiger, they'll have to pay far more than triple or even quadruple the current price."

Heinz looked forlorn.

"Oh, come on now, darling. Look at it this way, the value of your collection will increase in direct proportion to the decrease in the tiger population. You'll be able to move your stuff to Berlin, if you want, and charge admission. Homage to the great cat of Siberia that is no more. Think of it."

Heinz cleared his throat.

"If Klaus doesn't have some flaw we don't know about. Some secret that he's holding back. That worries me, it really does."

Mildly, Heinz said, "I don't imagine Klaus has any kind of deep, dark secret."

"It's the unexpected that's the most dangerous. If he'd only told us why."

Heinz said, "I have no idea what Klaus's problem might be."

"When CITES hired Major Khartoum, you asked to receive copies of his reports in case there was anything you could do that might be of help. Isn't that right? You know the details of Khartoum's conversations with the Russians and the people in Hong Kong and Vijay Sangrit in Bombay."

Heinz stared at his food.

"Then don't look so glum, darling. Getting depressed is not the answer. Cheer up. Enjoy. The legend of Faust is German, is it not, part of your cultural heritage? I bet you learned it as a schoolboy."

"*Ja, ja,* I know the story."

"Faust sold his soul to the devil for power and knowledge, something like that. Isn't that how it goes?"

"That's it," Heinz said.

"Then you should look at your situation that way. You live the good life—name the comfort and it's delivered. You have the money to buy whatever you want for your tiger collection. You have a beautiful wife. I let you have fun with the little Filipinas whenever you want. Young, lithe little beauties. Isn't that a situation men dream of? Meanwhile, you have the respect and admiration of conservationists around the world. You travel whenever and wherever you want, and you're wined and dined. They all think you're fighting the good fight on behalf of the endangered tiger. When the Siberian tiger goes under, maybe they'll listen to you and actually do something to save the Bengal tiger. You'll be a hero. Perhaps you can even write a book telling how you did it. Really, darling, sometimes you amaze me. What more could you possibly ask for?"

Heinz said nothing.

Lily smiled. "But, just like Faust, there is no backing out. You know that perfectly well, darling. It was made clear from the beginning. You were allowed to choose of your own free will, knowing the consequences in advance, and you chose. You're a big boy. A deal is a deal. We're holding up our end of the bargain, and we expect you to do the same. If you try to back out now, the Nine Dragons will pursue you to the ends of the earth and make you pay in ways you never thought imaginable. There is absolutely no escaping them. None. After they get through with you, mere death will be a blessed relief. Don't become obsessed over what might have been, darling. Enjoy what you have!"

Heinz Tepe's idea of digging a moat to preserve his view of the ocean was perfectly wonderful as far as James Burlane was concerned. The lack of obstruction meant Burlane could hide out in the brush between the house and the beach and use a parabolic microphone to record conversation on the patio.

Burlane, listening through earphones, adjusted the tape recorder that was hooked up to the parabolic. He wanted to make sure the conversation between Heinz Tepe and Lilly Tepe would play loud and clear. The Klaus they were talking about had to be Klaus Neumann.

Burlane didn't know who the Nine Dragons were, but he had a good idea. He'd have Ara Schott run the name by his sources in Interpol.

Tepe's CITES committee had hired him to run down the people who were buying poached tigers, and he'd done just that. But he had to have more than a tape recording to nail the Tepes and their friend Klaus. He'd have to break into the Chua food products warehouse on Mactan and take some pictures and steal a little evidence.

31

██████ The idea that it was possible for a solo hound to follow a spooked rabbit in a car without the rabbit getting wise was impossible movie foolishness. It was a difficult enough assignment with professionals in several vehicles switching places to give the rabbit a new look in his rearview mirror, but in heavy traffic even that was a chore. In the movie *Chinatown,* Jack Nicholson had smashed the taillight of Faye Dunaway's car so he could follow her in the snarl of L.A. traffic. But the best bet, in this age of sophisticated electronic spook and police gadgetry, was to put a tailing device on the rabbit's vehicle and follow the beeps.

James Burlane did not want to risk attempting to penetrate the security of Heinz Tepe's Mactan Island compound to put a tailer in place, but, judging from the conversation between Tepe and his wife the previous night, he didn't think the CITES tiger man was yet spooked; more old-fashioned methods would yet suffice.

The Philippines did not have a mass transit system in the western sense; it relied instead on jeepneys, a labor-intensive solution to moving bodies. The colorful vehicles ordinarily carried from sixteen to twenty-two passengers. Traffic was so bad in Manila there was seldom opportunity to get out of low gear; while not so bad in Cebu City and neighboring Mandaue City and Mactan Island, the impossible glut of vehicles was enough to make a westerner grind his teeth. During rush hour, Filipinos, as in the old circus routine of seeing how many clowns could fit in a Volkswagen bug, were unceremoniously squished into the jeepneys until they could hardly breathe, with hardy travelers clinging to the back. The drivers inched their vehicles forward, bumper to bumper, and as there were no rules to control exhaust or emission, veteran commuters often held handkerchiefs to their face in a losing effort to filter the noxious diesel fumes that covered the streets in a smelly pall.

The sheer number of vehicles in the streets was compounded by a cultural disdain for rules in general and traffic rules in particular. The rule of thumb was that a larger vehicle had the right-of-way over smaller vehicles, and all vehicles had the right-of-way over pedestrians. Burlane had observed drivers accelerate for the apparent sport of scattering pedestrians so presumptuous as to cross the street.

The result of this anarchy was that if a rabbit made it through a light and the hound didn't, the rabbit was lost forever. Burlane knew his chances of actually following Tepe anywhere depended on the time of day and luck.

At eight o'clock the next morning—allowing Tepe to have breakfast before checking out the house of the man named Klaus, presumably Klaus Neumann—Burlane parked his rented Toyota just off the road to Tambuli Beach Resort, which also served as the entrance and exit to the Tepe compound. From there, he was able to see both the main gate to Tepe's house and the road leading from Tepe's house to the Tambuli Beach Road.

An hour and a half later the gate opened and a Mitsubishi Pajero emerged. A Mitsubishi Pajero was the general vehicle of choice among Filipinos of means, although Burlane knew that sugar planters on the island of Negros felt they would embarrass themselves by driving anything other than a Toyota Land Cruiser.

Burlane kept an eye on the Pajero, and as it passed on its way west, toward the Cebu side of Mactan Island, he saw that it was driven by the doomed, tormented Heinz Tepe. Lily, the beautiful Lucifer, was not with him.

Burlane gave Tepe a reasonable distance and started following in his Toyota. Burlane had lucked out; between nine-thirty and ten traffic was as good as it was going to get. Ever so slowly the morning, noontime, and afternoon traffic gluts were getting larger and larger, until there would inevitably come the day when Cebu City would be like Manila or Bangkok, an unrelieved day-long snarl of vehicles.

He followed Tepe through Lapu-Lapu City, then across the bridge to Mandaue City, then right toward the mountains in the center of the island, then south past the Montebello Hotel toward Cebu City. High on his right sat the five-star Plaza Hotel, an overpriced, sterile phallus of a building standing high above Mandaue City and Cebu City, catering to Japanese tourists who wanted to travel without leaving Japan.

Burlane followed his rabbit around the provincial capital, then west past the district called Guadalupe, then higher and higher into the posh residential area above the city that was known as Beverly Hills. He was forced to run several red lights to keep up with the Pajero, but this was the Philippines; what were red lights for, if not to be ignored?

He followed Tepe up winding streets past cul-de-sacs with ranch-style homes and well-tended lawns that might have graced a middle-class suburb of an American city. Finally, Tepe parked his Pajero in front of a handsome house; Burlane still well behind him, and confident that he was still covert, parked his Toyota and watched Tepe dig out of his personal set of keys the key to Klaus's house.

When Tepe went inside, Burlane got out, hustled up the street, put an electronic tailer under his fender, and retreated back to his car. Ten minutes later, Tepe emerged and drove off. Burlane waited another five minutes and went to the house. There he picked the lock to the front door.

The inside of the house, just like the exterior, might have been a middle-class American home. It was air-conditioned and carpeted, and everything from the television set in the living room to the kitchen appliances was brand-name and high-tech.

But Burlane was most interested in what he found in the master bedroom—a handsomely framed and mounted circus poster. This was the same 12 June 1957 poster of Captain Prince–Cox's International Circus that he had first seen in Heinz Tepe's collection, and which he had lifted from the murdered Fritz Steiner's room in the McSherry Pension.

This one, like Tepe's, was also autographed, but a very much more personal autograph. It read:

To my son Klaus with much affection,
Lothar the Magnificent

So this was the man who bought the tiger bones! Heinz Tepe kept a watch on the sorehead conservationists. His wife stored the bones at her food warehouse on Mactan Island, and sold them to the Chinese manufacturers of traditional medicines. Such a wonderful setup.

Burlane decided he would give Tepe a bogus report to retain his confidence while he went about collecting further evidence.

He searched the house. Neumann was apparently a photography enthusiast, because he had several top-of-the-line cameras plus reflecting panels of the kind professionals used for portrait photography. But, curiously, Burlane could find no photographs.

In the bedroom there were metal screw holes in the ceiling and on the wall and floor, which puzzled Burlane. He decided they must be used to mount more photography gear.

Burlane, wondering about the lack of photographs, put voice-activated bugging devices in Neumann's bedroom and living room and in his telephones. These microphones contained diminutive transmitters—among the best available from Ara Schott's friends in the Company—that could easily beam Neumann's telephone conversations to a tape recorder in Burlane's rented house in Banilad. Unless Neumann had access to a professional with the gear to properly sweep his house, the listening devices would go undetected.

When Herr Doktor Heinz Tepe and the committee of conservationists had hired Burlane, they'd told him they didn't want a report that ended with a resounding maybe or might be or could be. They were willing to pay top dollar for solid, documented evidence that would legally nail the villains who were buying tiger bones and would draw proper public attention to the awful business.

James Burlane regarded himself as nothing if not a conscientious employee. As a young man, Burlane's daddy had been a moonshiner who used a thumping keg to remove the foul-tasting feusel from his rye whiskey, never mind that the racket it made could be heard for a half mile. He didn't want to have the reputation of peddling second-rate whiskey.

He told young Jimmy he should always do his damnedest to do the best work possible and always give a full day's effort for a full day's pay; the adult Burlane—who had Mixed Enterprises' reputation to protect—was determined to do just that.

When he'd returned to his rented house from recording the conversation between Lily and Heinz Tepe, he'd phoned Ara Schott, asking him to check with Interpol to see what the Nine Dragons was all about. By now Schott would have had a chance to make the necessary inquiries. Perhaps when Burlane got back, Schott would have had a chance to fax a reply.

32

James Burlane poured himself a hit of Tanduay rum and added a squeeze of *kalamansi* juice. His mind was on tigers and the familiar human standbys—deception and greed—and the master Sir James George Frazer, whose classic twelve-volume work on magic and religion, *The Golden Bough,* did for civilization what Sigmund Freud did for the individual imagination.

In hiring a professional to hunt down the buyers of poached tigers, Burlane felt his employers were revealing the human yearning—recorded in stories and myths through the millennia—for a hero, a mortal god who would do battle with the scumbag tiger poachers and prevail. Here, in this please-please-let-it-be-so fantasy land, the confrontations were uncomplicated struggles between good and evil, and the solutions were inevitably physical. Such was the attraction of heroes from Conan the Barbarian to John Wayne and the improbable movie triumphs of Sylvester Stallone, Chuck Norris, Charles Bronson, and Clint Eastwood. Save us, save us, was the unspoken cry! We're tired of high-minded speeches. Give us action! Do something!

And so, from the Duke to Clint, the heroes, standing tall above greed and lust and cowardice, did just that. The mortal gods delivered. In the old Westerns, the screenwriters even went so far as to provide white and black hats so there would be no confusion as to who was good and who was bad.

Burlane himself preferred the triumphs of a Sherlock Holmes, Miss Marple, or Perry Mason, who relied on logic to unravel vexing puzzles. But in the case of tiger poaching, he felt the last word—and the solution, if there was one—was to be found in the studies of a series of intellectuals running from Frazer through Karl Jung and Joseph Campbell.

After following Heinz to Beverly Hills, he set about to find some Frazer—perhaps a modern, condensed edition existed. He tried the National Bookstore on Mango Avenue, but the books there ran to best-sellers and whatever was new and fashionable. He found nothing in the bookstores by the University of San Carlos, but struck pay dirt in a bookstore just off Colon Street in downtown Cebu City, where a hodgepodge of books with yellowing pages lay stacked in unsorted heaps around the walls. Here he found Theodor H. Gaster's 1959 abridgment of Frazer's masterpiece, called *The New Golden Bough.*

This volume contained Frazer's observations on sympathetic magic and homeopathy, which Burlane thought likely went to the heart of tiger poaching. Burlane was glad it was not a new book because he considered Gaster a disgrace, together with the publishers, and did not want to support such enterprises. Gaster had seen fit—well after the book was in the public domain and therefore out of Frazer's heirs' control—to cut the master's lengthy, penetrating discussion of the genealogical relation between magic and religion. If Frazer was off the mark, Burlane felt, he was still entitled to his opinion. To edit the book so as not to offend Christians and yet leave Frazer's name on the cover was shameless publishing. Did Gaster not trust the readers to make up their own minds? Or were Frazer's conclusions too close to truths Gaster refused to acknowledge? If that were the case, why didn't Gaster write his own books and let others edit Frazer?

The honorable and open-minded scholar Joseph Campbell, noting the vast variety of religious and magical beliefs since the dawn of man, had, at the end of his popular television series, simply urged his viewers to "follow the bliss" whether it was a belief in science, magic, or religion. He did not prescribe the nature of the bliss. He let his viewers decide for themselves.

After studying thousands of myths in archaic societies around the world, Frazer had concluded there were two kinds of magic.

The first, homeopathic magic, was based on the idea that like produces like, that is, effect resembles cause. The second, contagious magic, assumed that once things have been in contact, they continue to act on each other forever. The Chinese belief in the medicinal properties of tiger bones was an example of homeopathic magic.

Frazer cited numerous examples of homeopathic magic. For example, the ancient Greeks believed if a person eats an eagle's gall, he will gain an eagle's eyesight; if a gray-haired Greek eats a raven, his hair will turn black. Native Americans on Vancouver Island spread the ashes of wasps on their faces to make themselves behave like wasps in battle. The same Native Americans believed that if a woman eats a wasp's nest, she will multiply like an insect. The East African Wajaggas believed if they tied the wing bone of a vulture around their leg they could run all day without tiring—just as vultures can stay aloft for hours with ease. The Cholones of Eastern Peru protected themselves against the bite of a poisonous serpent by carrying the tooth of a poisonous snake. Cannibals of New Guinea believed a warrior could gain courage by eating the heart of a slain enemy. And so on. Examples of homeopathic magic would take up a thick volume by themselves.

After reading Frazer's analysis of homeopathic magic, Burlane opened his copy of TRAFFIC Network's *Prescription for Extinction,* leafing through the statistics on the traditional medicines and the prices for animal parts other than the tiger's. There were twenty-two patented medicines that used antelope parts, including the straightforward *A Good Remedy for Colds,* manufactured by the dependable Tianjin Drug Manufactory, *Dendrobium Moniliforme Night Sight Pills,* manufactured by the same company, *Pills of Calculus Bovis for Lowering Blood Pressure,* and the wonderful *Margarite Acne Pills,* a product of Foshan Pharmaceutical Company in Guangdong.

The Chinese so believed in products made from bears, especially the gall bladder, that they had killed off most of their own, and were importing gall bladders from the black bear in the United States and Canada. TRAFFIC Network counted nineteen patented traditional medicines, including laryngitis pills, ear drop oil, and cold medicines—all made from bear's gall bladders. So prized were these parts that the Wuhan Factory in Hong Kong was willing to pay ten thousand U.S. dollars a kilogram for them. Other parts of the bear were held to be useful for treating acne and hemorrhoids. It was beyond Burlane how they figured this all out, but he was aware that cause and effect were irrelevant; logic was not involved. Faith was necessary. Belief.

Eight out of the ten products made from the poor leopard also contained musk deer, tiger, or ginseng—all Chinese standbys for a limp cock. The *Hindu Magic Pills,* made by the Wah Yan Hong Chemical Factory in Hong Kong, were no doubt marketed for the same purpose. The tenth medicine, *Bolus for Easing Tendons and Collaterals,* was made by the Chen Li Qi Pharmaceutical Factory in Guangzhou.

The musk deer—actually four species of deer ranging from Siberia to the Himalayas—was the source of seventy patented medicines. Here the major ingredient listed on the labels was either musk or musk gland. This wonderful musk had many homeopathic properties. The Chinese held it to be useful for arteries, hemorrhoids, rheumatism, laryngitis, and phlegm. Mixed with tiger bones, it was thought useful for the affliction of limp dick. The price for musk ran to a whopping eighty-four thousand U.S. dollars a kilogram, offered by TCM of Hong Kong. The medicine containing musk that Burlane liked best was the *Ta Huo Lo Tan Chinese Old Man Tea,* made by the Tientsin Herb Tea Manufactory.

The pangolin, also known as the scaly anteater, a heavily armored, toothless mammal of Asia and Africa—whose defense was to roll itself into a ball—was highly prized as a source of traditional Chinese medicine. The scales were held to be an antidote to poisoning, although *Prescription for Extinction* gave no prices per kilo.

Thirty-two patented medicines included the horn of the rhinoceros as an ingredient. Here again, Burlane found problems with acne, arteries, tendons, and laryngitis. As Andrei Bure had pointed out in Vladivostok, the demand for rhino horn had nearly driven the African black rhino to extinction.

Burlane felt sympathetic to the plight of fur seals, whose penises were coveted by the Chinese, although he found it difficult to get excited over the pressure put on plants ranging from wild ginseng to magnolia. Also, as was pointed out by forensics examinations, many of the medicines listing exotic animal parts contained no such thing; they were bogus.

The scamming by the manufacturers of traditional medicines wasn't surprising to Burlane, who was forever amazed at the simple-minded North Americans and Europeans—drooling over the cheap Asian labor to make toys or Christmas decorations—who were skinned out of fortunes because they were so stupidly trusting.

No amount of high-kicking kung fu artistry or blazing assault rifles could defeat the deadly march of traditional Chinese medicine. The Chinese did not have a system of research laboratories as in North America and Europe, where research scientists laboriously traced the effects of various drugs on the human body. They had instead traditional medicine based on thousands of years of ingesting various natural ingredients. Some of these medicines, including the famous ginseng, did indeed work. But most were the useless result of human faith in homeopathic magic.

From a western point of view, the belief in homeopathic magic was rank stupidity—totally without rational foundation—but Asians believed in it nevertheless. Their belief required a leap of faith, the same, as Frazer had coolly pointed out—to Theodor Gaster's annoyance, poor baby—as religious beliefs.

The only way to save the tiger from extinction, Burlane knew, was the politically unacceptable tactic of public ridicule coupled with trade sanctions. But for westerners to ridicule Chinese traditional medicine was unfashionably ethnocentric and impolite; trade sanctions were fine in the case of tiny Taiwan, but impossible to apply when western businessmen were lusting over the vast market of Chinese consumers. If President Bill Clinton had to back down from his demand for human rights in China, what chance did anybody have in demanding an end to tiger poaching?

To put it another way: if Gaster saw fit to protect his readers from the uncomfortable similarities between magic and religion, what chance was there that logic would prevail?

Burlane thought the conservationists, many of them caught in the grip of multiculturalism in the United States, lacked the heart and resolve necessary for a dramatic confrontation with the Asian belief in traditional medicine. Piety and self-righteousness were their strong suits, not courage.

Burlane could bust Heinz Tepe and Klaus Neumann, but—with such crazy prices being offered for gall bladders and penises—another organization would certainly appear to supply the manufacturers of traditional medicines. Where there was money, there was the will: where there was the will, a way would be found.

And the poaching would continue. The tiger bones, rhino horns, deer musk glands, seal penises, bear gall bladders, and the rest would be delivered, and the populations of tigers and rhinos and other endangered species would slowly diminish until they were gone. The tiger would disappear from Siberia, even without help from Heinz Tepe and Klaus Neumann, then from Sumatra and the Indochinese and Malay Peninsulas, then from the Indian subcontinent.

The twenty-first century was coming up. Sometime in the twenty-first century, the tiger would be no more.

In exhorting his viewers to follow the bliss, Joseph Campbell was certainly not thinking of the consequences of homeopathic magic—he was far too civilized to support the elimination of endangered species. Where was the bliss if the tiger was gone?

Burlane squeegeed the sweat from his forehead with the back of his hand. He poured himself another hit of Tanduay, squeezed some kalamansi into it, and sat in a gloom, staring into the humid night.

33

James Burlane, his mind on a mango shake spiked with Tanduay rum, was pawing through a bag of mangoes looking for the ripest ones when the knocking came. He opened the door and found himself face-to-face with one of the Germans he had met in the Missouri Bar. It was the genial Hermann Iversen, a fan of Bayern Munich.

Only now, Iversen, looking decidedly ungenial, was pointing an automatic pistol at him.

"Aw shit!" Burlane was annoyed at himself for having his mind on mangoes and not being more careful.

Iversen smiled. "Okay, my American friend. I would like to know just who in the hell you are. You want to tell me, please?"

Burlane, eyeing the pistol, said, "My name is Major M. Sidarius Khartoum, same as it was when we talked in the Missouri. My friends call me Sid, just like I said."

"Such crap."

"Oh, come on. Be honest, now. Fair is fair. I just bet you're not Hermann Iversen, wholesale liquor dealer either. A guy who holds up wholesale liquor dealers, maybe."

"I'm the one with the pistol, Major Khartoum, or whatever your name is."

"Are you a tiger poacher?" Burlane asked mildly.

Iversen looked disgusted. "I'm a German police officer."

"Oh, sure you are," Burlane said. "Tanking up on San Miguel in expat bars in the Philippines."

"Put the mangoes down please. Hands on top of your head."

Burlane put the mangoes down, saying, "The mangoes here are sensational. They're good dried, too, but they're better when they're fresh. Have you seen the dried ones in the market?"

"If you move your hands, I shoot." Iversen held out his box-tops for Burlane to read.

"Could you hold them a little farther back, please? I need my bifocals to read."

Iversen, with a half-smile, held his badge farther back.

Burlane, momentarily squinting, looked relieved. "Munich. Herr Oktoberfest."

Iversen stepped farther back again, looking puzzled.

"That was a joke, Herr Iversen. Reggie Jackson was a baseball player who came on strong in the World Series, hence he was called Mr. October. He once hit three home runs in one game in the World Series. Hit 'em on the first pitch. Was that ever something! There was this moron named Steinbrenner, the Yankees' owner, who had been giving the Reg a ration of the worst, and Reggie showed him a thing or two. Boy, oh boy, did he ever!"

"And you are, besides a bogus overseas buyer?"

Burlane shrugged. "I've got some identification, too, if you're interested."

"What kind of identification?"

"A card with a telephone number on it," Burlane said.

Iversen said, "Okay, let's see your card. Keep both hands visible at all time. Any quick or unexpected moves and I will pull the trigger."

Slowly, Burlane retrieved his Mixed Enterprises card and gave it to Iversen.

Iversen, pocketing the card without reading it, gave Burlane a pair of handcuffs. "One end around your right wrist and the other around the doorknob, please." He stepped back, waiting for Burlane to comply. When Burlane had handcuffed himself to the door, Iversen fished out the card and read it. "What is this?"

"It's a business card, as you can see."

"Mixed Enterprises?"

"I do mixed work." Burlane smiled. "If you call that number, you'll reach a gentleman in Montgomery County, Maryland. He will confirm the fact that I'm currently working for a consortium of conservation groups. They want me to bust an organization that is poaching tigers and smuggling their bones in the name of homeopathic medicine."

"Tiger poachers?"

"The population of tigers is plunging, and my clients don't like it one damn bit. They're furious, in fact. Or say they are."

Iversen studied the card. "Precisely who is your client, Major Khartoum?"

"The Convention on International Trade in Endangered Species, in Geneva."

Iversen looked impressed. "Now then, are you or are you not the guy who put the Captain Prince–Cox's circus poster on the wall of the Missouri Bar? The girls behind the bar said you were."

Burlane said, "Yes, I am. A good-looking poster it is, too, don't you think? Lothar the Magnificent. A tiger jumping through a hoop. I bet the tiger thought that was just peachy, having the magnificent Lothar pop a whip over his head."

"You want to tell me how you came by that poster?"

"A certain Herr Steiner was in the Missouri bar, looking for a man named Klaus Neumann, who used to transport big cats to zoos. Somebody murdered Steiner in his room in the McSherry Pension on Palaez Street. It's been in all the newspapers. But I bet you know all about him, don't you?"

Iversen said, "Herr Steiner was a securities dealer from Berlin who collected circus posters." Iversen cocked his head, watching Burlane. "Did you murder Herr Steiner, Major Khartoum?"

Burlane grinned crookedly. "For a fucking circus poster?" Had Iversen really asked such a question? "Give me a break. The tiger trainer on the poster is named Lothar Neumann. Klaus Neumann is related to Lothar the Magnificent, I bet. Has to be. Are you after Klaus Neumann, too?"

Iversen said, "You're the one who's handcuffed to a door, not me."

"Mmm. So I am," Burlane said.

"Tell me exactly how you came by the poster."

"I went to Steiner's pension to talk to him about tigers. The girl at the desk was reading a magazine. Without looking up, she said a Filipino had just gone up to see him. I went upstairs and knocked on his door. I could hear a television set playing inside. Suddenly the television set boomed and I heard a shot inside. I knocked again, but there was no answer. After a little wait, I picked the lock, and went inside where I found Steiner dead. I'm a freelance, not a regular cop like you, so I can bend the rules."

"And do."

Burlane cleared his throat. "On occasion, my methods are as mixed as the jobs I undertake, I'll admit that."

"I bet," Iversen said.

"I pawed through Steiner's stuff and found a magazine with circus posters in it, and the Captain Prince–Cox's poster rolled up in a cardboard tube. Lothar trained tigers. Steiner said Klaus Neumann captured them for zoos. I wondered if Neumann might not be the prick I'm looking for."

"Which is why you put the poster on the wall of the Missouri."

"Correct. I put it there as bait. A form of tiger blind."

"Since nobody saw you go in, you took a back door out."

"I left by the fire escape. Probably the same as the man who had killed Steiner."

"And who is, as you so elegantly put it, the 'prick' you're looking for?"

"I'm convinced that he's European or North American, very likely a German, if a captured Russian poacher is to be believed. I suspect he's employed by the smugglers to deal directly with tiger poachers all over Asia. I know he's a raging bastard who knows his tigers, and I want to put his ass out of business. I have to consider Klaus Neumann a suspect. Wouldn't you?"

Iversen, glancing at the card, said, "May I use your phone to call this number?"

Burlane smiled. "Hey, like you say, I'm the guy handcuffed to the door. You can do anything you want. Be my guest, by all means. I assure you, my partner will be pleased to help you any way he can."

Iversen looked at the card again. "And your partner's name is?"

"Ara Schott. He speaks fluent German, by the way, so you can jabber with him in your language if you want."

"He speaks German?"

"He's from a German-American family. The members of his family all learned to speak German as a matter of ethnic pride, although they might not have all the idioms down pat. If you prefer to call the German Embassy in Washington, tell them they should call the Company. Somebody there will confirm the bona fides of my partner and myself."

"The Company?"

"That would be the dreaded Central Intelligence Agency, Herr Iversen."

Iversen blinked. "The CIA?"

Burlane looked disapproving. "It's considered amateurish if not outright boorish to refer directly to the organization as I just did, or even use the initials, Herr Iversen. One never refers directly to the you-know-what. Never." He grinned, looking sheepish. "But when you find yourself handcuffed to the door you stretch the rules."

"You work for them?"

"Worked for them. Past tense. They sacked me some years ago. Do please phone Ara, Herr Iversen. If your talking to him will mean unfastening me from this door and put an end to your waving that thing in my face, I don't mind springing for the tab. No problem."

"You'll just charge it to your clients as expenses."

"That's right," Burlane said cheerfully.

As Hermann Iversen dialed for a long-distance operator, Burlane said, "I showed you mine. You want to show me yours?"

Iversen looked puzzled.

Burlane said, "I told you I'm after tiger poachers. You want to tell me what you're doing here? This is a trifle bit off your turf, you have to admit. Bavaria is somewhere thataway." Burlane motioned with his head.

Iversen frowned. "In due time, Major Khartoum. Please be patient. Operator? I'd like to make a long-distance call to the United States please."

Burlane said, "Once you unfasten me from this door, I can start peeling mangoes. I'll can make us some mango shakes. I'll spike 'em with Tanduay rum. They're delicious. Also I've got some *tanguigi* here, a delicious fish, and some shallots, fresh ginger, and sweet little pea pods. With those ingredients and some corn oil, couple of teaspoons of cornstarch, an egg, a few tablespoons of soy sauce and oyster sauce, a couple of hits of Chinese rice wine, and a smidgen of sugar and salt, I propose to make you the most mouthwatering fish you've ever eaten. They don't call me Wokman for nothing."

34

■■■■James Burlane began throwing chunks of ripe mango into his blender. "I had these shakes when I was through here on a job a couple of years ago. This time I bought a blender straightaway. I'll list it on my expense account under 'moral maintenance.' " Burlane gave the chunks a good hit of cold, bottled water from his refrigerator and punched the button.

Hermann Iversen said, "This is one place where bottled water is mandatory."

"You think this water is safe because I poured it out of a bottle with a fancy label on it?" Burlane looked amused. "Herr Iversen, you have a lot to learn about the Philippines. I'm just too lazy to go through the hassle of boiling water for five minutes. If I were a religious person, I'd pray to the cholera gods to leave me alone. For all we know, this is recycled carabao piss."

Iversen looked chagrined. "What a place."

"It's an adventure, that's a fact."

Watching the buzzing blender, Iversen said, "I liked your Herr Ara Schott. He seemed like an honest, straightforward man."

"He is. Ara has always been bookish. In recent years, he's become a computer nerd. He used to be director of counterintelligence at the Company, but he quit shortly after I was sacked, and we threw in together. We have different but complementary natures." Burlane turned off the blender and gave the mixture a solid hit of Tanduay rum. "The label said this is supposed to be five years old. Five minutes is more like it."

"I assume Major Khartoum is not your real name."

Burlane smiled. "It's a nom de guerre, correct. I felt I needed a new identity when Ara and I established Mixed Enterprises. My real name was . . . well, used, shall we say. So I made up a new one." He poured them each a white plastic glass of mango shake. The glasses had SELECTA written on the side. "These are ice cream containers, actually. The Filipinos can't afford to waste anything. The shakes wouldn't taste any better if I served them in crystal, would they?"

"They're delicious."

"Also you can drop a Selecta glass and it won't break. A lot of Filipino ice cream is made from carabao milk, which I think gives it a certain class. The Tanduay label says the rum is eighty proof, but that's horsepucky. The first thing I do is get the rice going. You watch, two knuckles of water to one knuckle of rice, that's how the Filipinos do it. They don't have *pesos* to waste on measuring cups." He rinsed the rice, measured the water, and got the rice cooking. "And you're here on what kind of business, Herr Iversen?"

"A serial killer they've been calling Tigerman. He killed a dancer here in Cebu a couple of weeks ago."

"I've seen the stories, yes."

"The German girl he killed was the niece of my good friend and police superior, Karl Bauer."

"And Bauer detailed you to run the killer down."

"That's right. Have you ever heard of a German firm named Kruger's International?"

Burlane shook his head.

"Kruger's trains lions and tigers for circuses and the movies and takes care of them in the winter. I didn't think of Kruger's until I was in Siberia, where the killer painted a girl like a white tiger."

Burlane, thinking about the head of a white tiger mounted on the wall of Heinz Tepe's collection of tigerana, set about cutting the fish into chunks about an inch long and an inch-and-a-half wide, which he threw into a plastic bowl. Iversen was obviously a first-rate cop, and Burlane liked him; he wanted to hear his story. Neumann wasn't going anywhere. What was the hurry?

R isa Sanchez's captor had rolled up the Oriental carpet that had covered the hardwood floor of his bedroom. Under the carpet there was a trapdoor over a large recess. From it he had removed the ankle and wrist restraints.

On the wall to one side of her was a handsomely framed circus poster covered with glass. Risa, wondering how long she would be required to hang by her arms, saw that the poster featured a tiger trainer, a large, blond man snapping a whip over tigers.

Directly in front of her there was a large mirror that went from floor to ceiling. In this mirror, she saw herself stretched tight, hanging by her wrists, her ankles anchored to the floor.

W hen Burlane was finished cutting the fish into chunks, he quickly peeled a thumb-size piece of ginger and chopped it finely. Then he retrieved a garlic press from a kitchen drawer and squeezed the juice from the ginger onto the fish. "I do too much rather than too little ginger because I love it. You'll just have to go with the flow."

"I like ginger," Iversen said, watching Burlane separate an egg and begin beating the white with a fork. "I went to Kruger's. They couldn't help me, but suggested I talk to the former owner of a defunct Munich firm that used to provide animals to zoos. There's where I struck pay dirt."

"All right!" Burlane dumped the egg white onto the fish and added a healthy slug of amber-colored fluid from a bottle. "This is Shaohsing wine, made from rice. Tastes like sherry." He gave the fish chunks a strong pinch of salt, a goodly pinch of sugar, a teaspoon of cornstarch, and stirred everything with a spoon. "There's the marinade. See how easy." He poured them each a new mango shake, and gave the shakes a generous hit of Tanduay.

Watching all this with interest, Iversen said, "Klaus Neumann used to work for this outfit. I learned that his father, Lothar, was a tiger master for a circus when a tiger ripped his throat open in a performance in Hamburg in 1957."

"Hence the significance of Steiner's poster. This is a wonderful way to cook fish, by the way. Elegant and delicious. Do you cook?"

Iversen shook his head no.

"You should pay attention so you can tell your wife how it's done, although fish is probably pretty expensive in Bavaria."

Klaus Neumann, gesturing to the circus poster on the wall, said, "You like it."

"Oh, yes," Risa said. " 'Lothar the Magnificent.' Who is that?" Her mouth was dry. She'd never been so frightened in her life.

"A famous tiger trainer," Neumann said.

"Is he still alive?"

"No, no, no. He was killed in 1957."

"Oh, I'm sorry," Risa said, hoping that if she were reasonable and interested in Neumann's obsession, he might release her from her bonds. "I like tigers," she said. "They had tigers in the Royal London Circus when it came through town last year."

Iversen, taking a sip of his Tanduay-spiked mango shake, said, "Lothar got his start at Kruger's International, which provided tigers to Captain Prince–Cox's International Circus. Kruger's also gave young Klaus a job when he finished school, but he moved quickly to Hesse's, and became their chief big cat man worldwide."

"A tiger lover," Burlane said.

"Or hater. It's hard to tell. The man at Hesse's mentioned that someone from Berlin was through looking for Klaus. This man was mentioned by a neighbor in Munich where Klaus grew up— the neighbor ran a local meat market just down the street. It turned out that Lothar Neumann's widow Bette had died recently and Klaus, her only offspring, had returned to tend to the small estate he had inherited. You want to guess when that was?"

"When Klaus returned to Munich?"

"Right."

"I'll just bet you a case of German beer that Klaus Neumann was in Munich the night Erika Bauer was killed."

Iversen said, "You'd win your bet. But Klaus didn't go to his mother's funeral. He just took care of the business and quietly vanished."

In a separate cup, Burlane mixed a half teaspoon of cornstarch, three tablespoons of water, a two-tablespoon dollop of oyster sauce, and a smaller hit of Kikkoman soy sauce. "This is the sauce I'll need later. By the way, the cheapie Filipino soy sauce you see on the shelves here is not the real stuff. It's a by-product of the production of monosodium glutamate, a four-day process compared to the several years it takes to properly ferment soy beans for the real stuff." He put a small pot of water on a burner and turned up the heat.

Neumann said, "It was a tiger that killed Lothar the Magnificent. He was my father."

"Your father?"

"He was the greatest tiger trainer who ever lived. There's no arguing that. It happened in Hamburg."

"I'm sorry," Risa said.

Neumann looked surprised. "Why should you be sorry? You didn't know him."

Risa bit her lip, but said nothing.

Klaus Neumann removed the poster of his father from the wall.

From the hidden recess under the floor, he retrieved six enlarged photographs of young women painted like tigers. Except for one tiger-girl, a dark-skinned Indian girl, the girls were stretched from ceiling to floor, as Risa was now. Their taut, slender bodies glistened under the light.

Burlane peeled another chunk of ginger and quickly cut it into a half dozen thin slices. When the water was boiling, he dumped in the pea pods. Watching the water, he said, "Why didn't Neumann go to his mother's funeral?" When the water returned to a boil, he drained the pea pods, and began peeling two huge cloves of garlic.

"The man at the meat market said Bette Neumann had been having an affair when Lothar was killed—everybody in the neighborhood knew it—and Klaus apparently hated her for it. After he went to work for Hesse and moved to Africa, he never came back."

"How about girlfriends?" Burlane asked. He began cutting the garlic cloves diagonally into slivers.

Iversen said, "He never had any girlfriends that the man in the meat market knew about, although it was impossible to tell if he had an outright dislike for women. But he was obsessed with cats; that much was clear. He earned a living putting them behind bars, remember."

"In zoos . . ."

"That's right. I talked to a psychiatrist who agreed it possible that I might have tumbled onto the killer. Of course, psychiatrists are psychiatrists, we all know that."

"Twentieth-century witch doctors," Burlane said. "Freud got all the attention, but Karl Jung was the one with the brains." He peeled two large, purple shallots and quickly chopped them up.

"Lawyers seem to be able to hire a psychiatrist to say anything they need to sway a jury. But the truth is all they can do is make an educated guess, same as us."

"Definitely worth pursuing, though." Burlane put his wok on the gas burner, and poured it a third full of corn oil. He turned the flame on high.

"That's what I thought, and Karl Bauer agreed."

Neumann said, "Women have such have graceful bodies, don't you agree? Sleek and feline. Like cats, they are. Like you. And those eyes of yours. Far more beautiful than the eyes of western women. A nice almond shape. And dark brown. Fabulous!"

Risa bit her lower lip.

Gesturing to the photographs of the tiger-girls on the wall, he said, "The two girls on the left are Indian and Indonesian, then a

German girl, then two girls in Siberia. The Filipina on the right was a dancer in the Silver Dollar, but I bet you know all about that. It was on television every day and in the newspapers. They're beautiful, aren't they? Lovely tiger bodies."

"They all have nice bodies," she said.

Neumann produced a giant white paw attached to a silver chain. There was a screw-in attachment at the end of the chain that he fastened to the ceiling above the bed. "That's the paw of a white Siberian tiger," he said, batting the paw with his hand so that it swung to and fro above the bed.

Burlane said, "This fish is highly prized by Filipinos. You watch what I do next, because it's important. If they found more of that tiger, a paw, say, could they match the hairs?"

"That's what they said. Then, supported by the murdered girl's father, a rich surgeon in Munich, I went to Mombasa, which is where Hesse's chief African field office was located. Neumann was based there. I talked to a guy there who had known him. He said Neumann was on the road most of the time—mostly to India and Indonesia and the Malay Peninsula, which is where the tigers are found. He said Neumann simply disappeared after Hesse's went under. He said Neumann was more interested in tigers than lions, which he considered boring."

Burlane took the lid off the rice, stirred it with a pair of chopsticks, and turned down the heat. "I agree. Lions run in prides. Tigers are spooky loners. Man-killers." Slotted spoon in hand, he dumped a handful of fish into his wok, into the roiling oil. "The Chinese calling this letting the fish 'go through the oil.' The idea is to give it about ten seconds at this stage so it's about half cooked." Burlane retrieved the fish chunks with his slotted spoon and dropped some more chunks into the oil.

Neumann removed photography gear from his closet and began setting up light reflectors around her. Then he screwed adjustable lights into sockets mounted on the ceiling.

As he worked, Neumann said, "You said you were interested in photography. I've got the best gear money can buy. I thought you'd be interested in how it works. Well?"

Risa wet her lips.

"Speak up. Would you like to see how it works?"

"Yes," she said softly.

Neumann smiled. "Ahh, that's what I like. Curiosity. A natural student."

Iversen said, "The last time my informant saw Neumann was when he returned to Mombasa to pick up his belongings, including the poster with his father on it. He said Neumann had fresh stories about having been in the Philippines, and, once, Neumann mentioned Cebu by name."

"Which is why you came here." Burlane retrieved the second batch of chunks from the hot oil.

"One step behind the poster collecter, who had also put in an appearance in Mombasa."

"Poor Steiner." Burlane poured the oil into a jar, leaving about three tablespoons remaining in the wok. He turned the heat down a tad.

Neumann retrieved brushes, a palette, and tubes of acrylic paint from the recess under the trapdoor. He began mixing paints on the palette. He had oranges and ochers and black and white on the palette. Tiger colors.

He said, "Before I take your picture, I have to paint you. You said you were interested in both photography and art."

Risa bit her lower lip.

Neumann smiled. "Body painting is far more fun than using a stupid canvas."

Iversen said, "I'd no sooner arrived than the Filipina dancer was found painted like a tiger and murdered. I hadn't been able to find any pictures of Neumann. I only have a general description, so I started taking photographs of German expats."

Burlane threw the slivers of garlic into the oil, stirring them with a wooden spoon. As the aroma burst forth, he said, "Doesn't that smell good?" He added the slices of ginger and the chunks of shallot, flipping them in the hot oil with the spoon.

"Yes, it does," Iversen said.

Burlane dumped in the half-cooked fish chunks and began flipping them with a spoon. As he did, he added a healthy dollop of Shaohsing wine. After about thirty seconds, he plopped in the pea pods, followed quickly by the sauce he had prepared earlier. In a few seconds, when the sauce had thickened, Burlane plopped the dish onto a plate. "See there, done." He checked the rice. "This is ready, too. Perfect timing and there you have it, just like downtown. A fish fit for a Chinese emperor, and we two turkeys get to enjoy it out here in the Philippines." Burlane retrieved his cassette player and punched the play button. "Listen to this," he said as he started setting the table for their meal. "Go ahead, sit. Eat. Listen. Enjoy."

Iversen, listening to the tape, sat and began eating.

Neumann, carefully laying a black stripe across Risa Sanchez's shoulder blades, said, "A Bengal tiger slashed my father's throat at a performance in Hamburg. For no reason. Took him by surprise. He bled to death with a tentful of people looking on in horror. I was just a boy at the time. Women are like that, you know, unpredictable."

"I—" Risa started to say something but thought better of it and closed her mouth.

Newman laid another stripe of black acrylic across his captive's back. "While my father was on the road with a circus, my mother was fucking a schoolteacher down the street. This poster is from my father's final performance. It's highly prized by collectors—the poster from Lothar Neumann's last performance. There's a duplicate of it in the Missouri Bar."

"People collect circus posters?"

Neumann dipped his brush back into the squiggle of black on his palette. "Oh, sure."

"Like people collect stamps?"

"And comic books and theater programs and first edition novels. You have a wonderful body, Risa. You're going to look beautiful painted like a tiger." Brush poised, he studied his human canvas.

Iversen, who had stopped eating, said, "Who are these people talking?"

Burlane turned off the tape. "Heinz and Lily Tepe. Heinz is a tiger consultant for CITES. He was the chairman of the committee that hired me, and he's been receiving all my reports. I've been to Siberia, Hong Kong, and India. He's been getting everything. Lily Tepe is Chinese. She's a Chua. The same family that owns two shopping malls here in Cebu City. Lily runs the Chua food company that sells Chinese products to overseas Chinese cities here in Southeast Asia as well as North America and Europe."

Iversen licked his lips. "The Klaus they're talking about is Klaus Neumann, isn't it?"

Burlane nodded. "I followed Tepe there this morning. Neumann lives in a house in Beverly Hills, a rich man's district that overlooks the city."

Iversen grinned. "Who or what are the Nine Dragons? Have you had a chance to find that out?"

"Ara Schott checked that out with Interpol. Nine Dragons is a Chinese triad based in Hong Kong, but with influence in all major overseas Chinese communities. They've long been associated with the Chua family, which owns not only its shopping malls in the Philippines, Taiwan, and Singapore, plus real estate in obscene amounts and food-processing companies, but also private power companies, fish canneries, and a brewery in Malaysia. They also own a fleet of fishing trawlers that operates out of Taiwan, which is how they likely smuggle the bones. Lily is in charge of a company that markets Chinese foods to overseas markets. The overseas shops that sell Chinese food ordinarily sell traditional medicines as well. That means she has contacts with the manufacturers of traditional medicines."

"The Nine Dragons are dragon lady's muscle." Iversen began to eat again.

"That's right. Ara's sources say one doesn't mess with the Chua family without a response from the Nine Dragons. If they don't buy you off, they'll break your daughter's neck. The wonderful Mrs. Tepe has a factory and warehouse on Mactan Island. I have to break into it to collect evidence." Burlane took a piece of the fish. "You know, it's the business of running the fish 'through the oil' that does it. A pain in the ass, but worth it. Incidentally, Klaus Neumann has an autographed poster of his father's last performance mounted in his bedroom."

"You've been in his bedroom?"

"After Tepe left Neumann's house, I broke inside and wired the place."

"You did?" Iversen blinked.

Neumann following Risa Sanchez's eyes to the tiger's paw hanging over his bed, said, "That came from a white Siberian tiger. The Chinese believe it brings good luck." He smiled. "And great sex! Fear makes women sexy. They're at their best when they know they're about to die. Take yourself, for instance, you're getting sexier by the minute."

Burlane retrieved a fist-size recorder from a bureau drawer. "I've got one mike in his bedroom, a second in his living room, and a third in his telephone. They're voice activated, and will beam me their conversations twenty-four hours a day. This gadget will record anything that's going on. Shall we listen in and see if your Mr. Tigerman has come home?" Burlane grinned.

"You listened to me tell you all this stuff knowing full well you had my man pinned."

"I think I have him. I don't know for sure. I wanted to hear your story. You do good work, Herr Iversen. I appreciate professionals." Burlane punched a button on the recorder and turned up the volume.

A man's voice: *"Does that tickle?"*

Silence.

"No sense squirming; You can't go anywhere. I asked you if it tickles. A nice little black stripe over your breast. I bet it tickles. It has to tickle."

"It tickles."

Burlane's mouth dropped.

"You'll be a pretty little tigress, you will. Such a sleek little body."

Iversen looked alarmed. "My God, he's painting another victim."

Burlane, remembering the photography gear in Neumann's house, dropped his fork. "I've got a young Filipina friend who interviewed for a job with a German named Klaus. That's her. That's her voice."

35

James Burlane and Hermann Iversen listened to the conversation in Klaus Neumann's bedroom as Burlane, grim-faced and dry-mouthed, wheeled his Toyota left onto Archbishop Reyes Avenue, a main thoroughfare leading from the uptown district of Lahug toward Beverly Hills.

Only to find himself stalled between two jeepneys in an impossible traffic jam in front of the Gaisano Country Mall on his right.

Above Reyes, on Burlane's right and extending to foothills of the ridge of low mountains in the center of the island, lay the subdivisions of Cebu's wealthy and influential. The higher up the greater the wealth, and the more likely the residence belonged to a Chinese-Filipino family. Klaus Neumann lived in the maximum rent district, directly behind the island's capitol building.

On the receiver, Neumann's voice: *"Such a lovely tiger girl you are . . ."*

This wasn't just Cebu City at rush hour, it was right up there with Manila or Bangkok. What caused the jam at this time of night was anybody's guess, but the most likely reason was a simple traffic accident in which, Filipino style, wrecked vehicles were left in place, damn the consequences, until the police arrived to take care of things. When one of the arterial streets was plugged, everything was plugged; owing to the hodgepodge of streets and neighborhoods, there were few detours that could handle major traffic.

"Don't make things difficult for yourself, Risa. Turn. Turn. A little more. That's a beautiful little tigress."

Stalled.

Burlane leaned out of the window and looked ahead. The traffic was locked tight as far he could see. There was no relief in sight.

What to do? Abandon the Toyota and try to call the police?

No. That was a joke, Burlane knew. The police faced the same traffic as he did, and even if the police did get through to Neumann's house in Beverly Hills, all he'd have to do was greet them at the door with a smile and a fistful of American dollars. Nobody would ever remember having received a call from Burlane. An emergency call? A girl in trouble? What call? What girl? Who says he made a call?

Burlane or Hermann Iversen would risk being thrown into jail themselves on charges creatively lodged.

They had to do something else. But what?

In his rear-view mirror, Burlane saw the aging Hell's Angels aficionado—the pony-tailed American oil worker named Barry—that he had met in the Missouri Bar. Barry was cruising along beside the road on his immaculate Harley-Davidson. In an emergency, Burlane would trust an ex-Hell's Angel before a necktied suit any day of the week. Burlane jumped out of the car and ran around in front of Barry, holding his hand up.

Barry, grinning, rumbled to a halt. "Hey, Major Khartoum. What's up?"

Burlane unzipped an inside pocket of his photographer's vest and gave Barry a handful of hundred-dollar bills. "A young Filipina is about to be murdered unless my parter and I get to Beverly Hills in the next five minutes."

Barry's eyes widened. "Say what?"

"Let us use your bike, and when this traffic clears up, you take my Toyota to the Missouri Bar. We'll meet you there in an hour or so."

"I was on my way there anyway."

"I'll lay some more money on you, if you want, no problem. But we've got to move and move fast."

Barry, looking at the money, grinned and stepped off the bike. "Hey, a lady in distress. No problem, man. Go, do your thing. And good luck."

Burlane gave him the keys to the Toyota and swung his leg over the Harley—with Iversen right behind him. "Thanks, man, we'll need all the luck we can get."

And Burlane was off, roaring up the edge of the road with the German detective holding on with one arm around Burlane's waist; in the other hand he held the receiver up to Burlane's ear with the volume turned all the way up.

There was no shoulder on the road, in the western sense of the word. And no sidewalks either. Archbishop Reyes Avenue was clogged with every kind of vehicle—from *carenderias* on one side of the road to *lechon* and fruit vendors on the other. And neither was Burlane the only one piloting a motorcycle. The street was a din of the hammer and pop of 150cc Yamahas and Kawasakis, moving between and around the stalled cars. They were as toys compared to Barry's enormous Harley, which throbbed through the traffic with a throaty rumble that was positively demonic in its power and purpose. Burlane understood why it was Barry's prize.

Burlane rode Filipino style—whoever was larger had the right-of-way; with Iversen clinging to him, swearing in German, Burlane bulled his way through traffic, pushing through pedestrians, bicycles, and smaller Yamahas and Kawasakis. If pedestrians or one of those little Japanese poppers didn't get out of his way, that was tough shit, partner. He had places to go and things to do.

Burlane bore to the right onto Escario Street. Escario was one of the main escapes from Reyes, and it too was crammed with traffic. As he drove, he and Iversen listened to the conversation coming from the bug in Klaus Neumann's bedroom.

"You see how it works? A photographer paints with light. I need proper light to yield the curves of your little tiger body."

They were now headed southwest, following the ridge of mountains in the center of the island. Straight ahead was the provincial capitol at the top of Osmena Boulevard, named for the political family that had been a power on Cebu for generations.

Behind him, Iversen said, "If we get there on time. He's mine. I want him for Karl and Inga Bauer."

"I understand. He's yours."

As they passed an office of Philippine Airlines on their right, the traffic began to ease; Burlane pushed the Harley hard, getting all the speed he could out of the traffic.

"You wonder what I'm going to do after I finish with the pictures? You know what I'm going to do. You've read about it in the papers. I can make it easy on you or hard. It's up to you."

At the capitol, Burlane took a hard right, and they began to climb, with the mountains and the posh Beverly Hills subdivision above them. Burlane, listening to the deadly conversation, drove recklesslessly, dangerously, swerving madly up the street. The road was not as crowded as Reyes had been, or the early part of Escario, but no street was ever entirely clear on Cebu. But the Harley was not a sissy bike. It had power, and when Burlane twisted the accelerator, it responded.

"Go ahead, stretch. I know it's been tiresome hanging from your wrists. I'll tell you how to pose. You might as well look good on your way out."

As they entered Klaus Neumann's neighborhood, Burlane said, "There's a picture window in front. No sense fucking with the door. The master bedroom is to the right."

"Go through the window."

"Fastest way. No sense fucking with the lock."

"Door on the right," Iversen said.

"That's it. I'll be right behind you. Cover your face when you go through the glass."

"Got it."

Then, up ahead, Burlane saw it in the dim light of a street lamp. "The one with the blue roof."

"I see the window," Iversen said.

"I think I should get some shots featuring that rump of yours. You have a sleek little butt, tiger girl. Turn to the left. More. More."

Burlane threw Barry's motorcycle on the ground as Hermann Iversen sprinted for the window that overlooked the city lights.

Iversen, without hesitation, put his arms around his face, lowered his head, and hurled himself through the glass.

Burlane, doing the same, was right behind him. When he got

to his feet, he saw Iversen meet Klaus Neumann at the bedroom doorway.

Iversen planted a kick in Neumann's crotch that would surely have shattered an oak. The kick literally lifted Neumann from the floor. Neumann fell to the floor screaming from the pain. He began vomiting as Iversen, swinging his foot with all the drive he could muster, delivered a second vicious blow square to Neumann's face, sending teeth flying and blood squirting.

Burlane pushed past the stricken Neumann to find the naked Risa Sanchez, painted like a tiger, weeping, but still alive and physically unharmed. Burlane unbound her and gave her a comforting hug and an affectionate tap on the butt. "The toilet's in there. Go wash that crap off." He felt her head nod yes on his shoulder, but she said nothing.

Behind him, Iversen swore at Neumann in German that was too fast for Burlane to understand. To Burlane, he said, "Now what do we do?"

"You'll never get him to Germany through official channels in this part of the world. Too much Chua money."

Risa, sobbing, went to wash off the tiger paint.

"What then?"

"We hire that dude Barry to hire us a *banka* and a crew. We worry about getting him to Germany after we get out of the Philippines. If you've got a DNA match and a witness, the Australians will extradite him. Chua money may buy Indonesian or Malaysian judges, but not Australians. I think Darwin would be our best bet."

Klaus Neumann, his head obviously still spinning, looked up. He wiped the blood from his mouth with the sleeve of his hand. On top of having had his testicles flattened beyond repair, his nose was broken, his lip was mashed and swollen, and he was missing his top and bottom front teeth.

Knowing what Neumann had done, Burlane, as a form of editorial comment, wanted to take a shot, too, as Iversen had done, but restrained himself. Enough was enough. A nice stretch in a German prison would be good for Neumann. Give him time to think about what a raging asshole he was. "He looks like a hockey player. Don't you think, Hermann?"

Neumann started to say something, but Iversen said, "Oh, shut up," in German and laid a third kick in the pit of Neumann's stomach, sending him sprawling on the carpet once again.

Iversen said, "Yes to the *banka* and Australia."

"You're talking pirate country between here and Darwin, and it may take a couple of weeks. I'll go with you, of course. I've been there before."

"Karl Bauer will be pleased. Thank you, Major Khartoum. I'll need all the help I can get in this part of the world."

"No problem," Burlane said. "Glad to be of help."

Later that night, James Burlane, Hermann Iversen, and their captive, gingerly feeling his swollen face and crushed testicles, sat silently in the *banka* as it slid through the darkness.

They were headed on their way southwest toward Mindanao, the first leg of their journey to Australia. They would follow the coast of Mindanao toward Zamboanga. At Zamboanga, they would turn due west, across pirate country, to the east coast of Borneo; they would follow the coast of Borneo south for the run through the Indonesian archipelago to Darwin, where they would begin the drill of extraditing Klaus Neumann to the German courts for having murdered Erika Bauer.

Iversen wanted Burlane to accompany him to Germany to meet Karl Bauer and Erika's father, Rolf, who had financed Iversen's investigation to Africa and the Philippines, and Burlane had agreed.

The civilized world was in agreement on the proper treatment of shits like Klaus Neumann. But justice in the matter of endangered species was another matter. Looking into the darkness, holding on as the *banka* ascended the crest of a sea wave and plunged into a trough of salt water, Burlane wondered who, if anybody, would have the courage to speak up on behalf of the tiger. Following the demise of the Marxist dream, political liberals were having a rough time facing the untidy truth that politics was, and always would be, the art of managing greed. Alas, there would be no perfect socialist man.

On one level, it might be said the tigers were being eliminated by the callous Chinese. On another level, Burlane felt, the tigers were being killed by westerners given to high-minded lectures and their own moral purity.

There was, of course, a way to save the tiger.

Among Burlane's reading in the literature was *Chinese Herbal Medicine Materia Medica,* by D. Bensky and A. Gamble, published by the Eastland Press, Seattle, in 1986. The authors identified 392 substances found by the Chinese to have pharmaceutical properties. Of these 88 percent were plants; 9.4 percent were nonendangered animal products or minerals. Only 2.6 percent were from endangered species.

If conservationists were really serious about saving the tiger, Burlane felt, they had only to rely on simple common sense. As they get older, the Chinese, like people in all cultures and on all continents, come increasingly to suffer the aches and pains of arthritis, bursitis, and other afflictions of the joints and bones. Their medicine was based on thousands of years of years of trial and error, so it stood to reason that they had learned something. Western research had established that plain old garlic was good for reducing the cholesterol level in blood. Red wine in moderation had its benefits. Eat your veggies, researchers said. Have another helping of carrots.

Burlane stood by the efficiencies of western clinical research. But he wished most fervently that the West would stop lecturing the Chinese; better to work a deal—help them manufacture and distribute cheap western medicines to replace those made from the parts of wild animals. Aspirin, for example—despite all the hype and advertising of competing compounds—remained a true miracle medicine and was unprotected by patents. It was an anti-inflammatory analgesic that thinned the blood, an aid to people with fat-clogged arteries.

Research had shown that the tiger penis wine on the market was really laced with ginseng. And if the Chinese remained bent on having tiger penises to bolster their sex lives why not use advanced western surgical techniques to produce barbed tiger penises from bull penises without the telltale surgical incisions? Burlane did not believe for a second that it couldn't be done. The idea was to save tigers, not prove who was right and who was wrong.

They don't happen all the time. Bad luck tries to prevent them. Unpredictable deities are forever conniving against them. And they are scorned by cranky and callous authors. But, fortunately for the human spirit, happy endings do occasionally occur.

One of these reassuring anomalies was the case of Marta Fuentes. She faithfully took the medicine made from milk vetch and it worked, or at least her heart pains went away. If the heart pains returned, she would go to Mr. Chen and see what else he might recommend.

Marta Fuentes was like millions of poor people in East and Southeast Asia who could not afford the fancy price of western medicines. A day that passed with her family fed and tucked safely into bed was a successful day. The future was now, not tomorrow. She did not have time to worry about tigers, even if she had known that tiger bones were prized as an ingredient in Chinese traditional medicine.

If an ardent conservationist from London or San Francisco went to Mrs. Fuentes's tiny house and told her most fervently of their concern for the future of tigers, she would have agreed. Such a terrible thing to kill the tigers.

Being a polite woman, and taught by her culture not to offend and to respect westerners, she would have suppressed her feeling: If westerners were as concerned about people as they were about tigers, they would do something to bring cheap medicine to people with such ailments as aching bones and bad hearts. Then maybe the killing of tigers would stop, or at least slow down enough for the species to survive.